Readers love the Cow series by SUE

Speed Dating the Boss

"I was completely caught up in the story from the first page to the last. It was compelling and just about perfect."
—Joyfully Jay

"It was sweet, it had just the right emotional engagement, no big dramatic misunderstanding… and interesting characters."
—Gay Book Reviews

Secretly Dating the Lionman

"Brown spins a lively, emotionally satisfying story with complex characters and explicit sensuality."
—Publishers Weekly

"It kept me awake at night reading to finish it quickly just so I could see what happened. The ending was very satisfying…."
—Bayou Book Junkie

Slow Dating the Detective

"The scorching sex scenes and sweet romantic moments will have readers rooting for Keenan and Nate's happily ever after."
—Publishers Weekly

"Sue Brown is gifted with a great talent for writing dialogue that is sharp and witty in all the right spots while still keeping the sweetness that I crave in a good romance novel."
—Love Bytes

By Sue Brown

Chance to Be King
Falling for Ramos
Final Admission
Gabriel's Storm
Last Place in the Chalet
The Layered Mask
The Next Call
The Night Porter • Light of Day
Nothing Ever Happens
The Sky Is Dead
Stitch
Stolen Dreams
Waiting

COWBOYS AND ANGELS
Speed Dating the Boss
Secretly Dating the Lionman
Slow Dating the Detective

DREAMSPUN DESIRES
The Fireman's Pole

FRANKIE'S SERIES
Frankie & Al
Ed & Marchant
Anthony & Leo
Jordan & Rhys
Frankie & Friends Anthology

THE ISLE SERIES
The Isle of… Where?
Isle of Wishes
Isle of Waves

ISLAND MEDICS
Island Doctor
Island Counselor

MORNING REPORT
Morning Report
Complete Faith
Papa's Boy
Luke's Present
Letters From a Cowboy
Letters From a Cowboy Anthology

Published by DREAMSPINNER PRESS
www.dreamspinnerpress.com

GABRIEL'S STORM

SUE BROWN

DREAMSPINNER PRESS

Published by
DREAMSPINNER PRESS

5032 Capital Circle SW, Suite 2, PMB# 279, Tallahassee, FL 32305-7886 USA
www.dreamspinnerpress.com

This is a work of fiction. Names, characters, places, and incidents either are the product of author imagination or are used fictitiously, and any resemblance to actual persons, living or dead, business establishments, events, or locales is entirely coincidental.

Gabriel's Storm
© 2020 Sue Brown

Cover Art
© 2020 Brooke Albrecht
http://brookealbrechtstudio.com
Cover content is for illustrative purposes only and any person depicted on the cover is a model.

All rights reserved. This book is licensed to the original purchaser only. Duplication or distribution via any means is illegal and a violation of international copyright law, subject to criminal prosecution and upon conviction, fines, and/or imprisonment. Any eBook format cannot be legally loaned or given to others. No part of this book may be reproduced or transmitted in any form or by any means, electronic or mechanical, including photocopying, recording, or by any information storage and retrieval system, without the written permission of the Publisher, except where permitted by law. To request permission and all other inquiries, contact Dreamspinner Press, 5032 Capital Circle SW, Suite 2, PMB# 279, Tallahassee, FL 32305-7886, USA, or www.dreamspinnerpress.com.

Trade Paperback ISBN: 978-1-64405-549-6
Digital ISBN: 978-1-64405-548-9
Library of Congress Control Number: 2019955836
Trade Paperback published March 2020
v. 1.0

Printed in the United States of America
∞
This paper meets the requirements of
ANSI/NISO Z39.48-1992 (Permanence of Paper).

Chapter 1
Gabriel

"Daddy, Daddy, look at me! Look at me! Mummy, Daddy's here!"

Leaving his mother by the picnic basket, Michael ran across the beach, his face alight with laughter, his pale blond hair whipped by the wind. Gabriel Pennant strode across the damp sand, inhaling the salty air with pleasure after a morning hunched over the keyboard. He deserved time on the beach with his family.

He was a freelance web developer, not a miracle worker. Some clients didn't understand he couldn't create Facebook for the price of a cup of coffee. But now it didn't matter. He could relax with Jenny and Michael and play hooky for the rest of the afternoon. He grinned at his wife and then ran across the wet sand, ready to meet his son in the middle of the beach and swing him on his shoulders.

He frowned. Something was wrong. The closer he got, the farther away Michael seemed to be.

"Come on, Daddy!" Michael held out his thin arms to his father.

Gabriel ran forward to catch him, but their fingers never touched. Michael was just out of reach.

"Daddy! Daddy!"

Now there was fear in Michael's voice, and his big eyes were wide and scared. He called and called to Gabriel, his voice echoing along the beach, but Gabriel was rooted to the spot, unable to help his young son.

"Daddy, where are you? Why aren't you here?"

Michael's panicked voice repeated over and over, but Gabriel was unable to help him.

"Gabriel?"

Still lost in his painful thoughts, Gabriel Pennant shivered in the chill wind that blew across the Cornish clifftops, and shoved his hands into the pockets of his thin jacket. Earlier in the day, the tourists and families had wandered past him, taking advantage of the late autumn sunshine. They vanished as the evening approached and the temperature dropped, but Gabriel barely noticed their disappearance. He was more concerned with what he saw out to sea. The sky overhead was still a deep blue, but storm clouds had gathered on the horizon. The wind had increased too and whipped his shaggy hair around his face. Gabriel pushed a sea-dampened lock behind his ears, but it was a futile gesture, as it was back in his eyes with the next gust.

"Why am I not surprised to find you here?"

Gabriel looked up to see his brother-in-law standing next to him. He'd been so lost in memories of Jenny and Michael that Gabriel hadn't noticed Toby's approach. "Hey."

"How long have you been standing there?"

Gabriel shrugged. "A couple of hours."

Toby snorted sceptically. "And the rest?"

Gabriel didn't bother to argue. Toby knew him too well. He'd been standing on the clifftop for at least four hours.

"There's a storm coming," Toby said.

"It's going to be a bad one." Gabriel had checked the local news before he left his cottage, although he grimaced at the blond weathergirl when she cheerily discussed the oncoming storm as though it weren't important, as though there were no consequences when the weather wreaked its vengeance on the people who lived by the coastline.

"Gabriel, you can't stay here all day."

"I won't," Gabriel lied. "I've got work to do back at the cottage."

He hoped Toby would take the hint and leave him alone, but to his surprise, Toby grasped his shoulder and forced Gabriel to look at him. Toby's worried expression touched Gabriel even as it exasperated him. "Gabriel, go home. They're not coming back."

Gabriel stiffened and pulled away. "Leave it."

"I can't. You're my friend, and I'm worried about you." Toby shook his head. "You'll stand on this cliff until kingdom come. They're *gone*. Jenny and Michael are dead. It's been over a year, and they're not coming back."

"Shut your mouth." Gabriel clenched his fists in fury, a heartbeat away from punching Toby square in the face. How dare he. How *dare* he. "Don't talk about them like that." He stopped, the lump in his throat preventing him from yelling his anger.

He didn't need reminding that his family was gone, torn apart by a freak storm. The last time he'd seen them, Jenny had got Michael to help her pack a picnic. They'd left Gabriel to work and gone down to play on the beach for the day. He remembered the moment he ran to the beach to find it empty, no trace of them left bar one of Michael's shoes.

Despite extensive searching, their bodies were never found. The search was called off, and their funerals were held. Gabriel wanted to scream that they weren't dead, that those were empty coffins, but he'd stood there, ignoring all attempts to console him as the priest spouted useless platitudes that comforted no one. He had never stopped searching for his family. Even if the rest of the world had given up on Jenny and Michael, he wouldn't.

Apparently realising he'd gone too far, Toby apologetically put his hand out, but Gabriel stepped back, out of his reach. Toby sighed. "I don't want to upset you."

"I'm not upset," Gabriel snapped, furious at the pity in Toby's eyes. He'd become only too familiar with that expression over the past year—pity and a touch of exasperation because he wasn't moving on with his life. As if he could move on. As if he wanted to.

Toby sighed and shoved his hands into his pockets. "Jenny wouldn't want you to live like this, spending hours staring out at sea. What are you trying to do?"

"You think I don't know they're dead?" Gabriel said, hating the catch in his voice on the last word. "You think I don't live with their deaths every single minute, every day?"

"I know you do. But all you do is stand here?" Toby asked. "Day in, day out? Hours and hours? You don't do anything except watch the sea."

"I work."

Toby snorted again. "Hidden away in the cottage. When was the last time you walked into the village or came around for dinner? You never talk to anyone except me."

"I've always worked at home," Gabriel pointed out. "Since we—I—moved to the village, I've worked at home. You know that."

"Yeah, but you used to visit us. Charlie keeps knocking on my door, asking to visit you. He thinks it's his fault you don't visit him or us."

Gabriel flinched at Toby's reproachful expression. Charlie had been Michael's best friend. Gabriel didn't want to say that seeing Charlie was like a punch to the gut, a reminder of what he'd lost.

Then he looked up and realised he didn't have to say anything. Toby understood only too well.

A rumble of thunder in the distance attracted Gabriel's attention. The dark clouds were much closer now, and the temperature had dropped. Gabriel shivered. "Get home, Toby, before you get wet."

"What about you?" Toby asked.

Gabriel pushed his hair back from his face. "I won't stay much longer. I'll just make sure no boats are in trouble."

"Is that why you spend so much time here?"

"I couldn't save Jenny and Michael, but I might be able to save someone else."

Understanding dawned on Toby's face. "You're looking for people in trouble?"

"No one was looking out for them. Not even me."

"Gabriel, you know no one could've saved Jenny and Michael. It was a freak surge. They probably didn't know what hit them."

The thought of Jenny and Michael swept off the beach by a wave, Jenny struggling to get back to the beach, Michael ripped out of her arms, their lungs filling with water. The thought of their empty eyes, their dead bodies sinking to the bottom—it was a nightmare that filled Gabriel's waking and sleeping hours.

Gabriel needed to be alone. "Go home, Toby. You don't have to comfort me. I'll go home soon."

Toby seemed to grasp he was on a losing wicket. He sighed again. "She was my twin. I miss her too." He walked away, ignoring Gabriel's harsh indrawn breath.

Toby was Gabriel's ex-brother-in-law, Jenny's twin brother. He had mourned the loss of his sister and nephew as much as Gabriel had. Gabriel knew that, but he couldn't take the weight of Toby's grief as well as his own. He could just about handle Toby's mother-hen tendencies. The man had no issue with scolding Gabriel for not taking care of himself.

The first cool raindrops splattered Gabriel's face, and the air was heavy with the promise of a thunderstorm. His cottage was hidden behind the trees, next to Toby's. They had been neighbours for over eight years. Their families had spent many hours walking the clifftops together.

He looked over the edge of the cliff—the urge to throw himself over was strong, but he'd resisted that compulsion many times—but the beach was still empty, choppy steel-grey waves trimmed with white foam crashing onto the sand. Gabriel looked out to the horizon. He couldn't see any sign of life, and he turned away. Toby was right. It was time to go home.

He'd barely taken one step when something in the sea caught his eye. He squinted at the waves, trying to focus on what had attracted his attention, but he couldn't see anything. It must have been a seagull. Gabriel was about to give up when he spotted it again and took a few seconds to realise it was a small white boat being thrown about by the waves. As he watched, the boat dipped below the water. Gabriel fumbled with his phone and was about to call 9-9-9 when he saw the boat dip once more. He cursed, knowing the Coast Guard wouldn't arrive in time, no matter how quick they were. He didn't even know if there was anyone in the boat, but he had to try.

Gabriel ran to the steep steps and hurried down as fast as he could, cursing out loud when he slipped on the damp wood. He flailed but managed to regain his footing and resume his downward descent, albeit at a slower pace. His wet hair got in his eyes, and he impatiently pushed it back, anxious to reach the dinghy moored at the bottom of the steps. Gabriel worked on automatic as he pushed the dinghy into the crashing waves, refusing to think about how slim his chances were as he steered toward the approximate place where he'd seen the boat. He had to find it.

Spray after spray drenched him as he combed the area, leaving his eyes raw and his body shivering from the cold. His sodden hair resisted all of Gabriel's attempts to stay out of his eyes. As he crisscrossed the bay, the rain only got heavier, and the dinghy was in danger of turning over in the roiling waves. *Where the hell is it?* If he didn't go back soon, he'd be the one in danger of drowning.

I'd be with Jenny and Michael.

The thought wasn't a new one. Gabriel had wrestled with the idea since the day he lost them. Toby would have killed him if he ever admitted it.

"Where are you?" His words were whipped away by the wind.

He was about to give up when he saw a flash of white to his left. Then it vanished once more. He squinted. Nothing. Then another flash of white. He changed course, hoping he'd get there in time.

The white fiberglass boat listed badly as Gabriel came alongside. It was larger than it had looked from the clifftop—one of the expensive models that he'd gazed at with a curled lip as the wealthy fair-weather sailors took to the waves on the weekends. Certainly not designed to be out in bad weather like this. He couldn't see anyone aboard.

"Ahoy there. Anyone aboard?" he called, but his voice was whipped away in the storm.

With difficulty, Gabriel managed to tie a rope to the listing boat and clambered over. Almost immediately he saw a figure lying by the steering wheel. He staggered over to kneel beside the body of a young man dressed in a shirt and shorts who didn't stir at his approach. The cause of his unconsciousness became obvious when Gabriel spotted the large lump on his temple and the blood trickling down his cheeks and neck. He placed his fingers against the pulse point of his neck. He was alive. The relief took Gabriel's breath away as the stranger's pulse beat steady and strong under his fingertips.

The boat dipped at a sharp angle, and a wave crashed over them both. Gabriel slid along the deck and grabbed a railing for support to avoid being swept overboard. Fuck! He had to get both of them off the boat now or they were going to drown. He shoved the hair out of eyes and looked at the unconscious man. There was no time to check for injuries. Gabriel turned him, noting the lump on his temple, and gathered him into his arms. He staggered to his feet and nearly lost his footing as the boat seemed to fall out from under his feet. Hampered by the deadweight of the man and the wind, the rain, and the lurching boat, Gabriel inched over to the dinghy. The boat dipped again, and Gabriel slammed into the side trying to protect the man from further injury. He took a deep breath, prayed the storm would give him a break, and transferred the man into the dinghy. Gabriel looked over his shoulder to below deck of the listing boat, but there was too much water. If anyone had been down there…. He shook his head, scrambled back into the dinghy, and cast off, leaving the white boat to its watery fate.

He pushed his hair back as the wind whipped it across his eyes again. Between his hair and the rain and salt water, Gabriel's eyes were red-raw and stinging. Even with the engine, the dinghy had to fight the waves, and it seemed to take twice as long as it should to get back to shore. Gabriel looked at his unconscious passenger. He was still huddled in the bottom of the dinghy and hadn't shown any signs of returning to consciousness. Hypothermia, shock. Who knew how long he'd been out there?

Gabriel breathed a sigh of relief as they reached the shoreline, and he jumped out of the dinghy to haul it up the sand away from the crashing waves. He eased one arm under the man's legs and the other around his shoulders and started to climb. Each step was a fight against the rain and the wind. It was a long way up and he was a dead weight in Gabriel's arms, not helped by the sodden weight of his clothes. Gabriel was a few inches over six feet tall and broad-shouldered, but despite his slender frame, the man was tall and difficult to carry as he was so lax. Halfway up, he muttered an unheard apology, and Gabriel transferred him over his shoulder. There was no way he was going to get to the top otherwise. By the time Gabriel reached the clifftop, he was puffing heavily and wishing he'd been to the gym more often. He hadn't bothered to lock his front door, and he shouldered inside with his burden and slammed the door against the howling storm.

The quiet inside was a blessed relief after the noise. Gabriel placed the man on the large sofa, and water soaked into the fabric from his long dark hair. Concerned for his furniture, Gabriel rushed into the bathroom and returned with a towel, which he tucked under the man's head.

Gabriel hesitated for a moment, then muttered. "You can't leave him soaking wet."

The man had to be undressed, or he'd get pneumonia. The white shirt was transparent, outlining his slender figure, and his shorts clung to his bare and blueish-looking legs. He needed to be warmed up fast. Gabriel struggled with the buttons on the shirt, sat him up to remove the shirt, and then wrestled with the shorts. Then Gabriel grabbed the afghan he kept over the back of the sofa and wrapped it around him. The man hadn't stirred, not even a whimper, and that worried Gabriel.

He dug out his phone, relieved to see it was still working after being in his sodden jeans, and scrolled down to the right number.

"Dr Maris." Toby sounded exhausted.

"It's Gabriel."

"Gabriel? Are you okay?"

Toby's concern was immediate, and Gabriel understood. In the months following Jenny and Michael's deaths, he'd fallen apart every time there was a storm.

"Toby, I need you here," Gabriel said.

"Of course," Toby said without hesitation. "I'll be over to you right away. Just hold on, okay?"

Gabriel held back an impatient sigh. Toby thought he was having a meltdown. "It's not me. I rescued a man. He's unconscious, and I need you to look at him."

"A man? Rescued where?" Gabriel could hear someone speaking in the background. "Gabriel's got a man. I've got to go over there."

"I haven't got a man," Gabriel snapped. "I rescued him from his boat."

"Where are you now? Do you need the Coast Guard?"

"I'm back at the cottage."

"I'll be there in five minutes," Toby said. "I can't *wait* to hear this story."

Gabriel disconnected the call on Toby's gleeful tone and looked down at the man. He looked young, maybe early to midtwenties. He had delicate features, although they were marred by the large bruise covering his temple. His dark lashes swept over his cheeks, and a spray of freckles were a sharp contrast to his pale skin. Uncomfortable at staring at the man, even if he wasn't aware, Gabriel picked up the clothes and headed into his laundry room. He stripped off his sweater and jeans, shoved all the wet clothes into his washing machine, and took the detergent pods from the top shelf where they'd always been kept out of Michael's reach. Shivering so much his teeth chattered, Gabriel dried himself off with a towel and then redressed in sweats and a hoodie. As he pulled it over his head, he heard Toby calling his name.

Even though he'd only had to walk around the corner, Toby was soaked through. He stripped off his coat and hung it on a hook by the front door.

"Hey. I hope you've got the coffee on. Where's your guest?"

Gabriel's breath caught as it did every time he saw his wife's brother. Jenny and Toby had been twins, and his features were almost identical. Sometimes—always—it hurt Gabriel just to look at him. "He's on the sofa, and I'll go put the coffee on."

"You left him alone?" Toby said disapprovingly.

"He's unconscious, and I needed to change." He led the way to the sofa. The man hadn't moved at all. "See, he's fine."

Toby snorted as he knelt by the unconscious man's side and took his wrist. "Is that your professional opinion, Dr Pennant?"

"Shut up."

"Get the fire started. It's freezing in here."

Gabriel huffed but did as he was told. He knew from experience that it was simpler just to do what Toby wanted. "Make up your mind. Coffee or fire?"

"You're a big boy. You can do both. His pulse is strong, and his colour is good," Toby observed.

"He's been unconscious since I found him. Shouldn't he be awake by now?"

Toby examined his head. "He's got a nasty bump on the back of his head as well as the bruise on his temple." He flashed a light in his eyes. "But his pupils are reacting, and he's warming up."

"Should we get him to hospital? What if he's got a concussion?"

"In any other circumstances, I'd say yes, but a tree fell a couple of yards out of the village. One of the old ones. No one's going anywhere tonight." Toby sat back on his heels and looked up at Gabriel. "He's going to need to stay here until the tree is cleared."

Gabriel stared at him in horror. "He can't stay here."

Toby frowned at him. "He'll have to, Gabriel. He's got nowhere else to go until the roads are cleared."

"Can't you take him? You've got beds in the clinic."

"I need to keep the clinic free for emergencies. You're not my first call this evening. Poor old Bob got hit by a falling branch."

"Is he all right?"

Old Bob lived a couple of roads away from Gabriel. No one was sure how old he was, and Bob wasn't telling, but he lived by himself without any assistance from interfering do-gooders. His words.

"A dislocated collarbone and cuts and bruises," Toby said. "He was very lucky and bitching about going home."

"Our John Doe is unconscious," Gabriel pointed out. "Isn't that an emergency?"

"John Doe?" Toby's lips twitched. "You going all cop show on me? *John* is safe, warm, and with someone who can monitor him. That's you, in case you didn't know." Toby got to his feet. "Call me if there's any change in his condition."

"You can't leave me with him." Gabriel's voice rose as Toby picked up his coat. His hands clenched into fists. "I can't do this."

The man had to go. Gabriel had found him, but he couldn't look after him. He couldn't look after anyone.

Toby must have caught Gabriel's panic, because his amusement slipped away and he squeezed Gabriel's arm. "You can, Gabriel. I know John's unconscious, but he's breathing just fine, and his lungs are clear at the moment. Just sit with him, and if his condition deteriorates, call me."

"Can't Damien sit with him?"

"Damien can't handle anyone who's ill. You know that."

Gabriel growled under his breath. Toby's husband wasn't known for his caring nature, which most of the time, Gabriel found amusing. Not now, though. "I thought you wanted coffee."

Toby shrugged on his coat. "The coffee is for you. I'll call you in an hour."

"Make it thirty minutes."

"*An hour*. Call me if you have to."

With that, Toby left Gabriel standing in the middle of his lounge, wondering what the hell to do next. He knelt down next to his unwanted guest. He was still quiet, but his colour was good, and he was breathing steadily. Gabriel touched his cheek with the back of his hand and was relieved to feel he was much warmer. His hair was still wet, and he thought about trying to dry it, but he decided to leave him as he was until he woke up. For the sake of his sofa, he fetched a dry towel and replaced the one under his head, noting for the first time the coppery glints in the long hair.

Then Gabriel made himself a cup of coffee—because he wanted one, not because of Toby—and then sat in the armchair by the fire, appreciating the crackling warmth and dry clothes. Drinking the hot coffee soothed his irritation and concern. Outside, the wind had arrived in full force and the rain was even heavier. In the distance he could hear banging, as though a door was unlatched, but he wasn't going to venture outside again until the storm had abated. He looked over at his visitor. John had been really lucky Gabriel had spotted him. In another minute he'd have left the clifftop.

He was almost dozing when the man moaned. Gabriel sat bolt upright and looked at John. He was still, and Gabriel almost thought he'd imagined it when John's eyes opened and he stared up at the ceiling.

"Hey." Gabriel knelt beside the sofa. "How are you feeling?"

John turned toward the sound of his voice. Gabriel watched as he tried to focus on him and then shrank back as he saw him, confusion and panic in his expression. He couldn't help noticing his stunning dark grey eyes were the colour of the sea that had nearly claimed his life.

"Where—?" His voice sounded rusty. "Kill me?"

What the hell?

"You're okay. You're safe now," he assured John, who still looked panicked. "My name's Gabriel, Gabriel Pennant. You're in my cottage. You're safe, I promise."

"How—how did I get here?"

"I found you on a boat." Gabriel rested his fingertips on the pulse at the man's wrist. It beat faster, but that wasn't surprising, as he was in a panic.

"A boat?" He stared at him bewildered. "I was in a boat?"

"It's okay," he soothed. "You just relax. We can talk about this later."

"Okay."

John closed his eyes and seemed to fall back to sleep. Gabriel waited, but he didn't stir, so Gabriel got to his feet and stretched. He picked up his mug and went to the kitchen to pour himself more coffee. Then he returned to the fireplace and resumed vigil over his sleeping guest. The colour in his face was better, his creamy skin less ashen than before.

It was another half an hour before John stirred, blinking as he woke. Gabriel put his mug down, and John focused on him, panic in his eyes.

Gabriel stayed where he was, not wanting to scare him. "You're all right," he said. "My name is Gabriel. You're in my cottage, and you're safe." He repeated the words from before, hoping John would understand.

"Gabriel," John said, his voice soft.

"That's right. What's your name?"

"Name?" John sounded completely confused by the question.

"Yes, you do have a name, don't you?"

"I—I don't know what my name is?" It sounded like he was asking Gabriel a question.

"It's okay," he said soothingly. "You've taken a bump to the head. I'm sure you'll remember your name soon enough." Gabriel didn't know what to do next. John was awake now. He was going to have to talk to him. "Does your head hurt?"

"Here." John pressed the area where the bump was and the colour drained out of his face. "Oh God." He clapped a hand over his mouth.

"Don't do that again," Gabriel said hastily. "I'll get you a bowl." He grabbed a plastic bowl from a kitchen cabinet and rushed back to the sofa. John was struggling to free his arms and sit up. "Here. Wait. Let me help you."

The afghan slipped, and John looked down at his bare chest. "Where are my clothes?"

Gabriel had forgotten that John was almost naked under the afghan. He grabbed the fleece on the back of the chair and tucked it around John's shoulders. "Your clothes are wet through. I didn't want you to get pneumonia… or wreck my sofa. They're in the washing machine."

John nodded, although he didn't stop staring at Gabriel as though he was wary about what he'd do next.

"Do you feel sick?" Gabriel asked.

"Only if I press the bump." Unconsciously, his hand went to it.

Gabriel gently pushed it away. "Not a good idea. Would you like a tea or coffee?"

"I—I don't know?"

Gabriel opened his mouth but shut it again. "I'll make you a coffee. You stay here."

John seemed about to argue, but he lay back, obviously exhausted, and he closed his eyes again. Gabriel escaped to the kitchen and phoned Toby.

"It hasn't been an hour yet." Toby sounded irritated.

"It's almost an hour, and he's awake."

"John?"

"No, my mother," Gabriel snapped. "Yes, John. Who else would it be?"

"Don't be smart with me, Gabriel Pennant. It's been a long and wet evening." Toby's tone was even sharper than Gabriel's.

Gabriel tucked the phone under his chin, cleaned out the filter of the coffee machine, and counted to five before he spoke again. "Where are you?"

"Back at home for five minutes. Do you need me to come over? I've got another couple of calls, but I could visit you first."

Gabriel was about to say "Hell, yes," but Toby sounded exhausted. "John's got a headache, and he doesn't remember who he is. What can I give him?"

"Okay, give him two paracetamol for the pain, and if he falls asleep, keep waking him up."

Gabriel groaned. "It's going to be a long night."

"Why should I be the only one to suffer?" Toby said. He yawned loudly in Gabriel's ear. "I've got to go."

"I'll call if there's a problem."

"You do that. I might not answer." Then Toby disconnected the call before Gabriel could say goodbye.

Gabriel shook his head. His brother-in-law drove him insane, and yeah, he loved the hell out of him even if he was a pain in the arse. Mechanically, he went through the motions of making the coffee for his guest. Milk, sugar? What the heck should he give him? He loaded up a tray with everything and waited for the coffee to drip through. Gabriel smiled wryly because he knew he was delaying the moment he had to face his unwanted guest.

Rain lashed against the kitchen window, and he sobered. John was lucky he'd been watching on the clifftop. No one had been looking out for Jenny and Michael, but today he'd been there for John. Gabriel closed his eyes, and for a moment, he felt as though Jenny's hand were on his shoulder.

"You were there for him, my Gabriel. You were there."

A whisper of her voice breezed through him, and for an instant, he smelt her perfume again.

"I love you, Jenny."

"I know."

There was a crash outside, and Gabriel was abruptly jolted from his memories. He stared out into the darkness, but all he could see was his reflection staring back at him.

Chapter 2
Sam

He must have dozed again, because he heard a noise and woke up, his heart racing and the blood pounding in him ears. He blinked and focused on a large, dark-haired stranger looming over him, an oval tray in his hands.

Don't kill me!

"It's okay. It's only me." The man put the tray down on the small coffee table.

He stared up at him, unable to comprehend his words. For a moment he panicked, unsure who he was. He struggled to his feet and took a step, desperate to get away, but he was tangled in a thick blanket, and he swayed. Hands gripped his arms through the blanket, and he panicked again.

"John, calm down. It's okay. I found you, and you're safe. You're in my cottage. My name is Gabriel. Remember?" It sounded like it wasn't the first time he'd been given that information.

It was his calm tone that finally penetrated the panic, and he looked up into Gabriel's light grey eyes. He'd got up in his panic, the afghan loosely wrapped around. Now he became conscious that he was almost naked in front of a stranger, and he clutched the afghan to him.

Why couldn't he remember anything? It was as though there was a black hole in his mind where his life should be. His heart started pounding so hard he felt it was going to burst out of his chest, and his breathing grew choppy.

"Sit down before you fall down. The last thing you need is to bang your head again." Gabriel manhandled him back onto the sofa, although his touch was gentle.

He wrapped himself up like a mummy, needing the protection from the world, even from Gabriel's kindness. Then, of course, he had to fight to extricate his arms when Gabriel offered him coffee.

"I don't know how you take it, and I don't suppose you remember?" Gabriel said.

He hesitated, then shook his head.

"Try it black," Gabriel suggested as he filled a mug not quite to the brim.

He took a sip and pulled a face at the bitter taste. Without a word, Gabriel took it back and added milk and sugar. This time the coffee tasted less disgusting, and he managed to swallow it.

Gabriel drank his coffee silently, his gaze focused on the fire, and he took the opportunity to stare at him without being noticed. Gabriel was tall and broad-shouldered and towered over him when they stood up. Gabriel had grey eyes too, but lighter than his, almost like ice.

Hey, he remembered he had grey eyes. Now he had to remember everything else. His host looked lost in his thoughts. From his sorrowful expression, they weren't happy thoughts. He wondered if Gabriel had forgotten he was there.

The lights flickered, and Gabriel seemed to return to himself. He stood and stared down at him. "We'll probably lose power at some point. I'll get you clothes while the lights are still on."

Gabriel disappeared, and he leaned back against the cushions, glad of a few moments to himself. The windows rattled as the storm battered the cottage. He shuddered, thinking of what almost happened to him.

Gabriel came back, looking angry, and threw a pile of clothes at him. He shrank back, not knowing what he'd done to make Gabriel so cross. "These should fit. I'll leave you to get dressed." Then he vanished again without saying anything else.

He was caught off guard by his anger. Gabriel had seemed kind and friendly before. Not wanting to make things worse, he hastily unwrapped the afghan and pulled on the long-sleeved T-shirt and sweatpants. He expected the clothes to be Gabriel's, as there wasn't any sign of a wife or husband, but these clothes were much smaller and well-worn. The T-shirt was a little tight across the shoulders, but they were infinitely better than trying to remain wrapped in the afghan and fleece. He was back on the sofa when Gabriel returned with an armful of logs. He looked relieved and angry to see he was dressed.

"Thank you for the clothes," he said timidly.

"It's fine." Gabriel glared at the fire as he poked it.

"What's wrong?"

"Nothing!" Gabriel viciously poked the fire and cursed as a spark landed on his hand.

He cowered. "You're angry."

"I'm not angry!" Gabriel snapped. Then he sat back on his heels and inspected the burn. He rubbed his temples. "I—I'm sorry. I'm being an arse."

"Is there a problem?" he asked. When Gabriel didn't turn his head, he said, "Is it something to do with the clothes? I'll take them off as soon as mine are dry."

Gabriel seemed to collapse in on himself, the anger fading away. "I don't expect you to do that. It's not your fault. It's just… the clothes were my wife's."

"Oh."

Gabriel must have realised he was taken aback, because he said, "Jenny was tall and preferred men's T-shirts and hoodies. My clothes would swamp you."

He wasn't sure how he felt about wearing Gabriel's wife's clothing. "Are you sure that's okay with her?" He didn't want to cause any problems for Gabriel with his wife.

"She won't need them." The anger was back, leaking through his attempt at patience.

He flinched away from the angry tone. "I'm sorry."

Gabriel huffed and turned to him, grief written over his face. "Jenny is dead. She and my son died last year."

"I'm so sorry." What else could he say?

He watched Gabriel stab at the fire, and he couldn't help the fear that coiled in his belly. Was he safe? Gabriel had saved him, but he obviously didn't want him there.

Gabriel dropped the poker and sat back in his seat. He looked defeated, as though the weight of the world were on his shoulders. "I didn't mean to frighten you, John."

He wrinkled his brow. "Why do you keep calling me that?"

Now it was Gabriel's turn to look confused. "What?"

"John. You keep calling me John. Is that my name?" It didn't sound familiar to him, but then, nothing sounded familiar.

Gabriel stared at him, and then his expression cleared. "Oh God, I'm sorry. It's John Doe, like unidentified bodies. John Doe. Get it?"

He did get it, although he didn't like the sound of it at all. "I'm not a John. And I'm not a body."

Although he very nearly had been. If it hadn't been for Gabriel, he'd have washed up somewhere for a passing stranger to find, and with no means of identifying him.

"But you don't remember your name?"

Gabriel's question broke into his morbid thoughts.

"No, but I'm not John." He was sure of that. It was about the only thing he was sure of.

"What else can I call you? I've got to call you something." Gabriel got to his feet. "Here, sign this."

He handed him a pen and paper. He stared at him blankly. "What?"

"Sign it. Don't think about it. Just sign it."

Maybe it was motor memory, but he scribbled something on the paper and handed it back. Gabriel stared at it for a moment. "Um… I'm not sure this helps." He gave him the paper. It was short and illegible, except for maybe an *S* at the start and maybe an *O* later on.

"I've no idea what it says."

"It was worth a try. I saw it on a cop show years ago. They couldn't work it out either, but it proves your memory is still there."

He had no idea how it was supposed to help, but Gabriel seemed excited about it and that was preferable to his anger. "Well, it's not John, anyway. What names begin with *S*?"

"Steve? Steven? Stan?" Gabriel suggested.

"I'm not a Stan," he said, somewhat indignantly.

Gabriel's lips twitched. "No, you're not a Stan."

Simon and Steven didn't sound right either, but then, nothing was right about the whole situation. He squinted harder at the paper. "I think the next letter is a *T*."

"Let's call you Steve until we find out what your name is."

"What?" He wrinkled his nose. He was so not a Steve.

"I've got to call you something, and if you won't accept John, then why not Steve?"

He pressed his lips together. Not Steve. "Call me Sam."

Gabriel squinted at the signature. "It doesn't look much like Sam."

Sam shrugged but wished he hadn't, because it set off his headache. "I don't know. That's the only name in my head that feels right. Not that anything feels right at the moment."

Gabriel held out his hand. "Hello, Sam. I'm Gabriel."

He shook it. "Thanks for saving me, Gabriel."

"You're welcome."

They were still holding hands when the lights flickered and died. They weren't in total darkness because the flames from the fire provided dancing shadows around the room. It could have been creepy, but somehow it was just warm and comforting.

Gabriel sighed and got to his feet. "I've got oil lamps in the closet."

"Does this happen a lot?" Sam asked. He shivered a little, as though the disappearance of the light had reduced the temperature in the room.

"Losing power? Yeah, the joys of living by the coast." Gabriel left the room, and Sam stared at the flickering flames. He returned a few minutes later with two lamps already lit.

"How do you feel?" Gabriel asked as he set the lamps on the small tables at either end of the sofa.

"My head hurts," he admitted.

"I'll find the paracetamol. Can you take it?"

"I don't know, but I'm willing to take the risk. My head is pounding."

Gabriel handed him two pills and water, and he swallowed them and grimaced at the taste.

"Sit back and close your eyes for a while," Gabriel suggested.

There wasn't anything else to do, so he took the advice and snuggled under the afghan. Sam fell asleep to the sound of the crackling flames muting the violence of the wind and rain outside.

VOICES DISTURBED his sleep. He recognised Gabriel's but not the other one, and he sat up, not wanting to be caught in a vulnerable position. Light streamed in through the window, but raindrops speckled the glass, and he could still hear the wind whistling around the cottage. He shivered as the night's events swept over him.

"Yeah, the power's still out all around the village. All the substations are out. Goodness knows when we'll get it back on. How's John?"

Sam frowned as the unknown voice called him John.

Then Gabriel spoke. "Sam."

"What?"

"His name is Sam, or something like that. I got him to sign a piece of paper."

"And it said Sam?"

"We couldn't read it, but Sam felt right."

Sam heard the doubt in Gabriel's tone.

"That's great!" At least the unknown voice sounded excited. "Now the police will have something to work on."

"He could've scribbled anything, and we wouldn't know if it's the truth," Gabriel pointed out.

Sam pressed his lips together as anger built inside him. Gabriel was virtually accusing him of lying.

"You think he's lying? Faking the amnesia?"

"We know nothing about him other than that I saved him from drowning," Gabriel said. "And I'm sure he's very grateful, but he could be faking the whole amnesia thing. We need to get him checked out. He could be a serial killer."

Oh, too much. "I'm not faking it. I'm not a serial killer," he called out, "And I'm not deaf."

There was a startled silence, and then Gabriel and another man, about Gabriel's age but shorter and with blond hair, entered the room. Both of them had the grace to look embarrassed. He glared at Gabriel, who flushed a deeper red.

"I'm sorry. I thought you were asleep," he managed, his voice gruff. "I'm sure you're not a serial killer."

"There's always a first time," he said tartly.

The stranger burst out laughing. "Oh Sam, I like you. You're going to be good for him."

Sam had no intention of being good for anyone. He just wanted to get out of here.

"Sam, this is Toby, my brother-in-law. He's also a doctor, and he just wants to check on you," Gabriel said. "Toby, this is Sam."

"It's good to see you awake," Toby said.

Sam glared at him. "I'm not faking the amnesia, and I'm not a serial killer. At least I don't think I am."

"How do you know?" Toby pointed out as he sat in the chair opposite him, although the grin on his face told him he wasn't being serious.

Of course, he didn't *know*, but wouldn't he feel it, inside him? "I've no desire to kill you. You,"—he stabbed a finger at Gabriel—"I'll reserve judgement."

Toby burst out laughing. "He's got you there. He's only just met you, and he already understands you."

Gabriel gave a wry smile. "Okay, maybe I asked for that."

"Maybe? You're lucky he didn't slap you around the face." Toby winked at Sam, and he smiled, although only at him. Gabriel was still in his bad books.

"I'm not a violent person," he said.

"As far you know," Toby pointed out. "*Joke*, it's a joke," he said as Sam turned on him.

"Shut up, Toby," Gabriel said. "You're the one who insisted I keep him here instead of taking him to your clinic."

Sam stared dubiously at Toby. "You did?"

"It wasn't like I had a choice. The roads are closed, and I needed the clinic free for emergencies. I knew you'd be well looked after by Gabriel." Toby rubbed his eyes, and Sam could see how tired he looked. "My brother-in-law may have the manners of a pig, but he's a good guy. He's always been a dick, but he gets better the longer you know him."

Sam furrowed his brow. "You're his brother-in-law?"

"His… um…."

"I told him about Jenny," Gabriel muttered.

Toby shot him a surprised look and then looked at Sam. "Jenny was my twin."

Sam could see the sadness and grief in his expression. Gabriel wasn't the only one in mourning. Sam didn't remember if he had any family, but he couldn't imagine what it would be like if a sibling, let alone a twin, died.

"We'll need to contact the police later this morning," Gabriel said. "Maybe someone's filed a missing persons report."

"Someone must know who I am." If he went out in the boat, wouldn't someone be worried when he didn't return?

"Of course they must. I'll make coffee while Toby takes a look at you." Gabriel must have caught Sam's dubious expression at being left alone with another stranger, because he smiled reassuringly and said, "Don't worry. Toby's a good doctor."

"And I'm much nicer than he is," Toby assured him.

Gabriel huffed and left the room, although Sam got the feeling it was mostly for show. He turned to see Toby eyeing him with frank curiosity.

"I'm fine," he said.

"Apart from the fact you can't remember who you are and you've got a killer headache?" Toby asked shrewdly.

Sam slumped back against the pillows. He thought he'd been doing a good job of hiding how much his head was pounding. "It hurts a little, but I'm not sure when I took the last pills."

"I'll ask Gabriel. Let me take a look at your eyes and take your blood pressure."

At his nod, Toby rested practised fingers on his pulse. Sam blinked when Toby shone a light into both his eyes.

"You're fine," he assured him, "although I'd like you to get a head X-ray, which I can't do at the clinic."

He disappeared for a moment, and Sam heard him talking to Gabriel, although their voices were low and this time he couldn't hear them. A minute later, Toby returned with a glass of water.

"You can take two more paracetamol."

Sam swallowed the tablets and leaned back, the throb of his head making him nauseated. "When will I get my memory back?"

Toby shrugged. "Who knows? In the cases I've come across, memories have returned in dribs and drabs."

"Gabriel says I was on a boat."

"An expensive one," Gabriel added as he came into the room with a tray. "Someone must be missing the boat."

"They might not realize it's gone in this weather," Toby pointed out.

Gabriel handed Sam a mug of coffee, already filled with milk and sugar. He didn't really want another coffee, but he didn't want to offend him by refusing.

Toby accepted his mug and took a sip with a sigh of pleasure. "God, I need this. It's been a long night."

The windows rattled as the storm raged on, and Sam shivered as he thought about what a lucky escape he'd had. A touch on his knee disturbed his thoughts, and he looked up to see Gabriel's concerned expression.

"Don't think about it. You're safe now, and we'll get you back home as soon as we can."

"I could've died." Sam could've kicked himself when he saw the pain on Gabriel's face and echoed in Toby's. "I'm sorry."

"It's okay," Toby said. "You've been through a rough night, and we're just thankful Gabriel found you."

He focused on Gabriel. "How did you see me?"

"I was on the clifftop. I was about to head back to the cottage when I saw your boat."

"You were standing on the clifftop in the storm?"

He gave a grim smile. "Yes."

Sam was about to ask another question when he caught Toby's warning look and decided to concentrate on his coffee. Then Toby yawned loudly, got to his feet, and stretched and rolled his shoulders.

"I'm off to see old Bob. Then I'm going to catch a few hours sleep before Damien pins me down to the bed."

Sam choked on his coffee, and Gabriel sighed.

"I'm sorry for my brother-in-law, Sam. He doesn't have a filter between his brain and his mouth."

Toby didn't look remotely cowed as he winked at Sam. "You'll get used to me soon. I'll bring Damien over later to meet you."

"Damien is your partner?" he hazarded.

"Husband. He's a bit of a dick, but I'll put a leash on him, and he'll behave."

Gabriel herded Toby out of the room. "Go away before you scare him off. Damien's not that bad."

"That's not what you usually say," Toby said.

"Just go."

Sam heard a rush of noise from the wind and rain. Then the door slammed, and there was peace again. Gabriel came back into the room and gave him a resigned look.

"I'm sorry, Toby's...."

"Unique?" Sam suggested.

"I was going to say something else, but unique will do." One side of his mouth quirked up. "How's your head?"

He rubbed his temples. The pain had muted from thumping rock to slow, aching jazz, but he was exhausted. "It's not too bad."

Gabriel shot him a knowing look. "Do you want another nap? You can use Michael's... the guest room."

Sam was about to say he was fine, but as though Gabriel had planted a suggestion in his mind, he yawned and flapped a hand over his mouth.

"Come on." Gabriel led him to a small bedroom at the back of the cottage, and his hesitation when he'd made the offer was explained the second Sam stepped into the bedroom. It had obviously been his son's bedroom, and it was equally obvious Gabriel hadn't touched the room since the day his son died, as toys and books tumbled over each other on the shelves. "The bedding is clean. I hope you don't mind dinosaurs. I know the bed is small, but I can sleep in it." Sam could picture the nights Gabriel had spent mourning his son in this room. "But if you'd prefer to sleep elsewhere…."

"It's fine," he assured him. "If it's all right with you."

Gabriel gave him that odd quirky smile again, and Sam ached at the pain in his expression. "It's okay. The bathroom is across the hall. Call me if you need anything."

Sam nodded and watched him walk out. He looked around the little boy's room and sighed. For a moment, he thought about asking to sleep on the sofa, away from ghosts, but exhaustion overtook him. He slipped under the duvet and closed his eyes. Despite his headache, darkness quickly crept into the corners of his mind, and he fell asleep, unaware of the storm battering its last breath against the cottage.

Chapter 3
Gabriel

Gabriel woke with a start, unsure why. He blinked and looked around, disorientated to find he'd been sleeping on the sofa. A cry pierced the silence and chased away the last vestiges of sleep as he shot to his feet, blood pounding in his ears.

Jenny!

There was another cry, and he frowned. It didn't sound like his Jenny.

"No! Why? No! Don't kill me!"

Sam!

He ran to the bedroom and flung back the door. The room was empty apart from the man in the bed, as it had been every time he'd checked on him. But this time he wasn't sleeping peacefully. Sam cried out again, begging someone not to kill him.

Gabriel recoiled, taken aback by the last sentence. Kill him? Who the hell was trying to kill him? Sam cried out again and smacked his hand against the wall. Gabriel moved swiftly to stop him hurting himself.

"Sam, stop! Wake up!"

"Don't hurt me. Please don't hurt me. Why can't I move?" He swung his arm and Gabriel caught it just before Sam smacked him in the face.

He captured both Sam's hands in his and they struggled. "Sam, you're safe. I promise, you're safe. Calm down." Sam opened his eyes and stared unseeing. Gabriel held on to him, speaking as calmly as he could, hoping his words would penetrate the haze he was in. "Sam, wake up. It's all right. You're safe now."

"Safe?" He sounded doubtful.

"Yes, you're safe, I promise." Gabriel traced soothing circles against his inner wrist.

"Don't kill me," he begged.

"I don't want to kill you. Just wake up now." Gabriel didn't want to let go of his hands, just in case.

Sam blinked rapidly and then looked at him and furrowed his brow as he focused properly for the first time. "Gabriel?"

Gabriel huffed out a sigh of relief and smiled. "Hey, you're awake now."

"Uh… is everything all right?"

"You were having a nightmare," Gabriel said.

He looked confused. "I was?"

"Yeah."

Gabriel searched for a way to ask what he'd been dreaming about, but before he could ask a question, Sam said, "Why're you holding my hands?"

"You nearly smacked me around the face." Tentatively he let go, as though he expected Sam to hit him again.

"I did?" He stared at his hands as though they weren't connected to him. Then he pushed back his tangled mess of bright copper hair. "I'm sorry for disturbing you."

He looked distressed, so Gabriel sought to reassure him. "It's okay. Can you remember anything about your dream?"

"No… no."

Gabriel wasn't sure he believed him. "You were begging for someone not to kill you."

Sam looked bewildered. "I don't remember."

Gabriel sat back, not wanting to push him when he'd obviously been so distressed. "Do you want to go back to sleep?"

As though his words were a trigger, Sam yawned and settled back down against the pillows. He closed his eyes, and Gabriel wondered if he wanted him to go away. Still concerned, he studied Sam for a moment. His red hair was in stark contrast to his pale skin, and his lashes swept over his cheeks.

Sam didn't stir again, and Gabriel left him to sleep and headed for his own bedroom. He needed a couple more hours sleep before he could face the day.

GABRIEL WAS disturbed a second time—not by voices but by loud knocking. He grumbled as he pushed back the duvet and headed to the front door. When he was two steps away, there was another round of thudding against it.

"Okay, okay, thumper. Quit doing that. I'm here." Gabriel flung open the door and had to duck quickly as Toby nearly thumped him on the nose. "Dammit, Tobes."

"Don't call me that," Toby snapped. "Thumper? Really? You took your own sweet time."

"I was asleep. You know that thing where you close your eyes and don't get up for several hours." Gabriel hastily stepped back as Toby brushed past him.

"Good for you. What do you want? A medal? Where's Sam?" Toby looked around as though he expected Sam to appear.

"I threw him out into the storm. Go look for him." Gabriel shut the front door with a snap and stalked after his visitor. "He's asleep. Go into the front room before you wake him."

As he turned, Toby had a smile playing about his lips.

"What?" Gabriel snapped.

Toby tilted his head. "Nothing. How is he?"

"Nothing my arse. You never mean *nothing*. What do you want?"

"I've come to see my patient."

"He's in Michael's room," Gabriel said reluctantly. He looked away as Toby's eyes opened comically wide. "What?"

Toby gently gripped his forearm. "Are you okay with him sleeping in Michael's room?"

Gabriel pressed his lips together. "I couldn't leave him on the sofa."

"He could've slept in your bed and you sleep on the sofa."

"Just leave it, Toby." Gabriel didn't need an inquest on where his guest had slept.

Thankfully Toby dropped the subject, instead hugging him swiftly with one arm. "I'll check on Sam, and you can make me a coffee."

"Why am I always making you coffee?" Gabriel grumbled.

"One, you never come over, and two, your tea is shite. Go, go." Toby shooed Gabriel towards the kitchen and headed into Michael's room, pausing to knock quietly at the door.

Gabriel grumbled under his breath the whole time he made the coffee, but by the time he placed a tray on his coffee table, his mood had improved. Toby still wasn't back, so Gabriel picked up his mug and went outside. The storm had blown over, and he sucked in the salt-tang of the sea air like a drug. Before he met Jenny, he'd been a city boy and had never visited Cornwall. Now he couldn't imagine living anywhere else.

He usually woke in the early morning and walked out to the cliffs to stand solitary vigil. Gabriel's stomach clenched as it always did when he thought about his wife and son. He and Jenny used to sit on the large rock at the top of the path, her slight body resting in his arms and her fragrant hair tickling his nose. When Michael arrived on the scene, he would sleep in the pushchair as Gabriel and Jenny traded kisses over a picnic.

Today he'd slept in, and there were more tourists on the cliff path. He said good morning to one or two who passed him, and then he took his place and looked out to the horizon. Sunlight sparkled on the tips of the waves as they chased across the sea only to break on the shore. Thanks to a strong wind, the sea was still choppy, and Gabriel couldn't see anyone in the water.

Footsteps crunching on the gravelled path disturbed Gabriel's reverie, and he looked over his shoulder to see Toby slowly ambling towards him as he sipped from the mug.

"Is he okay?" Gabriel asked.

"Sam is fine. He's remarkably resilient considering what he went through."

"Where is he?" Gabriel looked back to the cottage, worried about leaving him alone.

"He's gone for a shower. He knows we're out here." Toby sucked down a long swallow of coffee. "God, I needed that."

Gabriel saw the dark marks under Toby's blood-shot eyes. "Did you get any sleep last night?"

Toby yawned loudly. "Not more than half an hour at a time. But I'm off duty now. Dr Willis is on call, and I can go to bed."

"What're you doing here, then?" Gabriel asked in an exasperated tone.

"Checking on my patient."

Gabriel huffed. "I would've called if his condition had deteriorated."

"I meant you, dipshit." Toby turned to look at Gabriel. "You're the one I'm worried about."

There were so many ways Gabriel could have responded, but most of them involved curse words, and Toby was peculiarly sensitive to being sworn at. "What on earth for? I'm not the one who nearly died last night."

"You've got a strange man in your son's bed."

"You're the one who insisted I put him there," Gabriel pointed out.

"I just wanted to make sure you were keeping it together. I'm not blind to the fact I'm the only person you've allowed in the house since Jenny died."

"That's not true," Gabriel scoffed. He stopped as Toby raised an eyebrow. Damn, was it true? Gabriel thought back over the past year, but after the funerals, he couldn't remember any visitors. People had tried, but he'd sent them all away. Only Toby hadn't taken no for an answer. "It's only because I can't get rid of you. You're like a boil on my arse."

"Nice analogy." Toby snorted. "Thanks for that, Gabriel."

"You're welcome. Hopefully we can find out who Sam really is today, and he can go home." Gabriel slurped down the rest of his coffee. "I forgot to tell you, he had a nightmare. Kept saying someone was trying to kill him."

Toby furrowed his brow. "That doesn't sound good."

"I woke him up, but he didn't remember it," Gabriel said.

"I don't suppose it's something you'd want to remember. You should talk to him later."

It was Gabriel's turn to frown. "Do you think it's real or just a dream?"

"Who knows? We really need to get Sam to the hospital to get some X-rays. You can do that later when the road is open. The council said it should be clear by early afternoon. You can visit the police station at the same time and see if anyone has reported him missing."

"I've got work to do," Gabriel objected.

"Tough. He needs you," Toby snapped and then was overcome by another huge yawn. He handed his mug back to Gabriel. "I've got to sleep. I'll call you later."

Gabriel glared at Toby but managed a reasonably sympathetic "Get some rest."

Toby laid his hand on Gabriel's shoulder. "I know this is hard for you, but at the moment, Sam needs you."

A crunch on the gravel distracted Gabriel, and he looked over Toby's shoulder to see Sam picking his way towards them. He wasn't wearing any shoes, and he winced as the gravel dug into his feet.

"Jesus, Gabriel, you couldn't have found him some shoes?" Toby rushed over to help Sam with the last few steps until he reached the grassy section.

"I didn't think about it until I reached the gravel," Sam said.

"Shoes weren't the first thing on my mind last night," Gabriel pointed out. "Morning, Sam. How're you feeling?"

He smiled tentatively at him. "Better than I did last night."

Gabriel stared at him for a long moment, noticing his long copper hair caught by the light breeze and his dark, stormy eyes almost a deep blue-grey in the late morning light. He was jogged out of his study by a light cough.

"Well, I have to go, children. See you later." Toby beamed at Sam and gave an all-too-knowing smile at Gabriel. Without waiting for a response, he picked his way lightly across the gravel back in the direction of his cottage.

"Is he always like this?" Sam asked as Gabriel scowled at Toby's retreating back.

"Usually he's worse," Gabriel said sourly.

"You seem like an old married couple," he said and then, "God, I'm sorry, that was thoughtless of me."

Gabriel forced himself not to flinch at the pain of his words. "It's okay. We do bicker like that, even more than Jenny and I did. Toby's probably the only reason I haven't thrown myself off a cliff since the accident. He's yelled and stamped and made me live, even when all I wanted to do was be with Jenny and Michael." He stopped, unable to talk past the lump in his throat. Instead he looked at the horizon and thought about the number of times he'd stood in this exact spot, one breath away from taking the final step off the cliff. Gabriel startled as Sam laid a hand on his arm. He looked down at Sam's hand. He had fine, long fingers compared to Gabriel's and manicured nails, and there was a whiter band of skin where a ring used to be. Not the right finger for a wedding ring. Maybe he'd been robbed? Then how had he ended up in the boat?

"I'm so sorry," Sam said gently.

Gabriel gathered himself together and forced himself to smile. He shouldn't be the one worrying about him. From the way Sam's look eased, he was at least partially successful. "Would you like something to eat?"

Sam nodded. "I *am* hungry. Toast? I think I like toast."

"I can do toast. I've even got homemade strawberry jam."

"You make jam?"

At Sam's sceptical look, Gabriel laughed, and it eased the knot inside him. "You think I can't make jam?"

"I… er…." Sam searched for a way to extract his foot from his mouth. "It doesn't seem like something you'd do. I didn't mean to be rude."

Gabriel gave another chuckle. "It's okay. I can't make jam. Toby made it. It's his hobby. It helps clear his mind."

"In which case, it's probably safe to try it." Sam smirked, and they both laughed.

"Come on." Gabriel looked at the gravel. "Do you want me to carry you across the stones?"

Sam scoffed. "I can walk across gravel."

"It's up to you." He watched as Sam started back to the cottage, wincing at every step. "Stay there. No one is around to see you lose a little dignity."

Sam hesitated and then said, "Please. I was an idiot to come out without shoes on."

Gabriel picked him up, and Sam wound his arms around his neck. His nose itched as Sam's hair got in his face, but he felt light in his arms, so different from the previous night when he'd been weighed down by sodden clothes. Gabriel crunched across the stones to the grass near his cottage. "I'll carry you to the door."

"Gabriel?"

He growled under his breath and turned to see Sandra Whitely, one of his neighbours, looking at him, her eyebrows lost under her fringe. Gabriel set Sam down on a patch of grass free from stones and pasted a smile on for his neighbour.

"Morning, Sandra."

"Morning, Gabriel. You have… company?"

"Sam, this is Sandra, one of my neighbours. Sandra, this is Sam. He's… er… staying with me for a few days."

"Pleased to meet you." Sandra held out her hand and then narrowed her eyes, tilting her head to study Sam closely. "Are those Jenny's clothes?"

Sam glanced at Gabriel and then nodded. "Gabriel kindly loaned me these as mine got wet in the storm."

"You're staying at Gabriel's place?"

Gabriel gritted his teeth at the wealth of meaning implied in her voice. "Sam is visiting for a couple of days."

Sandra shot him an incredulous look. "You have a visitor?"

Gabriel growled under his breath. "Must go, Sandra. See you later." He put a hand at the small of Sam's back, guided him away from his nosy neighbour, and sighed with relief when he shut the door. "Dammit."

Sam looked over his shoulder at him. "Am I missing something?"

"They're not used to seeing me with guests," Gabriel said shortly. "I've not had many guests since Jenny and Michael died." None at all, according to Toby.

His expression softened. "That's understandable. I can't imagine you've felt like being sociable."

"No. But my friends think it's about time I moved on. I give it five minutes before Brian, her husband, is banging on the door."

He turned and shook his head. "They're wrong. You don't move on from something like that. You learn to live with it, but it's not something you leave behind. When my parents died I...." Sam stared up at him, his breath catching. "My parents are dead."

Gabriel saw the tears brim in his eyes. "I'm so sorry. You remember this?"

"I don't know how, but I know. I can feel it inside." He clenched a fist over his heart.

They stared at each other for a moment, and Gabriel felt a knot ease inside. It was a relief to be with someone who understood. Everyone had been sympathetic since his world fell apart, but now they were getting impatient with his grief, and he felt their impatience pressing down on him like a heavy weight.

He sighed and rubbed his eyes. "Do you want a coffee?"

"I hate coffee," Sam admitted. Then his eyes opened wide. "Wow, I remember that too."

Gabriel grinned at him. "What would you rather drink?"

"I don't know," he admitted with a slight laugh. "What do you suggest?"

"I think I've got tea bags somewhere." Gabriel went into the kitchen and opened a cupboard. He spotted a couple of boxes and let out a triumphant cry. "You're in luck. Normal tea or mint tea?" He held the two boxes out to Sam. "I have to confess I don't know how long they've been in there."

"I'll take the risk," Sam said. "I survived a storm. I can risk an old teabag." Gabriel did his best to hold back a wince as he took the kettle over to the sink, but Sam must have realised he'd touched a nerve, because he said, "I'm sorry, Gabriel. I seem to be saying that a lot today."

Gabriel shut off the tap and turned to look at him. "It's okay. You did survive. I can't hate you for that."

"I survived because of you," he pointed out.

"That's true." Gabriel switched on the kettle. "I guess it's all my fault. Milk and sugar?"

"Eh?"

"Your tea. Milk and sugar. Don't think, just answer."

"A little milk and two sugars," he said without hesitation. "I've no idea if that's right or not."

Gabriel looked in the box of tea bags. "You've got a few times to get it right."

Chapter 4
Sam

Sam took a tentative sip of the tea and grinned at Gabriel. "Perfect."

Gabriel raised a dark eyebrow. "How do you keep that figure if you drink tea with two sugars?"

"I...." He looked down at his flat belly and lean hips. "I have no idea."

"Well, if I catch you jogging along the cliffs, we'll know how."

He hadn't finished the mug when there was a knock at the door. Gabriel frowned, his thick brows knitting together. He stomped over to the front door and flung it open.

"Brian," he said, his lack of enthusiasm obvious.

Sam held back a smile. Gabriel had been spot on about his neighbours.

Brian—Sam judged him to be around forty—stood on his doorstep, shifting restlessly from foot to foot. "I... er...." His gaze landed on Sam, and his eyes widened. "You have a...."

"A guest. Yes. I have a guest," Gabriel snapped. "Brian, this is Sam. Sam, this is Brian Whitely, a neighbour. Is that it? Bye, then."

From Gabriel's angry tone, Sam expected him to slam the door in Brian's face, but Brian stuck his arm out and walked into the cottage, a broad smile on his face as he headed for Sam.

"Really pleased to meet you. Sam was it?" He held out his hand to him.

Sam looked for somewhere to put his mug and found a side table. Then he stood and took Brian's hand. From his vigorous handshake, he really was pleased to make Sam's acquaintance. "Pleased to meet you, Brian. You're Gabriel's neighbour?"

"We've been neighbours for years," Brian said. "Goodness, I didn't believe Sandra when she said Gabriel had a guest, but here you are."

After a moment of awkwardly smiling at each other, Sam withdrew his hand and looked around for his tea. "Sandra is your wife?"

"Oh yes. She and Jenny were friends at school." Brian's smiled faded. "Did you ever meet Jenny?"

Sam shook his head. "I wasn't lucky enough to meet her. I only met Gabriel yesterday."

Brian turned on Gabriel. "That was quick, man. I mean—"

Sighing, Gabriel rubbed his forehead. "Don't get ahead of yourself. I spotted Sam's boat in the storm. I saw it was in trouble, so I took the dinghy out."

"It was a good thing he did. I was unconscious, and my boat was taking on water. If it hadn't been for him, I'd have drowned." Sam shivered as he thought about it.

"Don't," Gabriel said gruffly and squeezed his arm. "You're safe now."

Sam caught Brian's wide-eyed curious expression and decided to focus on his tea. He had no idea how much Gabriel wanted to let on about him.

"Well, I—" Brian started, but Gabriel cut him off.

"Once the tree is cleared off the road, we're going to see about getting Sam home. Anyway, nice to see you again, Brian. Is that all?"

This time Brian took the hint and said, "I must be getting back. Nice to meet you, Sam."

Sam smiled. "And you, Brian."

Once the door was closed on his very curious neighbour, Gabriel rested his head on the wood and let out a long sigh. "The whole village is going to know now."

Sam drew up his knees and wrapped his arms around his legs. "I'm sorry, Gabriel."

"It's not your fault."

It would have been more convincing if Gabriel had managed to look at him instead of talking to the door.

"Gabriel, look at me."

Gabriel turned, reluctance oozing from him. If Sam had known him better, he would have walked over and taken him in his arms for a comforting hug, but he barely knew the man apart from his pain.

"At least my arrival will give the village something new to gossip about," Sam suggested.

Gabriel gave a bark of laughter. "You understand village life."

"It's the same everywhere." Sam paused. "At least, I think it is."

"You're right, and especially here." Gabriel sat down in his chair and expelled a long breath. "I love my neighbours, but you can't keep any secrets."

"It didn't help that Sandra caught me in your arms," Sam pointed out, grinning as Gabriel groaned. "By the time it gets back to Toby, I'll be wearing a silk dress and called Samantha."

Gabriel's face snorted. "Knowing Toby, he'd come over with fashion tips."

Sam stared, then burst out laughing. From what little he'd seen of Toby, he could imagine that too. "What was it like? Being married to a twin?" He saw the grief cross Gabriel's face and cursed his wayward thoughts. Then Gabriel gave a wistful smile.

"Well, I didn't have to worry about kissing the wrong twin."

"Obviously not."

"Toby was already going out with Damien when we met. He was cute."

"He's cute now," Sam said without thinking. "Wait, did you just say he was cute?"

Gabriel gave a wicked grin, and Sam's heart fluttered. Christ, the man was hot.

"I did."

"You're bi?"

"Yeah, but once Toby introduced me to Jenny, she was it for me. I took one look into her eyes and never looked at anyone else again. Toby was the same with Damien."

Sam couldn't imagine meeting someone who he wanted to spend the rest of his life with. Then again, maybe he was married. He looked at Gabriel's left hand. He still wore his wedding ring. Sam stretched out his hands. There was a lighter band of skin on the middle finger of his right hand as if a ring had once been there, but nothing on his left hand.

"What are you thinking?" Gabriel asked.

"If I've left someone behind. I don't think I wear a wedding ring." He stared at Gabriel. "I don't know. I don't feel anything. I can't remember anything."

He could feel cloying panic sweeping over him, his heart started beating faster, and for a moment, his vision blurred.

Someone tried to kill me.

The sharp tug of his hair trapped beneath his shoulders roused him from the cold darkness. His body hurt from head to toe, but as hard as he tried, he couldn't seem to move his limbs to wriggle into a better position. It was as though the connection between his brain and body had been severed. Whatever he was lying on was hard and uncomfortable, and a harsh disinfectant smell clung to the back of his throat.

He tried to open his eyes to make sense of what was happening, but his eyelids had the same heavy weights attached to them as his arms and legs. He fought to calm the rising panic that threatened to overwhelm him. There had to be a simple explanation. Perhaps he'd fallen and bumped his head. Maybe he hurt his neck, and that's why he couldn't move. All he needed was to attract someone's attention, but he couldn't freakin' move.

He couldn't move!

Sam tried to struggle as rough hands gripped his arms, but he was hauled over someone's shoulder as though he were nothing more than a sack of potatoes. Sickness rose in his throat, and Sam swallowed hard. The man reeked of sweat and cigarette smoke, which didn't help the nausea, and his cheek rubbed painfully against a coarse jacket as he bumped against the man's back.

"Sam, Sam, listen to me. It's okay. Just breathe."

He needed to calm the hell down and take deep breaths, but even that seemed like a struggle, and the acrid smell from the floor made him feel nauseated. Sam focused on his breathing. He tried to count, but it was hard to focus, and he'd miss a few numbers and start over again.

"In. Out. In. Out."

A voice, not his own, kept murmuring the same thing. A firm, kind, male voice. It didn't sound as if he wanted to harm Sam.

Sam slowed his breathing in rhythm with the voice and his breathing steadied and his heart slowed.

"Open your eyes."

His eyes were closed? He opened them to find Gabriel sitting on the coffee table, concern in his grey eyes and his hands wrapped around Sam's.

"Hey, welcome back," Gabriel said, a faint smile curving his lips.

"What happened?"

Sam was disorientated, still lost in fear and panic.

"I think you had a panic attack," Gabriel said.

"It felt so real." Sam shuddered and Gabriel held his hands tighter. It was grounding and Sam didn't want Gabriel to take his hands away.

"I think you're fine, but I'll get Toby to take a look at you."

Sam shook his head. "I'm all right. It's all a bit overwhelming, you know?"

"I know." Gabriel stayed where he was for a few minutes and then moved back to his chair.

Sam clasped his hands together, missing Gabriel's warmth. He shivered, and Gabriel noticed.

"Why don't you put the throw around your shoulders?"

Gabriel got up immediately and wrapped the afghan around Sam's shoulders, leaning in to smooth it down Sam's back.

Gabriel's face was so close. Sam looked up and held his breath. For an instant he thought Gabriel was going to kiss him, but then the man's eyes grew hooded and he took a step back. Sam reached a hand out to him. "Gabriel, I...."

"I... have to get milk." Gabriel rushed away, grabbing his wallet and hurrying outside, leaving Sam alone in the cottage.

Sam wrapped his hands around the cooling mug of tea, not sure whether to run after him and offer comfort or leave him alone, but he had no shoes, and rummaging through the wardrobes and cupboards while he was alone seemed wrong. He felt alone and vulnerable, and that feeling was alien to him. Sam didn't know how he knew that, but he did.

"You're lucky he's a good guy," he muttered.

He looked around for something to do, but the place was clean and tidy. Gabriel's bedroom door was shut, and it seemed like another barrier. He wasn't about to open it without invitation. Eventually, Sam sat down on the sofa and stared at his hands as if they would give him the answers to all his questions. They were soft, well-manicured, but with calluses on his fingertips, as if he did something specific that caused the hard skin.

He thought back to his panic attack. It had scared him, not being able to move.

"Was it real? Did it really happen?" he murmured. No one answered him.

It had *seemed* real. The smells, the sounds. Even the feel of the weave of the man's jacket on his cheek. How could he imagine that? Was he having dreams, nightmares, or flashbacks? How had he ended up on the boat? No matter how hard he tried, he couldn't remember that. It was so damned frustrating.

He was distracted by a deep rumbling sound and the mugs on the table rattled and one moved close to the edge. Sam pushed it back. What the hell was that? Gabriel! Was he all right? Sam leapt to his feet, ready to go and find him, but a wave of pain shot through his head and he sat back down, his head in his hands.

He wasn't going anywhere for a moment. Sam closed his eyes, trying to breathe through the pain. Okay then. He'd stay here until he could move and then look for Gabriel.

Chapter 5
Gabriel

Gabriel needed to get out of the cottage and away from Sam. His unwanted visitor was too much for him to deal with. He'd told Toby it was a bad idea to have anyone else in the house, and look what happened. He'd nearly kissed Sam, been so close to him he could smell the sweet tea on Sam's breath, the citrus scent of his shampoo in Sam's bright hair. Sam would have been horrified. The cottage was Gabriel's home, and he needed it back. Alone.

He shoved his hands into his jacket, put his head down, and strode as fast as he could without looking as though he were running. He didn't know where he was going, just that he had to be away from the cottage and temptation and he had to buy milk. Gabriel knew he was being childish. He could hear Toby's voice in his head, telling him to get over himself. When had Toby replaced his mother as his voice of conscience?

Gabriel had just reached the old coastal road when the ground shook so hard it almost forced him to his knees. He staggered and braced to keep his balance. Then he grabbed the low wall nearby to hang on to as he wondered if the earth was about to open up and swallow him whole in a thunderclap. He tried to focus, even as the world shook around him. The noise was ahead of him, not behind. Sam was safe in the cottage. Relief flooded through him before he pushed it aside. More shaking and intense noise. Gabriel stayed where he was until the shaking stopped.

He waited for a few seconds. The silence was as deafening as the noise had been. Then Gabriel heard shouting ahead of him and ran towards the voices. It was coming from around the bend.

Gabriel turned the corner and immediately saw the cause of the problem. Not just one tree this time. A landslip had brought trees, boulders, and tonnes of earth down onto the houses and road below. The road was blocked for several hundred yards. Gabriel tried to remember the sequence of houses along this stretch. It was the main road out of the village and was lined with small bungalows and cottages. If he remembered rightly, there were three or four cottages on this side. The landslide had effectively covered the bend of the road.

Gabriel's heart faltered. What if people were trapped in their houses? The village had suffered a tragedy just after the turn of the twentieth century when a catastrophic landslip engulfed half the village. No one was alive from that time, but all the locals had lost family, Toby and Jenny included.

Gabriel patted his pocket. Thank God he had the muscle memory to pick up his phone before his flight from the cottage. His first call was to Toby.

"Is Sam okay?" Toby said by way of greeting. "I'm getting my shoes on. What was the noise?"

"He's fine. There's been a landslip on the old coast road by Bert Wooding's cottage. It's large, Toby. I don't know of any casualties yet."

"Evacuate everyone to the centre. Damien can take care of them," Toby said crisply, and Gabriel nodded, unseen, as his brother-in-law went into take-charge mode. "I'll be there in five minutes. I'll get Damien to call the emergency services."

"Get the council and highways services here too. I don't know how stable the banks are."

"Damien knows what to do."

Gabriel disconnected the call and ran to join the people surrounding the slip. Old Mrs Thomas came out of her gate looking tired and confused as he jogged past. She was over eighty, and Gabriel was very fond of her.

"What just happened, Gabriel. Was it a bomb?" Her voice was shaky and her eyes wide and frightened.

Although he was anxious to see what happened, he stopped and took her shaking hands as she reached out to him. "It was a landslide, Mrs Thomas, by Bert and Elsie Wooding's place."

"Oh dear, are they all right?" She looked distressed.

"I'll find out," he promised.

One of her neighbours came out of her bungalow looking equally confused. Gabriel didn't know her name, as she'd moved into the village in the past year.

"What just happened? I thought it was an earthquake," she said. Then she spotted the landslip. "Oh my God. Is everyone all right?"

"I don't know yet," Gabriel told her. "You need to evacuate your house for now. Dr Maris has set up an evacuation centre at his clinic."

"Evacuate? Do I have to? I've got dinner on."

Gabriel stared at her. Her life was in danger and she was worried about dinner? "We don't know how stable the banks are. There could be more landslides. If that bank comes down it could cover the whole road."

A burly middle-aged man with dark grey hair joined them. He nodded at Gabriel. "Pennant, good to see you here. We'll need you." He turned to the woman. "Do what he says, Marion. The whole bank is unstable. The last thing we need is to lose more houses."

Marion looked frightened. "I'll turn off the oven, Tim. Where shall we go?"

"Take Mrs Thomas with you to Dr Maris's clinic," Gabriel said. "Damien is setting up an evacuation centre. Can you get her to go with you?"

With that simple task, Marion went from combative to helpful. "Leave it with me. Just wait while I turn off the oven." She vanished into her house and reappeared a moment later with her coat and a blanket.

Mrs Thomas stood between Gabriel and Tim, looking like a tiny bewildered owl. Gabriel held her hands and assured her everything would be fine, and no, it wasn't a bomb. Marion put the blanket and her arm around the elderly lady and walked away, promising a nice cup of tea and a nice shortbread once she got to that nice doctor's place.

Gabriel looked at Tim. "Thanks for backing me up."

"No problem. You've got the evac centre set up and emergencies on the way?"

Gabriel nodded. "Plus the council and highways agencies. Tell me what we've got?"

They strode back to the edge of the slip, Tim talking as they walked. "Three houses partially covered. The bulk of the rocks and dirt missed the houses, but those trees are threatening to fall. After that storm, the whole bank could come down. I've been telling the council for months it was unstable. That tree fell for a reason. The team from the council only left about an hour ago."

"Any casualties?" Gabriel asked.

"Not at the moment. That house—" Tim pointed to the middle house, partially buried under the weight of soil and boulders. "My wife says the family is away. She's going to call them. The other two we don't know. Bert and Elsie could be at their daughter's."

"We need to get the surrounding houses evacuated first. What about the houses on the other side?"

"I'm coordinating with my brother-in-law, working the other side of the slip. There are fewer houses that side, as it's almost at the edge of the village. That's my home." Tim pointed to a grey stone cottage on the side of the road, constructed much like Gabriel's own.

They reached the crowd of people by the slip.

Gabriel assessed the crowd, who were predominately elderly couples. They weren't going to be much help with any rescue attempt.

"People, Dr Maris is opening the clinic for an evacuation point. We need to get everyone out of their houses and to the clinic now!" Tim said. "If this slip blocked the road, a more catastrophic one could cover the homes on both sides of the road."

"We'll start knocking on doors," one of the older men in the crowd said. "Ellen, you're with me. Johnny, do the other side. Don't let anyone say no."

Johnny was a younger version of him and built like a brick outhouse. If anyone refused, he'd probably pick them up bodily and cart them over his shoulder to the clinic. Gabriel knew from experience some of the villagers were stubborn as hell.

"Who owns the cottage on the left?" Gabriel asked.

He'd known the previous owners, but they'd been elderly. From the toys and swing in the front garden, the place had changed hands without him realising. Life had gone on around him, and he hadn't even noticed.

"Shaun and Janice moved to be near their daughter. A young family own it now. I don't really know them. They keep themselves to themselves." Tim sounded faintly disapproving, and Gabriel remembered Tim was a man of the community. He liked to know what was going on in his village. Jenny had been like that—loved by everyone and always ready to help out.

"We know one house is empty. Bert and Elsie might be away. It's just this one."

Johnny jogged up to them. "My neighbour said she saw the mum going into the village about half an hour ago. I'm going to find her."

He loped away on his mission, and Gabriel felt some of the tension recede. All three houses possibly empty. How fortunate was that? They could wait until highways services arrived. If the slip had occurred a couple of hundred yards further on, more houses and local shops would have been affected and the casualty rate higher. This was the least occupied part of the road. If they managed to shore up the bank before any further slippage, it would be fine.

The crack reverberated like a gunshot. Gabriel instinctively ducked, and Tim cried out as a large tree split as though someone had swung a giant axe at it. It careered down the slope into the first house, crumpling one side as though it were cardboard. More stones and boulders and dirt piled down behind it.

The silence left behind was almost as shocking, broken only by a few smaller stones bouncing down the road.

"Fuck!" Tim uttered succinctly.

Gabriel agreed with that sentiment. He coughed, and the dust-filled air cloyed at the back of his throat.

He was about to suggest they move the hell out of the way of any further landslides when a woman in a long summer dress ran up the road, crying and screaming, "Where's my daughter? Where's my daughter?"

"Who's this?" he asked Tim.

"She lives there." Tim pointed to the cottage now barely visible under the weight of dirt and trees.

Gabriel caught the woman as she ran past him, heading for the cottage. "Stop, ma'am, you can't go in there."

She tore her arm out of his grasp. "My kid's in there." Fear was in her eyes and trembling frame.

Déjà vu coiled in the pit of Gabriel's belly. "You left your child in there alone?"

"Maisie didn't want to come with me, and I was only going to be five minutes." Her face screwed up as though she was about to cry. "I've got to get her out of there."

"Where was she?" Gabriel asked.

"I left her watching TV in the back room. We've got to get her out."

The back of the cottage had almost been completely demolished by the tree. Gabriel looked at Tim, who just shook his head slightly. If the little girl had been in the back room, there was little chance of her being alive.

"I'm going to call my brother-in-law," Tim said as he walked away, phone pressed to his ear.

Gabriel had heard the sirens and seen the blue flashing lights on the other side of the landslip, but there was no way they could get over here yet. The whole area was too unstable. But they had to get the little girl out fast. Tim was arguing with someone, and Gabriel guessed he was being told what Gabriel had just thought. No chance of a rescue yet.

"Maisie is in there. I've got to get her. Why isn't anyone helping me?"

The woman bolted towards the cottage, but Gabriel lunged forward and grabbed her, spinning her into Tim's arms.

"You take her. I'm going in."

"You can't do that. It's too unstable," Tim protested.

"Someone has to," Gabriel said grimly.

"You can't take that risk!"

"One more slip, and that little girl is…." He stopped, but he knew by Tim's pursed lips that he'd got the meaning. One more slip of earth and the cottage would be gone.

"If anything happens, you'll be caught in it."

Gabriel shrugged. "What have I got to lose?"

Tim grimaced, knowing what Gabriel wasn't saying.

It was a foolhardy risk of his own life, but he'd already lost everything that mattered to him. If the cottage came down on his head, he'd be with his family again.

Sam.

He pushed away the thought of the young man waking up alone. Toby would take care of him. He walked towards the cottage, shoved open the gate and passed an upturned plastic ride-along car that was half buried by earth and small stones. Gabriel trod carefully along the remains of the path as he assessed how best to find Maisie. The only reason the cottage wasn't completely demolished was its stone structure. If it were timber framed, it would be gone by now.

He stood still and listened intently, tuning out the sounds around him and focusing on the one thing he needed to hear.

"Maisie?"

Nothing.

Gabriel picked his way over the rubble around the side of the cottage, taking care with each footstep not to dislodge anything that could set off another slip.

He reached the back and sucked in a breath. The scene was even worse than it had seemed from the road. The back of the cottage had completely vanished, and the tree trunks had acted like two javelins and pierced through the floors. There was no chance a small child could have survived.

"Maisie?"

The silence haunted him. He remembered yelling for Jenny and Michael until his throat was raw and Damien had dragged him away from the beach, still screaming their names.

"Mummy?"

It was so quiet he barely heard it. Gabriel blinked. "Maisie? Is that you?"

Oh my God, she was alive. Where the hell was she?

"Yes. Where's Mummy?" The tiny little voice sounded scared.

"She's outside waiting for you, sweetheart. My name is Gabe. I've come to find you. Do you know where you are?"

"I'm in the little toilet. I can't open the door. It's stuck. I waited for Mummy to come back and open the door, but she didn't. I was scared."

Poor little mite. He was going to have words with her mum when this was all over.

Gabe studied the structure of the part of the house that wasn't destroyed. The cottages in the village had been built for the workers in the local mines and were the same basic structure. Over the years, some homeowners had converted the cupboard under the stairs into a downstairs bathroom. There was just space enough for a toilet and sink.

"Maisie, is the toilet under the stairs?"

"Yes."

Heaving in a shaky breath, Gabriel surveyed the area. The stairs were still intact, the tree having speared either side.

"Maisie, I'm going to come and get you, but you have to stay still, okay?"

"Okay, Gabe."

Gabriel looked at the slope visible behind the house. Tim was right. It wouldn't take much to bring it down, but if he waited for the emergency services, it could be too late.

He edged around the tree and to the stairs, careful of live electrical cables. The cupboard door was visible. He and Michael had always called the under-stairs cupboard Harry Potter's bedroom. The door was blocked by two large boulders, too heavy to carry.

"Maisie, I'm outside the door, but there are stones in the way."

"There weren't stones there when I went into the toilet." Maisie sounded puzzled. "Who put them there?"

Gabriel closed his eyes. The little girl had no idea of the devastation that had just been wreaked around her. "You just hang tight, Maisie. You'll be free in no time."

If he moved the stones, was he going to bring the roof down on top of him? He had no choice. There was just enough space to move them one at a time. He cleared the area to give the boulders room to move and put every ounce of energy he had into shifting the nearest one. At first he thought it was going to be impossible. Sweat ran down between his shoulder blades as he heaved, but then it moved, just a fraction. He pushed again, and it rolled an inch.

"Oh, you beauty," he cooed, wiping the sweat from his eyes.

Another heave and the stone was clear. The house shook a little. Gabriel froze, but nothing happened.

"Nearly done, Maisie," he said, although it was more to reassure himself.

"I want to see Mummy." Maisie sounded on the verge of tears.

"Very soon, sweetheart."

He took the chance and pushed the second one. It didn't budge, and he had a frustrating moment before he realised it was caught on the carpet. He sorted that, and the boulder moved more easily than the first one had. Then he tried the door. It was stuck, and he cursed under his breath. If he yanked hard, would it destabilise the stairs?

There was one way to find out. He wrenched at the door, and it opened, but everything creaked.

A little girl with long pale blonde hair gave him a watery smile that turned into a frown when Gabriel pushed his way into the bathroom.

He smiled at her. "Hello Maisie."

"What are you doing, Gabe? I want to see Mummy."

"Two minutes, sweetheart," he promised.

He heard a few crashes, but nothing moved. After a moment's silence, Maisie stared up at him with beautiful blue eyes. "Can we go now?"

"Yes, we can," he promised her. "Maisie, something happened to your house. I need to carry you out, okay?"

"Okay."

Gabriel eased open the door, grateful nothing had fallen in front of it. He picked Maisie up and headed out of the house as carefully as he could.

She stared around her, wide-eyed. "Did I do this? Is Mummy going to shout at me?"

He chuckled. "No, Maisie, you didn't do this."

Something stung his cheek, and he flinched.

Maisie pointed just under his eye. "The stone cut you."

"Bad stone," he growled, and she chuckled.

They made it back to the front garden without incident. He heard Maisie's mum's gasp and run towards them, and Maisie burst into tears, wriggling to be put down. As soon as it was safe, he set Maisie on the ground, and she ran to her mum, saying sorry over and over. Her mum wrapped her in her arms and cried harder.

"I bet that's the last time she leaves her to pop to the shops," Tim muttered to Gabriel.

Gabriel didn't disagree.

"What the hell did you think you were doing?" Toby said in an icy tone from behind Gabriel.

Gabriel turned slowly to see his furious brother-in-law glaring at him. "Rescuing a little girl."

"Are you insane? You went in there without equipment, without knowing if she was alive. You could have died."

The cottage collapsed without warning, and dust and stones shot up in the air as the building folded in on itself. When they could see again, the stairs were gone.

"If Maisie had still been trapped in there, she'd be dead," Gabriel said quietly. "I had to take the chance."

Toby grabbed him into a rough hug. "I could have lost you."

Gabriel felt him shake in his arms and held him close. His eyes prickled, and he realised, not for the first time, how much he loved his brother-in-law. "You won't get rid of me that easily."

Toby pulled back and stared into Gabriel's eyes. "You promise."

It was more than a throwaway promise. Gabriel knew what Toby was demanding.

"I promise, Tobes. I promise."

Toby hauled him closer until Gabriel protested that he needed to breathe.

Chapter 6
Sam

SOMETHING WOKE him. He was trapped inside his body again. Oh God, had they found him? Who were they? They talked over him as though he weren't there. Move, move! He tried to open his eyes, curl his fingers, do *something*, but nothing worked. His body was his prison again.

Nothing made sense. What had happened to him? Had he had an accident? Where was he? Who were these people? Was he being abducted? Fear threatened to overwhelm him again no matter how hard he tried to remain calm.

"This is wrong. Why do we have to do this?"

Who *was* speaking?

Sam tamped down the panic and tried to focus on what they were saying. He needed some clue, anything to make sense of what was happening.

"'Cause he told us to."

"But—"

"Shut up, Mitchell." The voice sounded angry.

Mitchell? Sam knew that name. It took a minute to think through the fog in his brain to identify the face. Mitchell. There was a Mitchell who worked for the management company as a security guard. Billy Mitchell, a big lout of a man with an ill-fitting suit and a permanent scowl. He made Sam feel uncomfortable, but he was good at his job. People stayed the hell away from Sam when Mitchell was by his side. Was this the same guy? The man carrying him felt solid and muscled. It could be him.

How had he ended up over the shoulder of a man who worked for the family? Had he been kidnapped? Was Mitchell rescuing him? His senses, dulled as they were, screamed that something was wrong. Was there a fire? He couldn't smell smoke, but he didn't trust his body to give him the right information.

Think! Think!

Someone touched his shoulder, and he screamed, desperate to get away from the people about to kill him!

"Sam, you've got to wake up. It's me, Toby. You're all right. You're safe."

Sam opened his eyes to see the doctor standing over him, a look of concern on his face. "T-Toby?"

"You were having a nightmare."

"I dreamt people were trying to kill me." He shuddered and wrapped his arms around himself.

Toby sat down on one of the chairs. "Is this something you remember?"

He shook his head. "I hope not. It's just a dream, but I've had it before."

"Gabriel mentioned it," Toby said, his brow furrowed. "I'll talk to you about this later."

"Is Gabriel here? He… left earlier, and I haven't seen him." Sam stumbled over what to say.

Toby's eyes narrowed, but he merely said, "He's over at my clinic."

Sam sat up. "Is he all right?"

"After he left you, he went for a walk. There was a landslide on the old coast road. He helped to rescue a trapped child."

The rumbling from earlier. Dammit, Sam should have gone looking for Gabriel.

"Oh my God. is everyone okay?"

"We've got two unaccounted for, but the little girl is safe. The two that are missing might be on holiday. We haven't had a chance to check yet."

"You said Gabriel was at your clinic?"

"He got hit by a stone on his cheek as he pulled her free. Gabriel's fine. He just needed the wound cleaned and to be given a tetanus shot."

"Does he make a habit of rescuing people?" Sam asked.

Toby's lips twisted wryly. "Our Gabriel used to be a bit of an action man, but you were the first for a while. He didn't have much choice this afternoon. He was right by the old coast road when it happened."

"Is he coming home?" Sam flushed, realising how presumptuous that sounded. This wasn't his home, and he had no claim on Gabriel's time.

"He's going to wait until he knows whether Bert and Elsie Wooding are trapped. Their neighbour thinks they went to their daughter's this morning."

"Is there anything I can do to help?" He didn't want to sit around, not when people were in need.

Toby gave him an approving smile. "How are you at making sandwiches?"

"What are sandwiches?" he asked.

Toby opened his mouth to answer, but then he caught Sam's sly smile. "You haven't lost your sense of humour, I see."

"I'm sorry." He grinned as Toby huffed and stood.

"Come on, then."

They got to the door before Sam stopped. "I haven't got any shoes."

Toby opened the tall, thin cupboard by the front door and pulled out a pair of brown suede walking boots. "These are a size eight. They were too big for Jenny. She never wore them. Wait, you'll need socks."

"I don't have any socks."

"Wait here." Toby ran over to Gabriel's bedroom, obviously not worried about the closed door. He returned with another T-shirt, and a sweater. He threw a pair of socks to Sam. "Gabriel is filthy. He'll appreciate the clean clothes."

Sam quickly put on the socks and boots, which were a little large, but at this point he didn't care. He just wanted to check for himself that Gabriel was all right. He didn't want to examine too closely why he was concerned for Gabriel's welfare, except that Gabriel had risked his life for him yesterday. That had to mean something.

As Toby led him down the path, he looked around curiously. The cottage seemed completely isolated, but then they turned a corner onto a narrow road that led to a row of cottages. Toby stopped at the first house and pushed open the gate. This one was bigger than Gabriel's—two stories, with an extension on the side. It was pretty, with a cottage garden he envied. Someone had obviously put a lot of time into it.

Toby caught the direction of Sam's gaze. "The garden is all Damien's work. He doesn't let me near it. I kill everything."

"I hope not," Sam murmured. "I thought you were a doctor."

Toby grinned. "Plant life," he amended. "I don't think I need to worry about whether you had the wits knocked out of you yesterday."

"Just my memory." Sam sighed, and Toby patted his shoulder.

"It'll return soon enough. Don't worry."

"I keep telling myself that." He ran his hand through his hair and winced at the tangles and wished he'd brushed it before they left. "Anyway, enough about me. Where's Gabriel?"

Toby studied him thoughtfully for a moment. Then he led him into the clinic. Sam paused on the doorstep of what was obviously the waiting room as the conversation died and all eyes in the room turned to him, although none of them belonged to Gabriel.

"Okay, okay," Toby grumbled. "Don't scare the poor man away. He's here to make sandwiches."

There was a rumble of laughter, and a man in the corner, covered in mud that was a sharp contrast to the pristine white dressing on his arm, said, "You mean you're letting Damien near him?"

"Ha bloody ha," Toby snapped. "Everyone okay? Any news on Bert and Elsie?"

The smiles were wiped off just like that and worry returned to their faces.

"Not yet," a man said. "I rang their Jeanie about an hour ago, but she's still not returned my call."

"They're not letting us near the road now," the man who'd spoken before said. "The experts—" There was a wealth of derision in his tone, "—think the whole road could collapse."

"I'll go and check in a minute." Toby turned to Sam. "Gabriel is probably with Damien. Follow me."

He opened a door with Staff Only written in big red letters and beckoned him through. The conversation died again, but this time Sam recognised one of the people despite the layers of caked-on mud and the oozing wound on his right arm. He stood and came over to him.

"Good, you're here," Gabriel said. "I'm so sorry for leaving you alone."

"That's okay. You've had a busy morning." Sam frowned as he saw his arm. "I thought you hurt your cheek."

Gabriel turned to show him the slight graze and bruise where the stone hit his face.

"You didn't have a damaged arm when I left you," Toby said.

Gabriel touched the cut and winced. "I went back to check on Bert and Elsie. I scraped up against some rocks."

"Sit down here, and I'll clean you up," Toby said, pointing to a stool.

"I'm—"

"Sit!"

To Sam's amusement, Gabriel sat. Toby opened a cupboard and brought out a first aid kit. Gabriel grimaced as Toby started to wipe away the blood.

"I hear you saved a little girl," Sam said to distract him.

"I don't make a habit of doing this. Most of the time, I just sit at my computer and work."

"Don't you believe it," Toby said. "He's got a superhero suit in his wardrobe."

"He's a hero to me," Sam murmured. then he flushed as he realised what he'd said.

Damien crowed, and though Sam couldn't be sure under all that mud, Gabriel looked like he was blushing too.

"You finally have one fan," Damien chuckled. He waved a sharp knife at Gabriel, who flipped him off.

Toby sighed loudly and turned to Sam. "Just ignore my husband. His sense of humour gets the better of him sometimes. You're done, Gabriel. It was just a graze."

"I could have told you that," Gabriel grumbled.

Toby cleared away the first aid kit. "Stop getting hurt. You're not my only patient today. You can take a shower if you want, and change." He pointed to the pile of clothes on the countertop.

Gabriel raised an eyebrow. "You been rummaging around in my bedroom?"

"Yes," Toby said. "Sam, I need to check on my patients. Are you okay alone with my husband? If he gets too much, just smack him on the nose like a puppy."

Sam turned his attention to Damien, who was studying him just as curiously. He was maybe in his thirties, tall, dark, very broad across the shoulders, and with a face weathered from hours in the sun—almost the complete opposite of Toby's lean physique and blond features. The reason for the sharp knife became evident when he looked at the two loaves of bread in front of him.

Sam felt a momentary panic at the prospect of being away from the two people he knew, but he nodded and smiled. "I'm here to help. What do you want me to do, Damien?"

Damien nodded approvingly. "You butter the bread, and I'll finish slicing this loaf."

Gabriel stood and came over to Sam. "Are you sure you're okay? I didn't intend to leave you alone for so long, but when I saw the landslide, I just couldn't walk away."

"Of course not," Sam hurried to reassure him. He felt guilty. Gabriel had been rescuing people, and what had he been doing? Taking a fucking nap.

"You two go away," Damien said, making shooing motions at Toby and Gabriel. "Me and Sam here have important work to do. Someone's got to feed the troops."

"I'll check on the site again. Then I'll have a shower," Gabriel said.

"Tell them to come here for a break," Damien ordered.

"Okay."

Gabriel disappeared out the kitchen, and Toby vanished back into the waiting room of the clinic.

Sam pasted on a smile, and looked at Damien. "Where do you want me to work?"

"You sit there." Damien pointed at a bar stool opposite to where he was slicing the bread. "I don't want you to fall over. Gabriel said you had a busy day yesterday."

"I wouldn't know," Sam said drily. "I don't remember anything about it except waking up naked in a strange man's cottage."

Damien chuckled. "Honey, you've just described my top fantasy. Unless the man was Gabriel of course, because eww."

"He's very handsome," Sam said, rushing to defend Gabriel's honour in his absence.

"If you like tall, dark, and moody," Damien agreed. "But he's like my brother."

"Have you known Gabriel long?"

"About ten years. You know Toby was Jenny's twin?" Damien's expression grew sad and not for the first time, Sam realised how many lives had been shattered by Jenny and Michael's deaths.

"Yes. I'm so sorry."

Damien blinked rapidly. "Me too. Me too. But this won't make the sandwiches." He used the knife to point at the sliced bread on the board. "Start buttering."

Sam did as he was told and worked his way through the loaf. Once Damien had finished slicing, he expertly loaded the buttered bread with various fillings and placed them on platters.

"You look like you've done this before," Sam observed.

"That's because I have," Damien said. "I make and sell sandwiches and cakes to shops and offices. I've got a van."

"This is a busman's holiday for you, then."

"I always provide food and drink if there's an emergency. Can you take these out to the waiting room? I'll fill up the flasks of tea and coffee for the guys working on the road. They always appreciate it."

"Sure."

Damien held open the door, and Sam brought in the trays to cheers from the muddy crowd.

"'Bout time," one of the men grumbled.

"You be quiet, Petey," the man next to him scolded. "You only help out for the free food and drink."

Petey ignored him as he grabbed a handful of sandwiches.

Damien rolled his eyes at Sam, who held back a smile. Back in the kitchen with the door safely closed behind them, Damien said, "Petey used to run the local search and rescue until he was injured. Even now, he's always first in line to volunteer."

"He was hurt on a rescue?"

"He slipped down a cliff trying to find Jenny and Michael."

One more life touched by their deaths.

Damien gave a sigh and seemed to shake himself. "Let's go make more. It's going to be a long afternoon."

Sam followed him and started the buttering process over again. Although he had a headache, he was glad to be there, doing something useful.

Now they just needed to know about Bert and Elsie.

Chapter 7
Gabriel

The adrenaline crash hit Gabriel the second they found out Bert and Elsie were safe and sound at their daughter's house, several hundred miles away. A cheer went up from the volunteers as one of the women relayed the news from their daughter. Gabriel felt he could breathe for the first time since he'd arrived on the scene. Everyone was alive, and there were no injuries beyond cuts and bruises. Homes were damaged, and the road would take weeks to repair, but no one had died, no one was lost. *Unlike before.* Gabriel shuddered violently and clutched on to the kitchen counter because his legs were shaking so hard. He breathed in and out, trying to slow his pounding heart, thankful no one had noticed his meltdown, and looked around for Sam.

He found him talking to one of the elderly women displaced by the day's events, who was waiting for her son to collect her. Sam had spent the afternoon working under Damien's benevolent dictatorship, and then sat talking to people, offering comfort where he could. Gabriel had spent most of the afternoon by the slip, but every time he came in, Sam was engaged in conversation. Watching him talk gently to old Mrs Thomas, he'd never have known about the ordeal Sam had been through.

Gabriel turned away, took a deep breath, and squared his shoulders. He was fine. Everyone was safe. It wasn't like Jenny and Michael.

"Let's go home," Sam murmured at his side.

Gabriel shivered. He hadn't even realised Sam had approached him. He shook his head. "I'm fine."

"Sure you are," Sam soothed, rubbing circles on Gabriel's lower back.

Gabriel scowled at him. Maybe his meltdown hadn't been as secret as he'd thought, but he didn't need Sam patronising him.

"Gabriel?"

Great, now Toby was studying him.

"I'm fine," Gabriel snapped.

His all-too-knowing brother-in-law gave him a look and turned to Sam. "Sam, take Gabriel home."

Gabriel huffed. "I don't need to go home."

"And yet I don't care," Toby said. "Go and rest. I'll be in to see you later."

Gabriel scowled at Toby, who blandly ignored him. Sam said goodbye to Mrs Thomas, kissed her gently on her lined cheek, and joined Gabriel and Toby.

"I'm ready," he said.

Gabriel opened his mouth to argue, but Toby pointed to the door. "Go."

There was a short delay because people weren't going to let Gabriel leave without hugging him and shaking his hand. They all knew the situation could have been far worse if he hadn't been on the scene as soon as he had. Toby allowed it to go on for a while, but then he pushed Gabriel out the door, and Sam followed him.

"Gabe?"

Gabriel turned to see a couple and a little girl in the man's arms.

The woman stepped forward. "Thank you for saving my little girl," she sobbed as she flung herself into Gabriel's arms. He looked a bit startled but gave her a gentle hug in return. Then it was Maisie's turn to hug him, and finally the man, who shook his hand fiercely, his eyes gleaming with unshed tears.

"I can never repay you for saving my family." The man paused. "We heard…. We're so sorry."

Gabriel nodded and said goodbye, needing to get away from everyone. Aware his hands were shaking from the adrenaline crash, Gabriel shoved them in his pockets as they walked back to his cottage. Sam walked quietly by his side. He seemed to be someone who didn't need to talk, and Gabriel was thankful. He couldn't have held a conversation if he tried.

As soon as they were back indoors, Gabriel rubbed his eyes and winced at the gritty feel. "I'm going for a shower. I need to decake." He'd spent so much time going back to check for Bert and Elsie, he'd not managed to take a shower at Toby's.

Sam nodded. He was looking tired too, his face pinched around the eyes and mouth.

"Are you okay?" Gabriel asked.

"My head's aching. I'll be glad to sit down," he confessed.

"You relax. I'll see you in a few minutes."

Sam mumbled something, headed for the sofa, and closed his eyes before he'd even settled.

Gabriel checked he was all right and then headed into the bathroom. He stripped off his T-shirt and jeans, shedding dirt everywhere. Then he kicked the clothes into one corner, not wanting to dump a load of grit into the hamper.

The shower felt amazing, and he groaned with pleasure as the hot water streamed down his face and back, easing his aching muscles. He soaked up the heat for a few minutes before he squeezed shampoo into his palm and massaged it into his hair. It took two washes to get rid of the gritty feeling, and even then, he was sure he'd be finding dirt for days.

When he got out of the shower, clean and warm, Gabriel realised he didn't have any clean clothes to change into. Cursing under his breath, he wrapped a towel around his waist. Sam was bound to be asleep. He wouldn't notice a seminaked dash to the bedroom. But when he opened the bathroom door, he let out an undignified yell. He was not going to term it a shriek. Men didn't shriek. But he did yell when he discovered Sam just outside the door.

"What the hell?"

Sam stared at him. "I… uh, sorry. I just needed a cup of tea. I went to put the kettle on, but it needed water, and I thought it might affect the shower, so I decided to wait until you finished."

"Didn't you have enough tea at Toby's?" he snapped. Then he realised he was being an arse again. He sighed and scrubbed through his damp hair. "I'm sorry. It's been a stressful day."

Sam gave a curt nod. "Yes, it has. Is it all right if I…?" He waved at the kitchen.

"Sure, sure. Could you make me a coffee? Black, no sugar."

He felt the knot of the towel dislodge, but he grabbed at it before the situation became more uncomfortable than it already was.

Sam's eyes stayed fixed on his. "Uh…."

Gabriel hurried away. *Goddammit.* Could this day get any worse? He shut the bedroom door behind him and leaned against it. Yes, it could have been a lot worse, he acknowledged. The village might be mourning the loss of many residents. He felt the towel slip, and it fell to the floor. Gabriel shook his head. He could also have flashed his guest, and he was damn glad that hadn't happened.

By the time he had dressed and attempted to tame his unruly hair, Sam had made the drinks and was back on the sofa, eyes closed again. Gabriel pressed his lips together as he saw the red-and-white-striped mug on the coffee table in front of him. That had been Jenny's special mug, a present from Michael for her birthday not long before she and Michael went missing. He clenched his fists, holding back the urge to shout at Sam for something he didn't know. That was why he didn't have people in the cottage. He couldn't handle these situations.

Gabriel forced himself to join Sam and sat in his favourite chair. He picked up the mug of black coffee and sipped at it. It needed a little more sugar, but otherwise it was perfect. Sam didn't move for a long while, and Gabriel wondered if he'd fallen asleep. Then he wondered if he ought to get Toby over to take a look at him. He still hadn't gone to the hospital as they'd planned.

Eventually Sam opened his eyes and blinked owlishly at him. "I'm sorry. Did I fall asleep?"

"Just for a few minutes. Is your head still hurting?"

"It's not as bad as it was."

Sam sat up and reached for his tea.

Gabriel couldn't take it. "Let me make you another cup of tea. That must be cold."

Before Sam had a chance to object, he took the mug into the kitchen. As the kettle boiled, he emptied the mug down the sink and quickly washed and dried it. Then he put the mug at the back of a cupboard he barely used, well away from the others. He returned with a fresh mug of tea and a strip of paracetamol.

Sam took the new mug without comment and smiled gratefully for the pain relievers. "I'll be glad when this headache goes for good."

"Give it time," Gabriel said. "You took a bad knock."

His lips twitched. "Are you channelling Doctor Toby?"

Gabriel smirked at him. "Did it work?"

"He's scarier than you are."

Gabriel chuckled because Sam was spot on. Toby could be an arrogant sod when he chose to be. "Are you hungry?"

Sam nodded. "I shouldn't be after all those sandwiches, but I am a little."

"It's times like this I wish we lived close to somewhere that delivered food."

"No restaurants in the village?"

"There's two. A fish and chip shop and a Chinese, run by the same family. But no delivery. Which would you prefer?"

Sam didn't have to think about it for too long. "Fish and chips."

"I'll make the fire. Then I'll go to the chippy."

Gabriel needed a few minutes alone to think. He also wanted to spend some time on the clifftop.

"Do you think anyone is missing me?" Sam asked suddenly.

Gabriel frowned at the unexpected question. "I expect so."

Sam bit his lip and stared down into his lap. "I hope someone is looking for me the way you look for your family."

Gabriel swallowed hard around the lump in his throat. He would never stop looking for them, but Sam was equally lost, not knowing who he was or where he came from. Where were his family if his parents were dead? Did he have siblings? Did he have a wife or husband or a girlfriend or boyfriend? Too many questions and no answers. In a way Sam was like a blank canvas, waiting for the shading to take place, filling in the pieces to say who he was and where he came from. "I won't stop looking until we find your family," he promised.

Sam smiled at him a little sadly. "Thank you."

He huffed and looked away. "I've had practice."

The silence in the cottage was painful but not overwhelming. They were both hurting, and for once, Gabriel didn't feel so alone. Someone else knew what it was like to hurt.

He sighed again and stood looking down at Sam. The lines of pain had eased, and his face didn't look so pinched. "I'll be back soon."

"I think I might have another nap," Sam murmured.

"You do that."

On impulse, Gabriel gently ruffled Sam's hair. Then he spent a few minutes laying the fire and getting it started. There was no real need for the fire, but it would ease the air of dampness left over from the storm.

When he looked around again, Sam was curled up, asleep on the sofa, his hands tucked under his cheek.

It was getting late as Gabriel emerged from the cottage. He checked his watch. He just had time to spend a few minutes on the clifftop before he went to the fish and chip shop. He stood in his usual spot, watching the lazy waves break calmly against the beach. The air was still fresh, heavy with salt and ozone and the remains of the wild garlic growing on the cliff top. The only sign of the violence of the storm was the amount of debris washed up on the shoreline. Tomorrow he would go down to the beach and pick through it to see if there was anything from Jenny and Michael.

He wished them goodnight as he always did and jogged down the path towards the village. His stomach rumbled in anticipation of the fish and chips. Food hadn't been a priority over the past year, but now he was hungry. That's what running on adrenaline did for him.

The Chinese restaurant/takeaway and the chippie were nestled side-by-side. Run by the same Chinese family who'd been there for decades, they were well frequented by locals and tourists alike. Gabriel inhaled the greasy smell of fish and chips with pleasure as he pushed open the door. The young girl behind the counter called out someone's order and handed over a large bag to a man Gabriel didn't recognise. He was in his thirties and had the pale-and-red look of spending too much time in the sun. A tourist, then. They exchanged smiles, and Gabriel moved up to the counter.

The girl's eyes widened. "Gabriel, it's good to see you."

It had been months since he'd come in for a takeaway. Gabriel smiled at her. "It's good to see you too, Mei. How's university?"

"I can't wait to get back," she muttered, shooting a quick glance at her aunt, who was frying fish.

Gabriel grinned sympathetically at her. "Not long now."

"Not soon enough," she snapped. "What can I get you?"

"Two haddock and chips. Both medium."

"Two?" she asked doubtfully as she handed the order to her aunt. "Oh, the cutie you rescued. Everyone's talking about him. How is he? Remembered anything yet?"

Gabriel refrained from rolling his eyes. News spread quickly through the village, especially after the day's events. "Not since this afternoon," he said cheerfully. "I'm sure it will be soon."

"I wonder where he came from?"

To Gabriel's great relief, another tourist came in and distracted her, and Gabriel made his escape to sit down on one of the chairs lining the small waiting area. He picked up one of the tabloids and scanned the headlines—politician caught in sex scandal, missing pop star, one of the royals pregnant again. Gabriel turned to the sports pages and read about the latest injury to a premiership footballer. He winced as he read about the tackle that had broken his leg and put him out for the rest of the season.

"Gabriel, it's yours. On the house. We heard what you did this afternoon."

The girl held up a bag. Gabriel thanked her and squeezed around a family who'd just entered. It was considerably darker as Gabriel picked his way along the path to his cottage, and there was no light from the windows. A stirring of unease made Gabriel hurry the last few hundred yards to the front door.

Inside, he flicked on the light and sighed with relief when he saw Sam, still asleep on the sofa. He chided himself for feeling so worried as he went into the kitchen to serve up the food.

"Sam, dinner," he said, placing both plates on the coffee table.

By the time he returned with salt, pepper, and ketchup, Sam had sat up and was rubbing his eyes. "I feel like I've been asleep for hours." The last words were swallowed by a yawn.

"Nearly an hour," Gabriel said. "How's your head?"

"Much better. This looks good." He grinned at him. "I expected dinner wrapped in paper."

"I would have, if it were just me," Gabriel confessed. "I didn't know if you'd object."

"Paper's fine," Sam mumbled around a mouthful of chips.

"I'll remember that for next time."

Next time? Why would there be a next time? Sam would be gone as soon as they reached the police and found out who he was. From the tight look on Sam's face, the same thought had occurred to him. Gabriel coughed and focused on his dinner.

The battered haddock and large chips were just what he needed, and he cleared his plate. Then he eyed Sam's plate, but he was eating just as quickly. For such a slender man, he wasn't afraid of piling away the food. There wasn't a scrap left by the end of the meal, and they both sat back and sighed in satisfaction.

"Do you want a drink?" Gabriel asked. He didn't want to move, but he felt it was polite.

To his relief, Sam muttered, "Not yet."

His eyes were closed again, and he didn't seem interested in talking. Gabriel stared into the crackling flames. Not for the first time, Gabriel thought what a restful person Sam was to be around. Jenny had been lively, a bundle of energy, always on the go, much like Toby. Gabriel smiled sadly, thinking of the times he'd pulled Jenny into his arms just to make her stop moving. He didn't know Sam that well, but he seemed to be calmer. They sat in silence for a long time, until finally, Sam sighed and opened his eyes.

"I'm sorry. I was going to clear away the plates. I didn't mean to doze."

"It's okay," Gabriel reassured him. "It's been a long day. I'm tired too."

Sam sat up and ran his hands through his hair. The copper strands glinted in the light from the fire. He yawned and rubbed his eyes. "I'm sorry."

"Go to bed. Tomorrow we'll go into town and talk to the police. See if we can find out who you are."

Sam pressed his lips together. "Yes."

Gabriel frowned. "Is everything all right?"

He ignored the question as he stood and stretched out his back. "I think I'll go to bed."

Gabriel had the feeling Sam wasn't as enthused as he'd expected. "Don't you want to go home?"

Sam slumped into the sofa. "Of course I do."

"You could try being a bit more convincing," Gabriel said drily.

"I had another nightmare," he admitted.

"Just now?"

"Earlier, when Toby came to wake me up."

"Do you remember it?"

He nodded, looking very unhappy. "I was on the floor. I couldn't move. It was like I was paralysed. Men were talking over me, but I could hear what they were saying."

"What did they say?" Gabriel prompted gently.

His lips twisted. "Same old, same old. They were going to kill me, but this time they kept talking about 'him.'"

"Did you get a name?"

"No. I got the feeling they didn't like him, but they didn't have a choice." He looked at Gabriel. "I got the feeling they liked me, but they were prepared to kill me because they were scared of him."

Gabriel's blood ran cold. That was a vivid dream. Gabriel knew nothing about amnesia beyond what Toby had told him, but he couldn't help but wonder if that were a memory, not a dream. He needed to talk to Toby. The day had been too busy to focus on Sam, but he was still recovering from his ordeal. He forced a smile. "When we go to the police station, we're sure to find out more about you. Whatever happens, Sam, I've got your back. I promise."

Sam nodded, but Gabriel had the feeling he wasn't convinced. He walked over to him, rested on his haunches, and tucked a knuckle under his chin to make Sam look at him. "I promise I have your back. Me and Toby, even Damien. We're here for you. I won't let you walk back into danger."

Long lashes swept down, hiding his stormy eyes. "You might not have the choice," he whispered.

"Trust me," Gabriel ordered.

Sam opened his eyes, and there was a world of confusion and pain in his expression. "You're the only thing in this whole mess I do trust."

Chapter 8
Sam

The stress and hard labour of the previous day must have worked, because Sam's dreams were blessedly nightmare-free, and he awoke free of the wretched headache that had been plaguing him since he woke in Gabriel's cottage. He opened his eyes and watched the model aeroplane overhead moving gently in the draft from the open window. In the distance he could hear the sounds of children laughing, and he wondered how Gabriel coped with hearing the sounds of happy families when he'd had his ripped so cruelly away from him. Why did he not leave here with all its painful memories? Sam sighed. Because Jenny and Michael had never been found. Gabriel clung to the fragile hope that someday they would be found.

As he sat up and swung his legs over the side, the relief from not having the headache was palpable. Sam ran his hand through his hair and grimaced at the gritty feel and the tangles that stopped his fingers in their tracks. He needed a shower, a ton of conditioner, and fresh clothes. He looked down at the grubby clothes on the floor. After yesterday's activity, they were ready to walk to the washing machine by themselves. Sam slipped on his shorts and T-shirt, unwilling to wear the dirty clothes again. He would have to be brave and ask Gabriel for something new, if Jenny had anything else suitable for a man.

There was no noise in the cottage, and the living room was empty when he poked his head out. Sam headed into the kitchen to find a note stuck to the kettle.

Working in bedroom for a couple of hours.
Sorry, got to deal with crisis for a client.
Help yourself to breakfast.
Clean clothes in utility room.
G

Sam read the note again. It was a confident hand with a strong *G*. He wasn't sure how he knew that, but he just did. He would leave Gabriel alone to get on with his crisis. First, he needed a shower. He started for the bathroom and then doubled back to the utility room to grab the clothes. It was one thing for Gabriel to wander around his home in a towel, but he was a guest. Gabriel had left him a pair of jeans and a pale green T-shirt and another hoodie. Not something he would have chosen for himself, another thing he knew, but beggars couldn't be choosers. He was definitely a beggar at the moment, with nothing to his name… not even his name.

The shower was blissfully warm, and Sam closed his eyes as the water streamed over him. He shampooed his hair a couple of times to wash out the grit and then conditioned it thoroughly, getting rid of every tangle. He grimaced at Gabriel's generic shampoo and conditioner. He couldn't remember the products he used before the accident, but he needed them now. What was all brooding wavy locks on Gabriel left him with a frizzy lion's mane. Maybe he should cut it. Sam pushed that thought aside. He wasn't going to be here long enough to do that.

He dressed and looked at himself in the long mirror in the bathroom. He looked good in the T-shirt and jeans, although they were tight for him. It felt good to be dressed in something clean, but he was starting to be spooked about wearing a dead woman's clothing, even if they were menswear. *If* he stayed, then he'd ask Toby for clothes. Toby was about his height and weight.

There was no sign of Gabriel, and he could hear a soft murmur of voices from behind the bedroom door. Briefly he contemplated offering a cup of coffee, but the closed door intimidated him. Instead, Sam made himself a cup of tea. He thought about breakfast but decided against it. His boots were by the door, so he put them on, picked up his cup, and headed into the morning sunshine.

The tang of fresh salt permeated the air, and he inhaled, relishing the air so fresh it was almost sharp. He followed the path to the clifftop and sat down on a large rock to look out to sea. He sighed in pleasure as he sipped at his tea and looked out to the horizon. There was barely a breeze, and the waves were gentle.

Shrieks of laughter interrupted his thoughts. Two young children ran along the beach, a man and a woman trailing after them. Sam felt a little stab to his heart as he watched them. He didn't have a family—no husband, no children. He wondered how he knew that.

"They look happy," Gabriel said, sadness permeating his voice.

Sam looked up to see Gabriel standing behind him, one hand wrapped around his mug. Gabriel was dressed in a white shirt that caught in the breeze, and tight jeans. His feet were bare, and he seemed not to notice the stones. He had a healthy growth of stubble, and from the way his dark curls tumbled messily around his head, he'd obviously forgotten to comb his hair. Sam's fingers itched to try and tame the mess.

"I was that happy once." Gabriel was still focused on the family, his dark eyes filled with pain Sam longed to take away.

"Do you think you'll be that happy again?" Sam asked softly.

Gabriel shook his head, and Sam felt unaccountably sad. "I don't think I deserve that kind of happiness again."

"Everyone deserves another chance," he protested.

You could have that happiness with me.

Whoa, where had that come from? Sam hastily tamped down those thoughts.

"I was lucky enough to have it once. Some people don't ever find their soulmate."

Sam swallowed hard and dragged his gaze away from the bereft man before Gabriel saw what must be plain in his eyes. Sam's quiet dreams would remain just that—dreams. Gabriel was still mourning his lost love. Sam held back a sigh, knowing he had enough problems of his own to deal with. It was time he found out who he was.

"Are the roads open yet?" he asked.

"No, but they're talking about later today or early tomorrow. They're still shoring up the banks."

Sam nodded. "If you've been working, I guess Wi-Fi and phone lines have been restored."

"It was patchy, but yes."

"We could call the police and see if anyone has been looking for me."

He wondered if he sounded as unenthusiastic to Gabriel as he did to himself.

Gabriel frowned. It was fleeting, but it was definitely there. "Okay. You can do it when you're ready. You don't have to rush."

Sam's heart warmed at his words. Despite his initial reluctance, Gabriel wasn't in a hurry to get rid of him. It was hard to explain. Sam should be champing at the bit to go back to his real life. Instead he felt safe here, his world contained between the cottage and the clifftop looking out over the bay. If they contacted the police, he would have no choice but to deal with the authorities and become whoever he really was.

"Do you want to go down to the beach?" Gabriel offered.

Sam looked at the sandy beach and then back at Gabriel. "Down there?"

Gabriel's lips twitched. "Down there."

"I...."

He wasn't sure how he felt about that. He'd nearly drowned down there. Gabriel's family had drowned. But it was a pleasant day with a light breeze and blue skies. Sam contemplated walking down the steps to the beach. The tide was going out, and he could walk along the beach to the rocks at the far end.

"Will you come with me?" he asked, holding his breath as he waited for the answer.

Gabriel nodded and held out his hand. "Leave the mugs here."

Sam let Gabriel tug him to his feet, and they headed for the wooden steps.

"Take care on the steps," Gabriel warned. "They're always slippery."

Sam peered all the way down to the bottom. "That's a long way."

"It is," Gabriel rumbled as he started down, not seeming to bother about being barefoot.

"You carried me all the way up from the bottom?" Sam was no skinny lightweight, and Gabriel had been battling wind and rain all the way up. "Christ, are you a superhero?"

Gabriel chuckled. "I hide my cape."

"But still."

"You were in no position to walk," Gabriel pointed out. "I put you over my shoulder and did battle with the elements."

Sam thoughtfully eyed Gabriel's broad shoulders. Being carried in a fireman's lift by a gorgeous man, and he couldn't remember any of it. Fuck his life. Then a new memory pushed in... of being carried over a man's shoulder, smelling cigarette smoke and sweat. He'd felt nauseated and unable to move. Sam gasped as he swayed under the weight of the memory. The man had tried to kill him.

"Sam? Sam? What's the matter?"

Strong hands grasped his biceps and shook him gently, then he was eased against a man's chest. Sam fought to get away from his captor, relieved his arms worked this time.

"It's Gabriel. Sam, it's Gabriel. You safe now. No one is going to hurt you."

Gabriel? Sam swallowed hard and inhaled lavender and citrus scents rather than nicotine and body odour. "Gabriel?"

A gentle hand caressed his head. "Yes, it's me. Are you back with me now?"

"I think so." Sam stayed where he was in Gabriel's arms, not ready to face the world.

"What triggered you?" Gabriel's voice was calm, as though he were comforting a small child.

"One of the men who tried to kill me used a fireman's lift. I remember not being able to move. I could smell him, but that was all. I couldn't move or speak." Sam's voice cracked on the last word.

They stayed where they were until Sam felt more stable. He looked up at Gabriel, feeling a bit foolish for being triggered by something so simple.

"I'm sorry."

"Nothing to be sorry for," Gabriel said. "Someone tried to kill you. You're allowed to be freaked out."

Sam didn't want to think about it. He stepped back and smiled at Gabriel. "Let's get down to the beach. I want to paddle in the sea and explore the rock pools."

"If I'd planned ahead, we could have brought the nets."

"Next time," Sam said.

Gabriel gave him a smile that warmed Sam through. "Next time. I've got crab pots and fishing rods too."

Sam eyed him speculatively. "You like catching fish."

"I do, but I throw the small ones back."

"I love sea bass cooked on a beach BBQ." Sam blinked. "Wow, I remember how I like my tea and how I like my fish."

"I like sea bass too," Gabriel rumbled. "Come on. You need to get your feet wet. You go ahead of me."

Sam took a deep breath of salty air, calmed himself, and descended the steps to the beach below, Gabriel's hand on his shoulder grounding him.

At the bottom of the steps, Sam sat down to take off his boots and socks. He was determined to get the feel of the wet sand between his toes.

Sam grinned as he stood barefoot on the sand and flexed his toes. "Fuck, this feels good."

"Roll up your jeans. We'll go paddling in the sea." Gabriel could have been five from the boyish grin on his face.

"I can't remember the last time I went paddling," Sam deadpanned.

They looked at each other and burst out laughing. Sam felt better just from that. Gabriel gave him a not-so-gentle shove towards the sea, and Sam stumbled. He swore at Gabriel and set off at a run. His head throbbed a bit but not enough to make him stop. The tide was as far out as it could go, and he had to negotiate small rocks and seaweed and puddles that left splash marks up his legs. He looked over his shoulder to find Gabriel on his heels. Sam ran faster, but Gabriel had longer legs and easily kept pace for them to finish neck and neck where the shallow waves gently broke on the beach.

Sam was out of breath. He bent over, hands on his thighs and tried to get his breath back.

"You need to exercise," Gabriel mocked. The man was barely breathing faster.

"Bastard," Sam said cheerfully as he stood, stretched his back, and rolled his shoulders. "You're right, though. I'm out of shape if I can't run across a beach. I guess I'm not a gym bunny."

Gabriel eyed him appraisingly, and Sam felt his cheeks warm even more under his appreciative regard. "You look just fine to me."

"Thanks," Sam said, hoping Gabriel would put the flush down to the exercise and not his reaction to Gabriel's praise. It was as though he'd never been given a compliment before. Not that he remembered, but he hadn't broken any mirrors so far.

"Uh.... Sam."

"Yes?"

Just then a wave crashed into Sam, soaking him almost to his knees.

Gabe jumped out of the way. "Too late."

Sam scowled at him. "You could have told me earlier."

"I could have," Gabriel agreed, his mouth quirking into a mischievous smile. "But what would be the fun in that?"

Sam huffed and shoved his hands in his pockets. "It's hard to believe there ever was a storm."

"Yes," Gabriel murmured, looking out to sea.

Sam cursed himself for his careless words and for putting that expression on Gabriel's face. "I'm so sorry."

Gabriel turned to look at him. "There's nothing to be sorry about. I've seen this bay in every weather; from sunshine to howling gales to snow capping the waves. It's beautiful here."

"You'll never leave here, will you?"

"How can I?"

Jenny and Michael were here. Sam understood. As long as the sea held the mystery of their whereabouts, Gabriel would remain, a stalwart sentinel of the cliffs.

Sam held back a sigh and squinted over to the rocks. The family they'd seen earlier were gone now. Time to explore the rock pools. "Race you to the rocks?"

"We won't have long now the tide is coming in," Gabriel warned.

"We'd better get there fast, then," Sam said, haring away.

Of course Gabriel overtook him, but it was fun while it lasted. The bastard perched against the rock as though he'd been there forever as Sam ran up to him.

"You took your time," Gabriel said.

Sam flipped him off because he deserved it.

Gabriel gave a wicked smirk. "Come on. Let's look in the rock pools for pirates' treasure."

Sam was about to make a jokey comment when he realised that must have been something Gabriel used to say to his son. "Have you ever found any pirates' treasure?"

"Just once," Gabriel said and winked at him.

It took a moment for Sam to realise Gabriel meant him. "I'm a pirate's treasure, am I?"

"I nearly found you on a sunken ship."

Sam flinched at the thought. Not the memory, because he didn't have that, but the thought of what he would have become if Gabriel hadn't found him. He flinched again as Gabriel caressed his cheek.

"I'm sorry. That was stupid of me." Gabriel's voice was soft and regretful.

"It's all right." Sam caught Gabriel's sceptical expression. "No, it really is. You saved me, and I'm alive."

Gabriel patted his shoulder. "You are, Sam from the storm. You're alive. Let's see if we can find more pirate treasure."

Sam let Gabriel haul him up onto the rocks to explore the myriad of pools. He had no idea if he'd done that before, but it didn't matter. Gabriel pointed out the crabs and sea creatures scuttling away as they lifted rocks to find the hidden treasures underneath. He was remarkably knowledgeable about the plants and animals, and when Sam remarked on it, Gabriel flushed and confessed that exploring rock pools had been a guilty pleasure of his.

"It's been a long time since I made the effort," Gabriel admitted, his gaze flickering out to sea as it always did when he thought about his family.

"Thank you for sharing it with me," Sam said, and Gabriel smiled at him.

When the waves started to lick around the rocks, Gabriel suggested it was time to depart. "The tide comes in a lot quicker than you'd expect."

Sam followed Gabe back to his shoes at the base of the steps. He passed a small dinghy and frowned as he looked at the name, Sweet Jenny. "Is this yours?" It was a stupid question. Who else could it belong to?

"Yes, although Toby and Damien use it occasionally."

"You went out in this to find me?"

The dinghy was so small. In stormy weather and fierce waves, it must have been terrifying.

"Don't think about it," Gabriel said.

Sam nodded, but it preyed on his mind as he sat on the bottom step and brushed the sand off his feet. He grimaced at the gritty feel as he rolled his socks on.

"I think I'm going to need another shower when we get home," he said without thinking.

Gabriel didn't say anything, and Sam wondered if he should apologise, but Gabriel led the way up the steps, and he decided to let it go, cursing his wayward tongue with each gritty step towards the top.

Chapter 9
Gabriel

Sam looked pale and drawn by the time he reached the top of the cliff. It took some prodding on Gabriel's part to get Sam to admit his head was pounding.

"Damn, I'm sorry," Gabriel said. "We should have taken it easy today, especially after yesterday."

Sam shook his head. Then he winced, and the colour drained out of his face. "Remind me not to do that."

"Don't do that," Gabriel said.

"Ha-ha, very funny."

"I thought so. Are you going to barf?"

From Sam's ashen face, he was going to be sick or pass out. Or both.

"Ask me in a few minutes."

Sam swayed, and Gabriel put an arm around his waist.

"Come on. You can lie down in the cottage and nap."

"For fuck's sake. I'm twenty-three, not three. I don't need a nap," Sam muttered. Then he stopped and looked up at Gabriel. "I'm twenty-three."

Christ, he was a kid. Gabriel suddenly felt ancient. "Congratulations. You make me feel old. When's your birthday?"

"Uh... ask me another time." Sam leaned against Gabriel. "Wow, I'm twenty-three."

"Another piece of the jigsaw falls into place."

"It's a big jigsaw."

Gabriel heard the defeated tone in Sam's voice. "Hey, a minute ago you were all excited because you remembered your age. Hang on to that."

"Okay."

It wasn't cartwheels-across-the-floor joy. but Gabriel would take it. He helped Sam into the cottage and guided him to the sofa. "Do you want to sleep here or in the bedroom?"

Sam snuggled into the corner of the sofa and closed his eyes. "Just leave me here."

Gabriel snorted. "Let's take off your shoes."

If Sam heard him, he didn't give any indication. Gabriel pulled off the shoes, grimacing at the pile of sand on his floor. Then he eased Sam's legs up until he was lying on the sofa. Gabriel covered him with an afghan and left him to sleep.

He stared at Sam for a long time, noting the dark smudges beneath his eyes and the faint lines of pain around his mouth and eyes. He should have been more careful with Sam. Toby would have his hide if he set back Sam's recovery.

Gabriel knew he should take the opportunity to work on his latest project for a couple of hours. He'd already lost a few days between the storm, Sam, and the landslip, but he couldn't tear his eyes away from the sleeping man, now on his side, hands tucked under his cheeks. Sam was beautiful, with strands of copper hair falling across his face and his creamy skin not so pale now he was asleep. Gabriel knew he was fast becoming ensnared by him.

Too soon! Too soon!

He couldn't push away his fears. It had only been a year. It was too soon to be falling for anyone, let alone a kid like Sam.

You need to contact the police and missing persons. The sooner he's gone the better.

Gabriel could get back to his life.

And the soul-sucking loneliness of your existence.

His damn mind needed to shut the hell up.

Ready to get to his feet, Gabriel paused as Sam made a noise. Sam seemed to be sleeping peacefully. Maybe it had been a noise outside. Gabriel stood, and Sam cried out, one hand flying out.

"Don't kill me. Don't kill me. Don't kill me." His litany trailed off into a sob.

Gabriel sat down next to him and captured Sam's flailing arms in a loose grip. He'd learned by now that just calling him didn't wake Sam up, and if he didn't grasp Sam's hands, he'd end up with a black eye or two.

"Hey, Sam, you're safe. It's all right. You're safe."

Sam tried to pull away from him, but Gabriel wouldn't let go. "Don't hurt me. Why do you want to hurt me? What did I do to deserve this?"

"Who's hurting you, Sam?"

But Sam didn't answer. He gave a heaving sigh, sobbed a couple of times, and fell back to sleep.

Gabriel stayed by him, still holding his hands until he was sure Sam wasn't going to wake again. Then he retreated to his desk to have time alone and recover his thoughts.

WHEN GABRIEL came out of his room, he noticed two things. One, it was dark. Where had the day gone? Two, the cottage was filled with the aroma of something good cooking. Gabriel could smell red wine and herbs, meat and lots of garlic. That was the extent of his knowledge. For a moment it was as though he'd stepped back in time to before his world turned to shit. Dinner was cooking, the radio was on in the kitchen, he could hear singing, and the cottage felt like his home again. Gabriel bit down on his bottom lip. This was temporary, he told himself. No point getting used to it.

He followed his nose to the kitchen to discover Sam, now dressed in a T-shirt Gabriel recognised as his, and Sam's shorts, his long hair tied back in a scrunchy and muttering to himself as he read a cookbook. The counter top... looked like a disaster area with vegetable peelings and spilled herbs everywhere. Gabriel sighed. He got dinner. He'd have to suck it up and do the clearing up afterwards.

"Reduce the sauce down. Reduce it to what?" Sam poked at the pan of bubbling liquid which spattered onto the hob and sizzled. "Isn't it reduced already?"

"You need to reduce the heat under the pan and let it simmer a while. The sauce gets thicker," Gabriel said as he moved forward. He turned the knob to reduce the heat on the hob, stirred the sauce, and inhaled appreciatively. "This smells good."

Pasta bubbled away on the hob, and if it was a little sauce-splattered, it didn't matter.

"I can't remember if I can cook or not," Sam admitted. "So I used one of the recipe books on the shelf. Is that okay?" He bit his lip as though he were worried Gabriel was going to shout at him for using one of Jenny's cookbooks.

"More than okay," Gabriel assured him. "I came out to see if you were awake and wanted dinner."

Sam reached into a cupboard and drew out a wineglass. They had been wedding presents from Jenny's parents. But Sam couldn't know that. He filled the glass with red wine and handed it to Gabriel. Then he picked up his own glass and clinked Gabriel's.

"Cheers. I hope I don't poison you."

Gabriel chuckled. "I hope so too. Where did you get the wine?"

"I went over to Toby's to ask where I could buy wine at this time of night. Damien gave me a couple of bottles. Some went in the sauce, and I had a glass for courage."

Gabriel sipped at it, deciding not to tell Sam he'd put a hundred-pound bottle of wine in his sauce. He certainly wouldn't tell Damien.

"I appreciate the dinner. I hate cooking for myself."

"I have a feeling I don't cook that much," Sam admitted, indicating the war zone of the countertop.

"It won't take long to clear up," Gabriel promised. Then he picked up a dishcloth by the sink. "I'll do that while you man the sauce."

Sam took the cloth out of his hand. "You take the wine and cutlery into the room. I'll clear up and serve dinner."

Gabriel did as he was told, taking a seat by the fire—Sam had got the fire started too—and sipped his very expensive glass of wine as he waited for dinner to be served. The wind had increased, and he could hear the occasional spatter of rain against the window panes, a contrast to the almost summery weather earlier in the day. He closed his eyes and let himself drift as he heard Sam singing 90s boy-band tunes in the kitchen.

Sam emerged fifteen minutes later, carrying two large bowls of pasta and sauce which he placed on mats on the coffee table.

Gabriel's stomach rumbled in appreciation. "This looks amazing."

"Just got to get the garlic bread."

Sam vanished into the kitchen. There was a clang and a muffled curse.

"Are you okay?" Gabriel asked cautiously.

"I'm fine," Sam snapped.

Gabriel grinned and waited.

"I hit my head on the open drawer."

"Has your memory returned?"

"Ha-ha, fuck you, Pennant." Sam returned with a plate of garlic bread and a red mark on his forehead. "I didn't make the garlic bread."

As Gabriel knew he'd had a pack in the freezer, the explanation was unnecessary. He picked up one of the bowls and cautiously took a mouthful.

"Damn, this is good."

More than good in fact.

Sam eyed him sourly. "What did you expect? I can follow a recipe."

Gabriel had shovelled in another mouthful and took his time to swallow and chew before he answered. "I use the same recipe, and this is better than I make it."

Sam nodded, seemingly mollified at Gabriel's compliment. "I liked cooking. I'm just not sure what to do."

"YouTube. There's a tutorial for everything."

"Two problems with that idea. No computer. No phone."

"So what did you do?" Gabriel asked.

"I called Damien," Sam confessed with a blush. "I did all the hard work, though."

Gabriel held back his chuckle, wishing he'd been there to see the forceful and feisty Damien teach Sam how to cook. Damien had tried to tutor Jenny once. It had not ended well. Gabriel had learned swear words he never knew existed that day.

They ate in comfortable silence for a few minutes, only breaking it when they both reached for a piece of garlic bread at the same time. Gabriel's fingers brushed the back of Sam's hand, and they looked up at each other.

"Sorry." Sam looked flustered. "Go on. It's all yours."

"No, you take it," Gabriel insisted.

It was ridiculous. There were several pieces of garlic bread left on the plate.

He handed Sam the piece, and their buttery fingers slid together. Sam gasped at the intimate touch.

"Thank you." Sam bit into the garlic bread, and a trickle of garlic butter smeared his lips.

Gabriel couldn't tear his eyes away from Sam's mouth, glistening in the low light. Sam licked his lips, an action that went straight to Gabriel's dick. He swallowed hard, looked down at his plate, and tried to focus on what he was supposed to be doing, which was not thinking about Sam's mouth wrapped around his cock.

The rattle of windows and the hard splash of rain were welcome distractions.

Sam looked up, concern written on his face. "Do you think we'll have another storm?"

"I don't know." Gabriel sat stock still, shock seeping through him as he realised that, for the first time, he hadn't spent the day watching the weather, watching the storm roll in, and checking the bay for anyone in distress.

"Gabriel?"

Sam's soft query barely broke through the distress building in Gabriel's head. He'd failed Jenny and Michael. Who else had he failed by not being there tonight?

"Gabriel, what's wrong?"

Gabriel put down his bowl with a clatter onto the coffee table. He didn't look at Sam, ashamed of his body's reaction a few minutes before. "I need to go."

Sam sat up and placed his plate on the table. "Go where, Gabriel? Where do you need to go?"

"Out. I need to look. To check. There might be someone in trouble." Gabriel stood, brushing the crumbs from his jeans.

"It's dark and raining," Sam said, getting to his feet too.

He was between Gabriel and the door. He was in the way. Gabriel was bigger and stronger than Sam. He could force Sam out of the way if he had to. But he didn't want to hurt him. He'd never want to hurt Sam.

"I've got to go," he repeated, hoping Sam would just get out of the way.

Sam stayed where he was. "You want to go to the clifftop."

"Yes."

"You want to check the bay."

"Yes," Gabriel snapped, his anger rising at the delay.

"It's pitch black outside. You won't be able to see anything."

"I can see distress signals." Gabriel pushed past Sam and headed to the door.

"You're going to stand on the edge of a cliff in total darkness during a howling gale."

"It won't be the first time. I'll take a torch."

He pulled out his thick waterproof jacket and sat down on the bench by the front door to pull on his boots.

"I'm coming with you," Sam said.

That penetrated the fog in Gabriel's mind. *Sam, out there?*

"No way," he said flatly.

"Why not? If you're going, I'm going. Two sets of eyes looking for trouble has got to be better than one."

"You have no idea what you're talking about. It's not a walk in the park. It's howling rain and wind."

Sam folded his arms, his expression mutinous. "I can see what it's like. I'm not blind."

Just then an enormous gust of wind seemed to rattle the cottage itself.

Gabriel gathered his wits and tried a different tactic. "I'm used to it, Sam. I know the dangers. You're still recovering from a concussion. If you slip and hurt your head, you could do more damage." He finished lacing his boots and stood. "I won't be long, I promise."

"You step one foot outside that door without me, and I'll call Toby."

Gabriel stared at him. "You wouldn't."

"Try me."

He couldn't believe it. Sam was threatening to sic Toby on him. From the stormy expression in his eyes, Gabriel could see it wasn't an idle threat. Sam would be on the phone the second the door shut behind him. Fuck.

"I've got to check, Sam," he pleaded. "Just for a moment. I have to."

"Then I'm coming with you."

Sam sat down on the bench and pulled on his boots. "Have you got a jacket?"

Mutely, Gabriel handed him his other coat. It swamped Sam, but it was the only one he had.

Sam shrugged it on and glared at Gabriel. "Let's go."

Gabriel picked up his powerful flashlight, opened the front door, and received a spray of rain in the face. "Stay close to me," he yelled over the noise of the storm.

He pushed his way out into the night, and Sam followed, pausing to wrestle the front door closed. He'd been out in far worse, but he knew the cliffs like the back of his hand. He knew what he was doing. Now he had to look after Sam, who could be taken by a strong gust of wind. He reached back and grabbed Sam's hand, and Sam held tight immediately.

"I won't let you go," he bellowed, not sure if Sam could hear him or not.

Sam tugged them to a stop and pulled Gabriel's face down to his. "You'd better not."

Then he took Gabriel's breath away by kissing him fiercely, cold lips on his. The kiss was brief, but Gabriel felt it lingering long after Sam pulled back.

"Let's get this madness over and done with," Sam said.

Gabriel led them out of the shelter of the cottage and into the night.

Chapter 10
Sam

He was officially a fucking idiot. Sam had been trying to prevent Gabriel going out, not get dragged out into the hideous weather himself. Even ducks were hiding from the storm. He couldn't believe his threat to call Toby hadn't worked. That was his trump card.

Rain pelted into his eyes, making it hard to see, and the wind seemed to whip his breath away. Sam was also trying to process the fact that he'd just kissed Gabriel. He licked his lips, tasting rain, salt, and Gabriel. He stuck his head down and pushed against the rain and wind, sheltering slightly against the larger bulk of Gabriel, who held his hand. The coat gave up any pretence of being waterproof after five minutes, and he was cold and wet and thoroughly miserable. When he got back into the cottage, he was going to take a long hot shower, climb into bed, and forget this day ever existed. And Gabriel. He was going to forget Gabriel ever existed too. The man was officially bonkers to come out in weather like this. Sam held tighter on to Gabriel's hand. For protection against the wind. Not because he wanted to.

Gabriel forged ahead, his torch showing a dim path ahead of them. He seemed to know where he was going, which made one of them. His hand was reassuringly tight around Sam's.

Sam felt the crunch of the gravel beneath his boots. A few steps and they were back onto grass and dirt. They were approaching the cliff edge. The wind was much stronger here, and Sam struggled to keep his feet. He didn't realise Gabriel had stopped until he ran into his back. Gabriel turned and put an arm around Sam, clamping him to his side, and Sam leaned into him, his heart thumping from nerves but also from Gabriel's proximity.

They stood for what seemed an eternity. Sam peered out across the bay, but he couldn't see anything but a dark void, no lights breaking the nothingness. If it hadn't been for the harsh noise of the crashing waves, he would have thought he was in a black hole. A wet black hole. Gabriel bent and his warm breath ghosted across Sam's cold ear.

"Let's go."

"Thank God," Sam muttered.

Going back was easier. The wind and rain were at their back. Gabriel forced open the cottage door and hauled Sam inside.

The silence was almost as deafening as the noise outside. Sam took a breath, ready to rip into Gabriel, only to be halted in his tracks when Gabriel started to laugh.

Sam stared at him. "What the hell?"

Gabriel clutched on to the door frame and laughed harder. He was a sight, his dark curls plastered to his skin, his coat dripping puddles around his boots.

Sam folded his arms and waited for Gabriel to share the joke.

"At least," Gabriel heaved, "you'll be able to take your own clothes off this time."

That was the joke? That was what Gabriel was having hysterics over?

"Are you sure you didn't get dropped on your head?" Sam asked sourly.

He tried to unzip his coat, but his ice-cold fingers refused to cooperate. After watching him struggle for a few minutes, Gabriel quit laughing like a hyena and came over, pushed Sam's useless fingers away, and unzipped the coat. Sam felt as though he were a kid being undressed by his dad. Gabriel pushed the coat off his shoulders, and Sam gratefully got rid of it, shivering as his wet hair dripped down his neck.

"I'll hang the coats up in the utility room and get a couple of towels," Gabriel said. "Sit down, and I'll take your boots off."

"I can manage," Sam groused.

Gabriel ignored him and headed into the utility room.

Sam had managed to untie the knot of the laces on one boot when Gabriel returned and dropped a towel on his head.

"What the—?" Sam spluttered as it obscured his view.

When he could see again, the angry words died away. Gabriel knelt at his feet, worried the other knot until it loosened, and then, with a bit of tugging, he managed to pull off his boots. Sam watched him, longing to run his fingers through the rain-swept dark curls.

Gabriel sat back with a satisfied huff and smiled at Sam. "You should go and have a shower. I'll make us hot chocolate."

Sam shivered, and while he wanted to shout at Gabriel, the thought of being warm and dry while he did it was intensely appealing.

Gabriel stood and pulled Sam to his feet. "Off you go." He took Sam's towel from him and used it to roughly dry his own hair. It stood up like a mane, and Sam smiled. "That's better," Gabriel said. "I was beginning to wonder if you'd ever smile at me again."

Sam growled and headed to his bedroom to pick up dry clothes, this time an old T-shirt of Gabriel's and joggers borrowed from Toby. He was getting tired of wearing other people's clothes. Then he huffed and told himself to get over it. If Gabriel hadn't saved him, he'd be fish food at the bottom of the bay, and no one would know where he'd gone.

The shower was hot and the water plentiful. The cottage had a combi boiler so he could have as long a shower as he wanted. But he reminded himself Gabriel needed to get warm too, and he got out when the cold had finally seeped from his bones.

He redressed, roughly combed his damp hair, and went in search of hot chocolate.

Unaware of Sam's presence in the doorway, Gabriel stood at the kitchen window, a mug wrapped in both hands. He wore a pensive look—not the sorrowful expression that he wore when he thought about Jenny and Michael, but something else. Sam wondered what he was thinking about. Rain lashed the window, and Gabriel jumped, startled from his thoughts. He turned and saw Sam in the doorway.

Sam pretended he hadn't been watching him and sniffed appreciatively at the fragrant chocolate intermingled with the red wine sauce from dinner. "That smells good."

Gabriel pointed to a cup topped with whipped cream and marshmallows. "It's all yours."

"What were you thinking about?" Sam asked before he could stop himself.

Gabriel sighed and ran his hand through his hair. It was still damp from the rain. "I was thinking that Toby might be right."

Sam blinked. That was the last thing he expected to hear. "Toby is right about what?"

"That I need to rejoin the world again. I can't stay here forever."

"Are you ready to rejoin the world?" Sam kept his tone light, not wanting to spook Gabriel.

"Not yet," Gabriel admitted, and Sam's heart sank. "But being a hermit and spending all my days on the cliffs isn't helping me either. I was thinking about seeing a counsellor. Toby's been trying to get me to see one since the funerals."

"I think...." Sam paused to pick his words carefully. "I think you need to know someone is on your side, someone outside of your family. Someone who isn't Toby," he added just to make it clear. He was relieved when Gabriel laughed instead of getting offended.

"That's exactly what Toby said." Gabriel leaned against the kitchen counter and smiled at him. "I think he just wants me to offload on someone else's shoulders rather than him."

"Toby would listen to you until the end of days if that's what you needed, but he's sensible enough to know you need something more than he can provide."

Gabriel gave a rumbling chuckle. "At least a counsellor wouldn't tell me to fuck off."

Sam joined in with the laughter and then took a long swallow of his chocolate. Smooth and sugar slid down the back of his throat. "This is good."

"Is it? Jenny was a real snob about chocolate." Gabriel gave a wry smile. "You must get sick of me talking about 'Jenny this' and 'Jenny that.'"

Sam shook his head. "I don't mind. It makes her more real to me. She's not some mythical being, but a person, a woman who loved you and her family."

"She loved us, and now she's gone."

"But you and Toby and Damien keep her alive."

"Maybe too much." Gabriel shook his head and forced a smile. "I'm going to have that shower, and then I think I'll crash for the night. I'm exhausted."

Sam nodded, not wanting to push Gabriel when he obviously had some hard thinking to do. "I'll clear up the coffee table and damp down the fire. I'll see you in the morning."

Gabriel nodded, walked past, and then stopped and turned to face Sam. "Thank you," he murmured.

Sam looked up at him. "What for?"

"For making me realise there's life again."

"You're welcome," Sam whispered.

He closed his eyes as Gabriel brushed his lips in the gentlest of kisses. Then he was gone, soft footsteps out of the kitchen, and Sam was alone.

"You're welcome," Sam whispered again.

IF SAM had a nightmare, he didn't remember it in the morning. He woke up to bright sunshine and the sound of seagulls squabbling noisily outside the window. As he scratched his armpit and decided what to do next, he watched the plane that hung overhead bob gently in a draft. A fierce rap on the door made him jump.

"Hi Sam, are you awake?" Gabriel asked.

"I am now," Sam said dryly.

"Sorry."

Gabriel didn't sound sorry, but he did offer Sam a cup of tea, a bacon sandwich, and a promise of sitting on the rock before all the tourists arrived for the day.

Sam had been there long enough to appreciate the quiet time before the world woke up, so he said he would be there soon.

"Okay."

Footsteps faded away, and Sam squinted at the clock on the bedside table. 6.20 a.m. What the hell?

"Some people like sleeping," he yelled.

"Stupid people," Gabriel yelled back.

By the time he emerged dressed in the T-shirt and joggers from the previous night, Gabriel and breakfast had vanished, presumably to the rock. Sam's stomach growled at the smell of bacon.

Gabriel was on the rock, his legs crossed, and for once, not looking outwards. He was talking to Toby, who from his clothing and bright-red face, had been out running.

"Morning Toby," Sam said as he sat down next to Gabriel.

"Morning sunshine. He won't let me eat your bacon sandwich."

"Go home and get your own," Gabriel growled.

Sam rolled his eyes and handed half of his sandwich to Toby, who crowed and bit into it.

Gabriel glowered at Sam. "What did you do that for? He'll be unbearable now."

"I'm always unbearable," Toby said smugly. "At least someone loves me."

"Yeah, and he's at home."

Toby winked at Sam and strolled away, chomping noisily on his sandwich. Sam picked up his half and ate it before Toby came back to claim it.

"There's more bacon in the fridge," Gabriel said.

Sam smiled at him. "Thanks."

The bay was beautiful, all white-capped waves in an iridescent green. In the early morning sunlight, it looked almost magical. It was a world of blues and yellows, the faded green of summer all shiny after the previous night's storm. He would miss this when he left, and he was grateful to Gabriel for sharing it with him. He leaned against Gabriel's shoulder, pleased when Gabriel didn't move away.

They stayed where they were until the sun was higher in the sky and the sound of kids laughing and shouting brought a tension to Gabriel's shoulders.

"Let's go inside," Sam suggested.

Gabriel nodded jerkily, and they got to their feet. Sam brushed sand off Gabriel's arse, provoking a snort from him.

"Thanks," he said.

"You could do the same for me," Sam suggested and stuck out his arse just as two young kids ran towards them. "Hold that thought," he said.

Gabriel quirked a smile and flexed his hand as though he were doing just that. "I'll do that."

Sam gathered up the mugs and strolled towards the cottage with a smile, dodging another family with an old-fashioned pram with the tiniest baby Sam had ever seen. He couldn't imagine taking care of anything or anyone that small. "What was Michael like as a baby?"

"Loud," Gabriel said, and he sounded more amused than sad. "He spent the first four months of his life crying. Jenny started to think she was doing something wrong."

"What changed?" Sam asked.

"Solid food. Jenny's mum said he was hungry. Everyone told us it was too early, that babies shouldn't have solid food until they were six months old, including Toby. But Jenny's mum insisted Michael was hungry and fed him baby rice. It's like wallpaper paste. He gobbled it up. We saw the first smile on his face that wasn't wind. The problem we had then was preventing Jenny's mum from overfeeding him."

"So she was right? He was just hungry?"

Gabriel gave a wistful smile. "It seems so. He was always happy with a spoon in his hand and dinner in his hair."

It was at times like this that Sam felt very alienated from Gabriel. He couldn't remember whether he'd ever wanted kids or not, but somehow he didn't think so. He was young and maybe he would change his mind. He looked over his shoulder at the young couple walking close together pushing the pram. They were a family.

He looked at Gabriel. How did he live, watching the happy families day after day? The force of what Gabriel had lost hit Sam like a blow to the gut.

A hand landed on Sam's shoulder. "It's okay, Sam. Breathe." Gabriel's voice was gruff.

Sam looked at him with wide eyes, not even trying to hide his freak-out. "How can you cope?"

Gabriel shrugged. "The alternative is walking off the cliff."

"That doesn't make me feel any better," Sam snapped.

"What do you want me to say?"

"I—I don't know." Sam stormed ahead, ashamed of his anger at Gabriel when it was Gabriel who'd suffered the horrible loss.

Gabriel stopped him as they reached the cottage. "Stop. Why are you so upset?"

Sam glared at him. Then he deflated like a pricked balloon. "I don't know. I don't know."

He blew on strands of hair covering his face, and Gabriel pushed them back and tucked them behind his ear.

"I hated seeing families for months. It tore me up inside. But life goes on, Sam. They didn't know my pain, and what could I do? My family is gone. That's not their problem."

Sam licked his dry lips. The salt air had left them chapped and cracking. "You're so brave."

"No, I'm not. Just putting one foot in front of the other day after day."

Sam ached at the dark pain in Gabriel's eyes. He longed to take it away, to enfold Gabriel in his arms and hold him until the pain subsided. "I wish I could help."

"You are a revelation," Gabriel murmured.

"I am?"

Gabriel nodded, and a shy smile lit up his face. Sam was entranced.

"I didn't want you to stay, but Toby insisted, and I thought, it's just for one night. And you made my house a home again. It's been so empty since Jenny…."

"I know." Sam filled in the sad silence.

"I know it's been just a few days, but I feel alive again in a way I haven't for months."

"I was so scared when I woke up and I didn't know who I was or where I was. I'm still scared, but you're here." Sam felt as though they were in a cocoon. He could hear the laughter and shouts of people around them, overlaid by the shrillness of a crying baby. But none of that was important. There was just him and Gabriel, sunlight dappled through the trees, baring their souls to each other. "Gabriel."

He reached up to cup Gabriel's jaw.

"Don't."

Chapter 11
Gabriel

Sam froze.

Seconds ticked by, and neither of them drew breath. Then Gabriel licked his lips.

"I'm sorry." He wanted Sam's mouth on his even as he blurted out, "I can't." The hitch of his breath betrayed him even in his refusal. He wrapped his hands around Sam's biceps intending to wrench him away.

"Gabriel."

He stilled as Sam whispered his name with such longing that it stopped Gabriel's world.

"It's okay," Sam assured him.

No, it wasn't okay. He shouldn't be feeling like this. This wasn't… this wasn't… he didn't….

Sam's kiss in the rain had taken him by surprise. But this was a slow lead in and gave his brain time to think. Too much time.

Sam was so still Gabriel wasn't even sure he was breathing. Gabriel knew if he walked away, Sam wouldn't follow him. It was Gabriel's decision, and he hated that.

He licked his lips. "Jenny…."

"I know."

But he didn't know. How could he when Gabriel didn't know himself?

Sam brushed away a stray tear from his cheek that Gabriel hadn't even known was there. "You're not ready for this."

For me.

Gabriel heard the words even if they were unspoken. He ran his hands through his hair. "It's too soon."

Sam nodded, and the kindness in his expression made Gabriel feel worse than before. "I understand."

"Jenny...." *Fuck!* He needed to be able to say more than just her name.

"She was your life."

Sam was killing him with his understanding. If he'd been angry, Gabriel would have had something to rail against.

"She was," Gabriel agreed, "but she's gone, and so is Michael."

"You need more time."

"Stop!" The force of his exclamation took Gabriel as much by surprise as Sam. He placed one finger over Sam's mouth and felt the soft, dry lips beneath his fingertip. "Just listen." Sam nodded, wide-eyed above his closed mouth. "Okay." Gabriel paused as he struggled to find the right words. "I never found their bodies. Jenny's and Michael's, I mean. I know they're dead. I feel it here." He took his hand from Sam's mouth and placed it over his heart. He heard Sam's indrawn breath and nodded. "I prayed for a long time for their bodies to be returned to me, but now... I just want them to be at peace together."

"You look out for them every day on the clifftop," Sam said, barely above a whisper.

Gabriel shook his head. "I know they're not coming back. I just feel closer to them there."

"I'm sorry for trying to kiss you again. It was wrong."

Gabriel did what Sam had intended to do. He cupped Sam's jaw and stroked his thumb along the bristles. He needed Sam to stop feeling guilty and *listen*. "Since Jenny died, I've not looked at another woman or man. You know that. I've barely been out of the house or talked to anyone. Then suddenly you come into my life, delivered by a storm, for Christ's sake, and my emotions are all over the place. I don't know what to think or do or say. You still haven't got your memory back. You could be married, for all I know." He saw Sam's stricken expression and knew the same thing had occurred to him. "I can't kiss another man's lover. I'm not made that way."

"I know."

"I need time, and you need to regain more of your memory."

"I don't feel like I'm married, if that helps."

Gabriel gave a wry smile. "I need more proof than that. To fall for you and then to lose you after losing Jenny.... It would be too much."

He saw the understanding dawn in Sam's eyes. Then Sam took a step back out of Gabriel's hands, and Gabriel felt the loss even as he felt the relief. He didn't want to admit even to himself that he already had tumbled head over heels for Sam.

"I need to find out who I really am," Sam said.

"You're a tea-drinking, twenty-three-year-old, non-serial killer. We know that much." Gabriel aimed for levity, but from Sam's clouded expression, he missed by a mile. Sam's next words confirmed it.

"And someone tried to kill me."

Gabriel frowned and chewed on his bottom lip. "You think that's real? Not just a nightmare?"

Sam shrugged and shoved his hands in his pockets. "If it's just a nightmare, why do I keep having the same one over and over?"

"I don't know," Gabriel admitted. "That's why we need to find out more about you."

"If people are trying to kill me, I'm not sure I want to be found."

He looked scared, and Gabriel longed to erase that expression by taking him in his arms. But he couldn't. Not yet. He didn't want the comforting gesture to be misinterpreted when he'd just rejected Sam's kiss.

"You have a home with me as long as you want," he assured Sam.

Sam shook his head. "I can't stay here forever. We won't know anything until we find out who I am. Call the police. Let's see if anyone has reported me missing."

"Are you sure?" Gabriel asked.

"I'm sure."

Gabriel nodded and opened the cottage door. His cell phone was on the coffee table. "I'll call 101."

Sam raised an eyebrow. "You don't think a missing person is an emergency?"

"You were an emergency," Gabriel agreed. "Now that you're safe, I've downgraded you to a routine case." He kept his tone light, but he was aware they were circling each other, their voices flat as they discussed the situation. He pressed his lips together firmly. First, he needed to find out who Sam was.

"THAT WAS... anticlimactic," Sam observed fifteen minutes later, as they sat on the rock on the clifftop again, both of them nursing hot drinks. By mutual consent they had retreated back outside. In public there was less chance of the electric moments between them which were becoming all too frequent. Gabriel looked down in his mug and swirled the cooling liquid. He had drunk more coffee since Sam had arrived than he had in the previous month. He was going to have to go shopping soon to replenish his stores.

"They're busy," he said, aware it was lame.

Sam was right. It had been so routine. Gabriel had given the information to a woman, and Sam had assured her he was okay and not being held against his will. He tried not to snicker at Gabriel's loud snort, and they promised to send a police officer when the village was accessible again. The call was over, and Gabriel suggested they take a drink out to the clifftop. Sam had looked so lost, and he just wanted to take him in his arms, but that way lay danger. Better to put emotional distance between them.

Sam frowned as he stared out to sea.

"What are you thinking?" Gabriel asked hesitantly.

Sam took a long while to answer, but eventually he sighed. "I don't know how I feel about the fact no one has reported me missing. Does no one give a fuck about me enough to even make a report to the police?"

"You don't know your real name," Gabriel said, "or where you lived, or anything to give the police something to match. Give it time."

"How much time?" Sam snarled. "I need to know who I am."

A thought occurred to Gabriel, and he didn't want to mention it, but he had to, just in case it triggered something in the mists of Sam's cotton-wool memory.

"I don't want to upset you, but there might have been someone on the boat. Below decks was flooded, and I didn't have time to check before the boat sank."

It had been a close enough call as it was. He didn't think he'd ever tell Sam just how close they had both come to drowning.

Sam ran his fingers through his long hair and winced as they got caught in tangles. "I hadn't thought of that. God, does that make me selfish? I didn't even ask if anyone else was on the boat."

"You've been kind of busy." Gabriel smiled at him.

Sam didn't smile back. "I might have had family on the boat."

Gabriel thought of the gut-wrenching loss in his heart every time he thought of Jenny and Michael. "Do you feel like you've lost anyone?"

The silence stretched between them for long moments before Sam answered. Gabriel listened to the screech of the seagulls overhead and the waves breaking on the beach below.

"No. I feel like the boat was meant to be my grave. Whoever put me in the boat wanted me dead."

"You don't think it was an accident? You took the boat out and got caught in the storm?"

Sam shook his head. "I'm sure it was deliberate. I don't know how I know, but I'm sure."

There was an uneasy roil in the pit of Gabriel's belly. How could anyone want to kill the vibrant man sitting next to him?

"You're not going anywhere until I know you're safe," he said firmly. Sam said nothing. Gabriel turned to look at him to discover Sam looking down at his mug. "Sam?"

"Sam. I don't even know if that's my name. I don't know anything."

Sam almost shrieked the last words, and seagulls huddling close by in hopeful anticipation of food took flight, accompanied by outraged squawking.

Gabriel didn't want to tell him it would take time. He'd heard that over and over from well-meaning people. It would take time to get over Jenny's and Michael's deaths, but one day the sun would shine again. He'd wanted to shout at them that they didn't know what they were talking about. How could they know what it was like to suffer a tragedy like his?

But the sun was shining again, and its rays shone on the man next to him, his copper hair lighting up the world around him.

And that scared Gabriel.

Sam flashed a strained smile at him. "I'm sorry."

"There's nothing to be sorry about," Gabriel said automatically.

"Yeah, there is. If it weren't for you, I wouldn't be here. You're my anchor. The world might want to kill me, but you'll keep me safe."

Panic swept over Gabriel. "I can't be your anchor."

He'd been that once and failed. He'd not been there when his family needed him the most, and they'd been swept away by the sea. Gabriel *wasn't* strong. Sam couldn't rely on him to be his rock. What if he failed again?

Gabriel stood, needing to get away from Sam. He'd made a mistake taking care of Sam when he was unconscious. He should have insisted Sam stay at Toby's house. "I need to go."

Sam looked up at him. "I'll be here when you get back."

No. Sam needed to leave. Gabriel needed his heart—his life—back. He needed to be on his own. But he didn't say any of that as he strode away. He'd have that conversation later.

Chapter 12
Sam

Tears prickled Sam's eyes as he watched Gabriel hurry away from him, and he swallowed around the sudden lump in his throat. It was ridiculous to be upset at Gabriel's shutdown, but he couldn't help but feel the sting of rejection again.

He caught sight of Gabriel's mug, abandoned on the rock. It was a good analogy for Sam's existence. Sam had nothing. No one. Not even a friend to report him missing. He choked back a sob as a couple walked past, hand-in-hand. Their intimate gesture highlighted how alone he was. As soon as they were out of sight, Sam wiped his eyes with the back of his hand. Tears weren't going to help him. He'd made the mistake of thinking Gabriel would be there for him, and Gabriel had offered to keep him safe, but that was just because he was obliged to. He had no choice until he could offload Sam onto the authorities.

Gabriel was a broken man. Sam knew that. He was still mourning the loss of his family, and just because they'd shared a few moments together didn't mean Sam could ask for anything more. What he wanted and what he could have were two different things. Sam needed to find out who he was and get back to his real life. Gabriel needed more time to grieve, and Sam had to give him that.

He leaned over the clifftop and saw that Gabriel had reached the beach. Sam watched as Gabriel strode towards the water's edge, his hands in his pockets and the wind whipping the hair into his face. Gabriel didn't bother pushing it away, probably knowing it was futile.

Sam wondered how he could bear to be down there, knowing that was where his wife and child had died? Maybe he felt closer to them on the beach. Gabriel paused and turned to look up at the clifftop. He didn't wave, and Sam didn't move, didn't acknowledge him. Gabriel turned his back on Sam.

Sam pressed his lips together, the hurt pricking him again. "Why did I have to meet you now?" he murmured.

Even as he said the words, he knew how ridiculous it was. Gabriel had plucked him out of the sea in the middle of a storm. Would they have met under other circumstances? It was unlikely. A chance meeting with a stranger. One with amnesia and believing someone was trying to kill him. The other still mourning his dead family. It wasn't a match made in heaven.

"Morning."

Sam looked up, his hand guarding his eyes and squinting against the sunlight. "Toby."

Toby stood over him, dressed in a thin, light blue V-neck jumper, dark jeans, and Doc Martens that needed a polish. He eyed Sam, who squirmed under his knowing gaze.

"You look stressed," Toby said finally.

Sam sighed, knowing Toby saw far too much and wasn't going to let it go. "Just thinking it's time I found my way back into the world."

"What did he say?" Toby sounded resigned, but also worried. Who was he concerned about? Gabriel or Sam?

"What makes you think—?"

"He's my brother-in-law, Sam. I've known him for over a decade. You're up here, he's not."

"I said the wrong thing, and he ran away."

Sam pointed to the beach where Gabriel stood with his back to them, his dark hair whipping wildly in the wind, his hands shoved in his pockets.

Toby nodded. "He always goes down there to think."

"Do you ever worry he won't come back?"

The moment the words hit the air, he wanted to take them back.

"Yes." Toby's simple reply tore at Sam's heart.

"I'm sorry, I shouldn't have asked."

Toby sighed and sat next to Sam. "Budge up."

Sam wriggled along the rock and gave him space. Toby was silent for a long while before he spoke.

"For the first six months, I expected to walk into the cottage and find it empty. He was determined to be with Jenny and Michael again, and if he didn't find them alive, then he would join them in death."

"Yet he's still here," Sam said.

Toby looked at him, his expression lost. "For a long while, I thought Gabriel believed Jenny and Michael were still alive."

Sam didn't want to ask, but he had to know the answer. "And now?"

"I think," Toby sighed, "he was looking for a reason to live."

"What happens if he never finds it?"

Toby gave Sam a pointed look. "What makes you think he hasn't?"

"He's not ready for a relationship yet."

"Did he say that?"

"Kind of." Sam was shocked to see a grin appear on Toby's face. "What?"

"Do you realise what you just told me?"

"Uh…?"

"Gabriel is thinking about a relationship. Sam, he's barely spoken a word to anyone since they died, and now you're all he can think about."

"I think you're jumping fences here."

"Am I?" Toby challenged.

"Yeah, you are. For Chrissake, we met three days ago." Sam felt the anger rising inside him. "I don't even know who I am."

"He saved your life three days ago, and that's just temporary."

"I might be married," Sam protested.

"And now we come to the heart of the problem. Let me guess, you made a pass, and he said no."

Sam felt his cheeks burning. "Something like that."

"Gabriel wouldn't go near you if he thought you were with someone else."

"So he says. Problem is, I don't know if I am."

Toby eyed him speculatively. "We need to find out who you are."

Sam held back the *well duh* on his lips. "What do you suggest?"

His fear, although he hadn't said it out loud, was that he'd never get his memory back. Toby had assured him it would come back in time. The head trauma hadn't been that severe.

"We could drop you on your head. You might get your memory back." Toby gave him a vicious grin.

Sam rolled his eyes. "Did they talk to you about your bedside manner when you were training to be a doctor?"

Toby waved his hand. "I skipped that class."

"It shows," Sam said dryly. "What happens if I never get my memory back?"

"Don't start jumping fences, young man. First, you get an X-ray and a CAT scan. Then we find out what's going on with your noggin. Are you still getting bad dreams?"

Sam had been expecting him to say *headaches* and stumbled over his response. "No... yes."

"Which is it?" Toby asked.

"Yes," Sam admitted. "Every time I go to sleep." He'd started to dread closing his eyes, because the same dream happened over and over.

Toby didn't seem surprised. "Have you talked about it to Gabriel?"

"He's the one who wakes me up."

"That's not what I asked."

Sam shook his head. "Not really. He has to calm me down, and by that time, the last thing I feel like doing is talking about the dream." He wrapped his arms around himself as though he were trying to ward off the nightmare that haunted him.

"Have you tried hypnosis?"

"In the last three days?"

Toby frowned and then realised what he'd said. "You're not going to remember, are you?"

"Do you think it would help me to remember the dream or who I am?"

"Your memory will return. It's already started to give you pieces of your life."

"By telling me someone is trying to kill me?" Sam could think of better things to remember.

"I think your brain warning you of potential danger is a damn good thing."

Sam watched Gabriel as he paced along the cove. He hadn't looked up once since that first time. "I should leave him," he murmured. "It's not fair to put him in danger."

Toby followed his gaze. "Gabriel would never flinch from danger. You couldn't be in safer hands."

"He doesn't want me here," Sam said, feeling the truth of that statement like a blow to the heart.

"If he didn't want you here, he'd have thrown you out after the first night. You've been good for him. He hasn't laughed since the day Jenny vanished. Not a single smile. But you've made him feel, and he's running scared. This—" Toby pointed to Gabriel. "This is just Gabriel panicking about the new emotions inside him. He's wrapped himself in his loss for so long he can't cope."

"I can't replace his family."

"No, you can't," Toby said brusquely, "and I'm not expecting you to."

Sam shot him a knowing look. "No? Because I get the opposite impression from the way you're pushing us together."

Toby sighed and ran his hand through his hair. "I'd like to see Gabriel happy again."

"What about you?"

Toby frowned. "What about me? I'm happy."

"Are you?" Sam asked.

"I'm happily married. I've got a great job. Why wouldn't I be happy?" Toby looked genuinely confused.

"And you spend all your time making sure Gabriel doesn't jump off the cliff."

Sam hated the way Toby flinched, but he wanted it out in the open. He needed to know Toby was coming from a place of love and not just offloading the problem in his life to Sam.

Toby's expression darkened. "I will spend the rest of my life taking care of Gabriel if necessary. You'll leave in a couple of days. I'll still be here."

"What about Damien?"

"What about him?" Toby snapped, his fists clenching.

Sam hadn't intended to make Toby so angry. He just wanted to clear the air between them. An elderly man with a backpack looked over at Toby's raised voice. Toby subsided back onto the rock.

"He thinks I coddle Gabriel," Toby admitted. "He thinks I need to let Gabriel move on with his life."

Sam hummed, not wanting to provoke Toby further.

Toby's sigh was resigned. "You think he's right, don't you?"

This was one of those trap questions. Whatever Sam said would be wrong. He hunted for the words that would convey what he meant without hurting Toby.

"I think without you, Gabriel would probably not be here now," he admitted. "I've never met anyone so lost and deep in grief."

"How do you know?"

Toby was teasing, but he had a point. How did Sam know? He turned to see Gabriel making his way back to the stairs.

"I feel it inside." Sam touched his heart.

"You like him, don't you?" Toby asked softly.

Sam decided not to prevaricate. "I do."

"Then we need to find out who you are."

"What if I am with someone?"

"Then you'll know, and you'll go back to your man, and Gabriel will start again."

"You really need to work on that bedside manner," Sam said wryly.

Toby shrugged. "Get used to it."

Sam drew his legs up to his chest and wrapped his arms around them. Leaving Gabriel made him feel sick. No matter what Gabriel said, he was the only anchor Sam had. There was no one else Sam could rely on, except maybe Toby.

Gabriel emerged at the clifftop and walked over to them. He glowered at Toby. "Why are you here?"

"Seeing my patient." Toby pointed at Sam, and Gabriel seemed to relax.

"He's fine," Gabriel said.

"So he says."

Sam waved at them. "Hi. I'm here."

They both ignored him, instead locked in a staring competition Sam didn't understand. To Sam's surprise, Toby broke the gaze first. "Don't be a dick, Gabriel."

"He's not," Sam said heatedly, rushing in to defend him.

Toby snorted, and Gabriel gave a soft laugh. "Yeah, I am. To you, not him. I'll always be a dick to him."

"He will," Toby agreed.

Sam held back the comment that they bickered like a married couple. "How about neither of you are dicks."

Gabriel sat down beside Sam and leant back, propped on his elbows. He raised his face as though he wanted to bask in the sun and closed his eyes. He was almost touching Sam, his warm length pressed up against him, grounding him. It didn't matter what Gabriel said, he was Sam's anchor, and without memory, family, or friends, Sam desperately needed that.

He looked over and saw Toby watching them closely. Toby winked.

"I care for him," he mouthed.

For once Toby didn't come back with a smart retort. So quietly that Sam barely heard him, he said, "I know."

TOBY MADE his excuses and returned home, leaving the two of them alone. Then Sam was left to his own devices when Gabriel muttered something about having to work and vanished back to the cottage. Sam stayed where he was, not sure what to do. He wasn't sure if work was an excuse or real, but the breathing space would do both of them some good. Being near Gabriel was an emotional roller coaster, and he could do with getting off for a while and recovering his breath.

He watched the waves crash and break on the shore below. It was hypnotic in its regularity. While he was in the cottage, the sound of the sea had become a background noise, noted but mainly ignored. Finally he realised he was just avoiding returning to the cottage, and he wandered back slowly. The bedroom door was closed. Gabriel had shut him out again.

Sam was left unsure what to do with himself. He wandered around the cottage, looking at the bookshelves full of novels and CDs. Whoever had been the reader in the family seemed to prefer crime and thrillers. Sam wasn't sure if he'd read any of the books. None of them seemed familiar to him. He contemplated reading one, but he couldn't muster much enthusiasm. Then he wandered into his bedroom, thought about a nap, decided against it, and was about to walk out when he spotted something that made his heart sing tucked to one side of the wardrobe. Sam pulled out a three-quarter size guitar, battered, and covered in dust. He plucked a couple of the strings.

Could he play the guitar? Sam had no idea, but he was going to find out. First it needed a damned good dust. He went on the hunt for a duster which he found under the sink in the kitchen and took his time cleaning the guitar. By the time he'd finished, the guitar looked slightly cleaner, if still battered. He wondered who it belonged to. It looked too old to be Michael's which meant it was either Gabriel's or Jenny's. So he studied it and found a *GP* etched in child-like letters on the casing. Gabriel Pennant. Sam smiled and caressed the strings, feeling as though he were caressing the man himself.

He sat on the sofa, quietly plucking the strings, and winced at how out of tune it was. Then he took his time tuning the strings, sure he had done it before. This was something he intimately knew how to do. He looked at his fingers. The calluses made sense. Finally it was tuned to his satisfaction, and he laid his hand against the strings. What could he play? What did he know?

Play from the heart.

He started playing something. He didn't even know what it was at first, but the notes rippled from beneath his fingers. It made sense. For the first time since he'd woken up on the sofa, this made sense. He reached into himself to pour his heart and soul into the melody.

The last note and the music died away. Sam felt drained, as though he'd run a marathon.

"That was beautiful."

Sam looked up to see Gabriel leaning against the doorjamb, his dark eyes locked on him. He couldn't read Gabriel's guarded expression. "I'm sorry. Did I disturb you?"

"No. Yes. But it doesn't matter. It was a welcome distraction." Gabriel walked over to Sam and sat down in his chair. He was dressed in a hoodie and faded jeans, his feet bare and his hair tousled as though he'd been running his hands through it constantly. He pinged all of Sam's buttons, and his closeness was distracting.

"I know I should have asked before I played it." Sam quickly made the apology.

Gabriel leaned forward, and Sam thought he was going to snatch the guitar out of Sam's hands, but instead he just ran his fingertips over the wood.

"I never thought I'd hear it played again." Gabriel wore a faint half-smile as though remembering something that gave him pleasure.

"The guitar was yours?"

"Yes, although it's been years since I last picked it up, and I could never play like you. Michael had just started to learn because he wanted to play my guitar."

Sam looked down at the guitar. "It seems it's something I know how to do."

"You don't just play it, you own it."

Sam warmed at the obvious admiration in Gabe's eyes. "Yes, I do, don't I."

"Can you play anything else?"

"I don't know. Do you know what I played, then?"

Gabriel's lips twitched. "Even I recognise 'Hello.' Did you remember it?"

"Yeah, I remembered as I played. I can remember Adele."

It didn't make sense to Sam. He just knew his fingers could put the notes together and his brain supplied the information. He closed his eyes, started to play, and faltered at first, but that might have had more to do with Gabriel's nearby presence than his fingers. Gradually he gained confidence, and by the end, was flying over the notes as he had before. He opened his eyes as the last note died away.

Gabriel watched with flattering attention. "You remember that?"

"'Course. Not going to forget a classic like 'Bridge over Troubled Water.'"

And that was how the afternoon progressed. Sam would play, and Gabriel tested him on the name and artist. It turned out Sam's taste was eclectic, from seventies rock to K-pop that Gabriel had to look up because he didn't have a clue. But they both seemed to have an affection for female artists.

When Sam's fingers started to bleed, Gabriel called a halt. He declared it was time for dinner and he was going to cook.

Sam eyed him dubiously. "Are you sure?"

Gabriel rolled his eyes. "I haven't poisoned myself yet, Gordon. I can put together a cottage pie."

"What's cottage pie?" Sam furrowed his brow. "Who's Gordon?"

Gabriel stared at him and burst out laughing, a warm rumbling sound that did strange things to Sam's insides. "Put the guitar down and come and peel potatoes. I'll tell you all about Gordon Ramsay."

THE COTTAGE pie wasn't bad at all, although the potato could have done with more mashing. As they had both had a go at mashing the potatoes, they declared it a joint success and a joint failure.

After dinner they retired to the fireside, and Gabriel spent a lot of time staring into the flames. Finally, Sam could take no more.

"What's bothering you?" he asked.

"The road out of the village is open now. They did the last repairs this morning."

Sam felt as though he'd just taken a step off the cliff. "Oh."

"We could drive out to town tomorrow and finally get your head X-rayed." Gabriel wouldn't meet Sam's gaze.

"That—that sounds good," Sam managed.

"Yeah."

Sam stared into the flames too, not sure how to interpret Gabriel's unenthusiastic response. He swallowed around the dry lump in his throat. "We should go to the police station too."

"Yeah." Short, and even less enthusiastic.

"Gabriel?"

Gabriel sprung to his feet, taking Sam by surprise. "I'm going to bed. It'll be a long day tomorrow. Make sure the guard is around the fire before you go to bed."

The bedroom door shut behind him, and Sam was left on his own. What the hell just happened there?

He stayed where he was for a long while, confused and yes, angry. Was Gabriel so anxious to get rid of him? So anxious to go back to his solo existence?

A tear slipped onto Sam's cheek, and he impatiently dashed it away. He felt completely and utterly alone in the world, his only link shut away behind the wood door.

Chapter 13
Gabriel

The cottage was still quiet when Gabriel awoke, or rather when he got up. He'd lain awake most of the night, staring up at the ceiling. With some hard thinking to do, his brain wasn't going to let him sleep until he'd processed his feelings for Sam.

By dawn he was no nearer untangling the knotted web of emotions he had for the young man. He was tired, confused, and lacking in caffeine.

Gabriel put on a pot of coffee and contemplated going out to the rock to watch the sunrise, but a light spatter of rain discouraged him. In the end he retreated to his bedroom to work. The distractions of the last few days had put him behind schedule, and a few hours of solid concentration was no bad thing. He switched on the computer, took a long slurp of coffee, and started work.

He had no idea how long he'd been engrossed in the project when a knock at the door made him jump. "Yeah?"

"Are you awake?" Sam asked.

"Yep."

"Do you want a coffee?"

"No thanks."

Gabriel had finished the pot of coffee and was lightly buzzing.

"Breakfast?"

"Already done that."

It had been an overripe banana and a packet of crisps, but it was all Gabriel could find to snack on.

"Just what time did you get up?"

Even through the door, Gabriel could hear the amusement in Sam's voice.

Gabriel looked at the clock. It was nearly ten o'clock. He'd been working for almost five hours.

"Too early," he said. "Hold on. I'll come out."

"You don't have to."

"I want to."

Gabriel saved his work and pushed back his chair. A short break would do him good. He stood, stretched out tired muscles, and went to the door. Sam stood outside, looking adorably sleep rumpled and sporting bright bed hair.

"Sorry to have disturbed you," Sam said, worrying his bottom lip.

"Not a problem. I needed a break."

"Sure I can't get you a coffee?"

Gabe shook his head. "I drank an entire pot."

Sam chuckled as he headed into the kitchen. "So you're wired now."

"Something like that."

"Are you planning to work all morning?"

The road through the village was open again, and they'd planned to drive to the police station in the afternoon as Gabriel had said he had work to do in the morning.

"I don't have much more to do. I managed to get most of the work done, thanks to the coffee. What did you have in mind?"

From the way Sam bounced on his toes, he could have been the one consuming the caffeine. "This is my last day. I want to do something."

"Like what?"

"I want to go for a walk."

The last time Gabriel had looked out the window, it had been raining, but now sun streamed through the windows and he could see the blue skies topped with the occasional fluffy cloud. He turned to see Sam's hopeful gaze. It was tempting to ask Sam to go for a walk by himself because he was close to finishing the part of the project that required all his attention, but then he absorbed Sam's words. It was his last day. Gabriel damped down the disappointment he was already feeling and smiled. "Okay, then."

"Are you sure you can take the time?" Sam asked.

"I've been working for nearly five hours. I've done a full day already." Gabriel rolled his tired shoulders. "A walk will do me good."

He sat next to Sam as they put their boots on and jostled and laughed as they got in each other's way. Gabriel couldn't remember the last time he'd had so much fun doing something so mundane. They tugged on jumpers because Sam said the breeze was brisk. Gabriel's was a dark mossy green, and Sam wore a charcoal grey sweater that had been bought for Gabriel but never worn because it was far too small for him. It suited his colouring, and Gabriel liked the way his copper curls spilled across the darkness of the jumper.

"Ready?" Gabriel asked as he finished tying his boots.

Sam grinned at him like a small child, and for a moment, Gabriel saw the echoes of Michael in Sam's excited expression. Michael had always been racing to get out of the door the moment anyone suggested a walk. "Can't wait."

"You're like an excited puppy," Gabriel drawled to distract himself from memories of his son.

"It's all right," Sam said. "I've been house trained. I won't pee on your rug." Then he burst out laughing at Gabriel's horrified expression.

Gabriel shook his head. "Where your mind goes."

Sam tapped his forehead. "It's still empty up there. Say one thing, and it rattles off in a million different directions."

"Including puppies peeing on carpets."

"You were the one who mentioned puppies," Sam said as he bounced out the door.

Maybe Gabriel needed to shut the hell up. He watched Sam race ahead of him and narrowed his eyes. Sam was... off, somehow. As though he were acting excited rather than actually being excited.

He knew Sam was nervous about the visit to the police station. He'd been cocooned in Gabriel's world, and now he was going to have to face reality. This was pure adrenaline and nerves. Maybe the walk would get rid of some of the excess energy and calm him down. Gabriel hoped he did before they faced the local police. He grimaced as he thought of that prospect.

"Why are you making faces?" Sam asked as Gabriel joined him where they met the gravel path.

"Just thinking about work," Gabriel lied.

Sam shot him a look as though he didn't believe his explanation, but he didn't push Gabriel further. He sucked in the sea air as they crunched over the path. "I should have got you to take me for a walk before. I don't know why I didn't ask."

His grin was infectious, and Gabriel found himself smiling and relaxing in his company.

"I don't really go for walks," Gabriel admitted, thinking about the confines he'd put around his life. "I'm either working, on the clifftop, or walking along the bay. And being annoyed by Toby, of course."

"Well, now's your chance to show me more than where you live." Sam sighed. "It's so beautiful here, Gabriel."

"It is." And for once Gabriel didn't feel a kick to his gut. His little world *was* beautiful. It was why he and Jenny had stayed here for so long, even though it was so isolated. "Okay, I'll play tourist guide. Which way do you want to go?"

Sam looked both ways along the coastline. "That way." He pointed left, towards Perranporth.

"Come on then. We can get an ice cream at the coffee shop."

Sam's eyes lit up, and Gabriel was reminded of Michael once more. "That would be great. Have you got any money?"

Gabriel felt his pockets. Empty. "Uh, no. Stay there."

He jogged back to the cottage and took a moment to hunt for his wallet as it wasn't where he usually stored it. He was about to jog back to Sam to ask if he'd put it somewhere, when he found it in a small bowl next to where he stored his keys. Logical, but not where he would have expected to find it.

Sam wasn't where he expected to find him either. Gabriel found Sam standing next to their rock, his face up to the sun. He stopped and just watched him for a moment. Sam could have been a model in a magazine, he looked so perfect. Even the secondhand, not-quite-fitting clothes didn't detract from his natural beauty. He'd acquired colour in his face from the sun and the wind, and he looked a far cry from the drowned rat of a few days before.

"Communing with the sun?" Gabriel asked as he joined him.

Sam didn't even open his eyes as he said, "Waiting for you to hurry the hell up so I can get my ice cream."

"I'd have been quicker if I'd known where my wallet was," Gabriel pointed out.

Sam blushed just a little. "Oh yeah, sorry. I moved it when I dusted."

Gabriel stared at him. "You dusted?"

"You didn't notice? Damn, I should have done a better job."

"I... damn. You didn't have to do that."

Sam shrugged. "A small payment for you saving my life and hosting me."

"No payment needed."

"You can still buy me that ice cream, though."

"You're on."

They ambled along, and Sam chattered excitedly as he saw more than just the bay infecting Gabriel with his enthusiasm. Gabriel's interest in the flora and fauna of the rock pools extended to the wild plants growing along the cliff tops, and he pointed out edible plants and enthused about the wild garlic found in springtime.

"For someone who doesn't like cooking, you know a lot about edible plants."

"Jenny was interested in the local plants she could use for cooking, and I wanted to please her." From the moment he met her, he'd known he would spend his entire life wanting to please her.

Sam didn't respond, and Gabriel turned to see the wistful look on his face.

"Sam?"

"Jenny was very lucky to have claimed your heart."

A familiar lump formed in Gabriel's throat, and he had to swallow back the tears. "I was the lucky one. She loved me just as fiercely."

"You deserve it," Sam said so quietly Gabriel barely heard him. "You really deserve it."

Gabriel swallowed back a lump in his throat and looked around. They were on their own, the cliff path was empty, and the only people in sight were far in the distance. He never expected to be having a heartfelt conversation about his entangled emotions on a clifftop with someone he barely knew, but he was beginning to think there was a reason Sam had been dropped into his life—to have these conversations. God, he'd done nothing but talk about his feelings for a year. He was sick of it. Now he wanted to do something different. He turned to Sam, took his courage in his hands, and threaded their fingers together. "I think I'm starting to understand that."

Sam looked somewhat startled at Gabriel agreeing with him. "That you deserve to be loved fiercely?"

"I thought love was a one-time deal, Sam. I thought that was it for me. I'd found my soulmate, and once she was gone, I was destined to be alone." Gabriel had seen his future, and it had stretched out interminably. He'd been convinced he would end up as a lonely old man, still standing watch over the bay.

Sam nodded as though he understood, although Gabriel didn't know how he could, because he barely understood it himself. "And now?"

"Now I think that I can love and be loved again. It won't be the same, but it doesn't have to be. I'm not looking for a replacement for Jenny."

"What are you saying?" Sam asked, his voice cracking.

Gabriel stared into Sam's stormy-grey eyes and begged, "Please let me kiss you."

Sam's expression was troubled. "There's nothing more I want than to kiss you, but are you sure it's what you want? I don't think I could kiss you and then take another rejection."

"Yesterday was never about you. You know that."

"It's not you, it's me?" Sam smiled, but the laughter didn't reach his eyes.

Gabriel cursed himself for putting the sadness in Sam's eyes. "Something like that." Gabriel looked at their joined hands. "I was never rejecting you."

"Just the idea of an us." The idea of an *us* again after so long had been a terrifying idea. "It doesn't seem so frightening now."

Sam blinked, his long lashes fanning over his eyes. "You mean that?"

"I mean it."

"Then show me."

Gabriel could do that. His emotions were still on a roller coaster and he didn't have a clue what would happen next, especially to Sam, but he was ready to show Sam exactly how he felt about him.

"You're so beautiful," he murmured, his fingers carding through Sam's hair to cup his head.

"You're just biased," Sam said shakily.

"I am."

Gabriel contemplated Sam's mouth for a moment—lush, full, a little chapped by the weather but ultimately kissable.

"Don't tease," Sam pleaded.

"Not teasing. Just thinking."

"Thinking what?"

Gabriel wrapped his free arm around Sam's back and inclined his head. "The best way to kiss you."

"Stop bloody thinking. Just do it." Sam growled and reached up for Gabriel's mouth.

"Not this time," Gabriel whispered as he pulled back.

Thwarted in his attempt to kiss Gabriel, Sam furrowed his brow. "Not this time what?"

"I'm kissing you this time."

Sam's arms wrapped around his neck. "Yes, please."

Gabriel closed the distance between them and nibbled on Sam's full bottom lip. Okay, so maybe he was a bit of a tease. Sam melted into his arms, and then Gabriel needed more. He pressed his mouth to Sam's, feeling it lush and alive under his. Sam was passive, taking Gabriel's order/plea to heart and not trying to control the moment. Gabriel kissed Sam gently and licked along the seam of his lips until Sam's mouth opened for his.

Sam pressed himself flush against Gabriel, almost on tiptoes in his anxiousness to be close to him. Gabriel wanted to cup his arse and hold him closer, but even in his haze of pleasure, he was still conscious they were in public. The kissing wasn't going to stop, though.

He explored Sam's mouth with lazy contentment—tongue, teeth, lips again. Gabriel was aroused but not unbearably so. He was more interested in learning the feel of Sam from his soft mouth to his hard, lean body against him. From the strength of Sam's arms around his neck, Sam felt exactly the same way. All the pent-up energy Sam had been showing was being poured out through his kiss. It was overwhelming to be the focus of all that energy.

They broke their kiss to breathe and rested their foreheads against each other. Gabriel stroked down Sam's sun-heated back, and Gabriel felt it was almost as intimate as kissing. Sam unlocked his arms from Gabriel's neck and took the slightest of steps back.

"Wow," Sam said somewhat breathlessly.

"Wow," Gabriel agreed.

They stared at each other, wide-eyed and breathless, and Gabriel had a sudden urge to put Sam over his shoulder again and haul him back to his cave.

"Your eyes go almost black when you think about fucking me," Sam murmured.

"In a moment," Gabriel said. "I have some more kissing to do."

He put one finger under Sam's chin and kissed him again, demanding Sam's full attention. Sam gave it to him willingly, trading him kiss for kiss, filling his senses, making him unaware of his surroundings until a shout penetrated the haze he was in.

"Storm Maitland?"

Chapter 14
Sam

"Storm Maitland?"

It was the first word that caught Sam's attention. All of him was involved in Gabriel's kiss, the touch of his lips slightly chapped by the wind and rain, the taste of coffee and peppermint, and the soft feel of his jumper beneath Sam's hands.

"Who's Storm Maitland, Lisa? Is he a friend of yours?"

"For God's sake, Mum, you're being embarrassing."

It was obvious to Sam their moment together was over. Reluctantly, he drew back from Gabriel, still thrumming with thwarted desire. He gave him an apologetic smile and turned to see four people staring at him—a man with a bright-red nose and cheeks, a woman wearing a floppy straw hat, and two teenagers. He noticed the family similarity between the kids and the adults. Then he saw the shocked, openmouthed expressions of the teenagers. The man and the woman looked quizzically at their kids.

The teenage girl, maybe sixteen or seventeen, took two steps towards them and stopped; her expression wary. "Are you Storm Maitland?" She wore a mustard coloured floral dress and strappy shoes, more suitable for a night out than a walk on the cliffs.

It sank in she was aiming the question at him. Before he could ask what she was talking about, the boy beside her answered.

"Course he is. He looks just like him. Didn't know he was gay."

She rolled her eyes at her little brother. "Course he's gay. Everyone knows that."

"They do?" Sam murmured.

Gabriel stiffened and moved so he was between Sam and these strangers. "You know who he is?"

His voice was harsh and unfriendly, and the two kids looked back at their parents for reassurance. They moved closer to their children, their expressions changing from quizzical to wary.

"What's going on, Lisa?" the woman asked. She had the same honey-blond hair that her daughter had, although Sam was pretty sure hers was out of a bottle.

Lisa pointed at Sam. "He's Storm Maitland, the pop star who went missing a couple of days ago. You remember. He was on the news. It's been all over Twitter."

Sam's first thought was amazement that his name really was Storm, not Sam, and his second was utter panic.

"What are you talking about?" Gabriel snarled, and Sam's panic lessened as he realised he was going to have to speak to the family before Gabriel frightened them away.

He stepped around Gabriel and smiled at the girl, hoping to reassure her and calm the deep scowl on Gabriel's face. "Hi Lisa. You know more than me at the moment. I banged my head in an accident." He turned to show her the bruise on his temple. "I can't remember much except I like tea and I hate coffee."

She pulled a face. "I hate coffee too. You've got amnesia? That's so cool."

Unless you're the person who can't remember a thing.

Sam gave a wry smile. "It's a bit frustrating. You say my name is Storm Maitland and I'm a pop star?"

At least now he understood why he could play the guitar.

Lisa blinked. Then she pulled out her phone and scrolled furiously while her brother looked at Sam as though he were a unicorn. "Here." She thrust out her phone.

Sam drew closer and looked at the screen. Gabriel peered at it too. It was the BBC news with the headline, Pop Star in Mystery Disappearance. Underneath was a picture of someone who looked very much like him.

"May I read it?" He held his hand out, and after a moment, Lisa reluctantly gave up her phone.

He scanned it, and Gabriel read over his shoulder.

Storm Maitland, 23, a singer-songwriter on the brink of mega-stardom, has been missing for four days, his record company revealed. He disappeared after dinner on Thursday, September 8 and has not been seen since. Coldstar Records is offering a reward for any information leading to Maitland's safe return.

Gabriel snorted in his ear. "You could be a lost dog."

Sam thought the same thing. His record label was missing him? What about family or friends?

"No one knew where you were," Lisa said uncertainly.

Sam snorted. "I didn't know where I was. If it hadn't been for Gabriel here, I'd have drowned."

"You saved him?" Lisa gave Gabriel the kind of dubious I-don't-think-so look teenage girls were notorious for.

Sam nearly burst out laughing, which wouldn't have gone down well with either Lisa or Gabriel. "I was lucky he saved me, but you found me."

"Lisa should get the reward," her brother said.

Sam blinked at him. "What?"

"She found you, so she should get the reward, not him." He pointed a sandy finger at Gabriel.

"Alfie, don't talk nonsense," his mum said.

Alfie pressed his lips together in a mutinous fashion. "It says there is a reward for whoever has information. Look!" He pointed to Lisa's phone.

Sam held up his hands. "I'm sure there'll be a reward for Lisa. First, we need to contact the police and my record company to let them know I'm safe. Lisa, I'm going to call the company, but if you leave me your phone number, then I'll get the reward sent to you."

Lisa started to recite her number, but her mother stepped forward.

"She's not giving her phone number out to a strange man. I don't care how famous he is," she said as Lisa protested. "You can take mine."

Sam nodded, not wanting to get involved in any safeguarding issue that could blow up in his face on social media. He might not remember who he was, but that sort of thing had to be tricky, didn't it?

He was aware of Gabriel almost vibrating next to him, and he smiled up at him apologetically, aware the man was as ashen as though he were ready to pass out. "I don't have a phone. Could you take Lisa's mum's number?"

It took a moment, but then Gabriel nodded and pulled out his phone. A few taps, and he handed it to Lisa's mum. "Put your number in here."

She looked as reluctant as Gabriel, but she did as asked. Sam exchanged an apologetic look with Lisa.

"How much?" Alfie demanded.

Sam blinked. "How much what?"

"How much is the reward? Is it a million pounds?"

"Don't be so stupid." Lisa shoved him hard and he stumbled, but he recovered quickly and launched himself at his sister with a loud yell.

To Sam's amusement, Gabriel put himself between the warring teenagers and Sam. "It's okay," he whispered. "I think they want to fight each other, not me."

Gabriel grunted and didn't move an inch. *Wonderful, ridiculous man.*

If they'd been on their own, Sam would have drawn Gabriel into his embrace and kissed him again until they were both breathless.

Lisa's mum huffed, and she looked embarrassed at her offspring's behaviour. "For heaven's sake, you two, cut it out." She looked at Sam. "I'm so sorry."

He grinned at her. "It's okay. But I think we'll go back to the cottage now. I've got a lot to do."

Alfie looked up from trying to punch his sister. "Don't forget about the reward, or I'll put it on Twitter."

"You haven't got a Twitter account," Lisa said scornfully.

"Have too," he yelled.

"Have not."

They launched at each other again, and Sam tugged at Gabriel's jumper. "Get me out of here," he muttered.

Gabriel turned on his heel and guided Sam away without another word. Sam's ears were ringing with the shouts from Lisa and Alfie, and he could feel a headache brewing at his temples.

"So… you're a famous rock star," Gabriel said as he strode back to the cottage.

Sam had to hurry to catch up with his long strides. "So it seems," he agreed somewhat breathlessly. He would have preferred being dragged back for a morning of sweet fucking than this angry march.

"Huh."

When Gabriel didn't elaborate, Sam looked at him. "Huh?"

"Didn't see that one coming."

"Me neither," Sam said honestly.

Gabriel carried on walking. "You played my old guitar, and you didn't remember anything about being a rock star?"

Sam thought about it for a long moment. There was nothing in the void of his memories, not even a hint that he'd been a musician, let alone a celebrity. "Not a thing. Even when I played the guitar, it was muscle memory rather than actual memory. I knew I could do it, but I couldn't relate it to anything in my life."

They crunched over the gravel. Just before they reached the cottage, Gabriel's phone rang. For one awful moment, Sam thought it was Archie demanding the reward again, but Gabriel said, "It's Toby."

"Don't… don't tell him yet," Sam begged. He just needed a moment alone with Gabriel to process what was going on. Even Toby would be too much.

Gabriel raised an eyebrow, but he nodded. "Hey, Tobes." He listened for a moment. "Yeah, okay, but later, yeah? Sam's got a headache. No, nothing serious. He's going to lie down for an hour. Yeah, sure. Come over later. I'll call you when he's awake."

Sam expelled a long breath when Gabriel disconnected the call. "Thanks."

"The headache isn't a lie, is it?" Gabriel asked shrewdly, and the anger seemed to drain out of him.

He leaned against the wall by the door and shook his head. "I should take a couple of paracetamol."

"Come and sit down," Gabriel said as he opened the door and gently pushed Sam through. Then he shut the door on the rest of the world. "I'll get the tablets. You close your eyes for a moment."

Sam felt he could breathe again now they were on their own. In here, he was safe with Gabriel. Outside the door, he was suddenly a whole new person and someone he didn't know. Storm Maitland. Who the hell was he?

"Hey."

Sam looked up as Gabriel cupped his jaw. "Uh…."

Gabriel stared down at him, his eyes dark and intense. "It's okay, Sam. You don't have to do this by yourself."

"Promise?" He knew it sounded weak, but he was a heartbeat away from a panic attack. His hands were clammy, and blood pounded in his ears.

"I promise. We'll find out who you are together."

Gabriel's deep-thunder-in-the-distance voice soothed him, and when Gabriel drew him into his arms and pulled him against his chest, he felt even better. Sam leaned his cheek against the soft jumper and soaked up the lavender and spices he'd come to associate with Gabriel. He swallowed hard. This might be the last time he was held by Gabriel. Once he made that call to the record company, he'd be sucked into his old life. Tears pricked at the back of his eyes. He wasn't ready for that yet.

Sam raised his head, dashing the tears away with an impatient hand. "I should call people. Do I call the police again? 'Hey, you remember me. I'm the famous pop singer who went missing.' My record company? Do I have any family? I still don't know who tried to kill me."

"One thing at a time," Gabriel said. He steered Sam to the sofa and sat down beside him. "The problem is that what we don't know is still far more than what we do know."

"We have a name… my name."

"Let's start from there. I'll get my laptop and tablet. I'll make tea and coffee, and we'll do research."

"How long do you think Alfie will give us before he starts yelling about rewards on social media?" Sam asked dryly.

Gabriel's lips twisted. "You have to admire his persistence, if not his motives."

"He's right, though. Lisa recognised me. If there is a reward, she deserves it."

"Let's find out if you really are Storm Maitland before you hand over half your fortune."

Sam blinked at the thought. "Just the idea I have money is amazing. I have nothing at the moment. Not even the clothes I'm wearing are mine."

"When we call whoever, they can bring you some of your own clothes." Gabriel stood and looked down at Sam. "You're not alone, Sam. You have me and Toby and even, God help you, Damien."

Sam curled his fingers and held back the urge to fall at Gabriel's feet and beg him not to send him away. Dammit, he was supposed to be a musician, not a drama queen. "It's good to know," he said huskily.

Chapter 15
Gabriel

Gabriel was grateful for a few minutes alone in the kitchen to process his thoughts. He'd felt icy to the core the moment he realised someone recognised Sam. He wasn't ready to have the world intrude on him, but now it looked as though he didn't have a choice. He went through the motions of making tea for Sam and coffee for himself, knowing that in a few moments, Sam would confirm his true identity, make a couple of phone calls, and their time together would be over. As he poured the boiling water over the coffee granules, he wondered if this time together had been some kind of sick joke the cosmos was playing on him. He sucked in a breath.

"Get over yourself, Pennant. This is about Sam, not you."

Five minutes later, steaming mugs on the coffee table, Gabriel typed in *Storm Maitland* and tapped Enter. He held his breath as he waited, damn sure that Sam wasn't breathing either.

"Bloody hell," Sam said.

Gabriel expelled a noisy breath. "Well, that answers that question. Now we know who you are."

Sam's face stared out at them, his copper hair gleaming under the lights, an electric guitar in his hands under the headline Pop Star Missing on His Birthday.

"My God, this is me." Sam reached out with trembling fingers to touch his face on the screen.

"You're exactly who they said you were. And look, your name really is Sam." Gabriel pointed to Storm's wiki entry, which gave his real name as Samuel Adam Maitland.

"No wonder it felt right," Sam murmured. "And my birthday was five days ago."

Christ, he was only *just* twenty-three.

Gabriel clicked on one of the many articles and scanned it briefly. It didn't tell him much other than that Storm's set at Reading Festival had been a success. He tried another article, this time an interview with a tabloid newspaper. The image was of Storm, sat on the dock of a lake, wearing denim shorts and a tight white T-shirt, his feet dangling in the water as he played an acoustic guitar.

"I have a brother." Sam sounded strangled. "He's my manager."

"He must be worried about you," Gabriel said quietly.

He could focus on Sam's brother and how anguished he must be feeling. That was normal. This… this was not normal. Every article, every image, was like a slap in the face. He couldn't deny Sam's identity anymore. He'd always known this moment would come, and Sam would find out who he really was, but not for one moment did he think Sam would be famous. He'd imagined…. Hell, he had no idea what he'd imagined, but not this. There was no way Sam would stay in his life now. Gabriel looked at the images. He'd toured the world, been invited to premieres, shaken hands with Prince Harry for God's sake. Storm Maitland was on his way to being an A-lister.

"Gabriel?" Sam's voice cracked.

He turned to look at Sam, expecting to see relief, and instead saw the utter terror in his eyes. Gabriel recognised that fear. He'd felt it himself when he reached the beach where his wife and son should be and found only one of Michael's shoes. He'd felt that fear when the coastguard returned with no news, time after time. And the knowledge that he would be alone forever when he realised Jenny and Michael were surely dead was all-consuming. That fear consumed Sam now. He was looking at a stranger on a screen who was supposed to be him.

"It's okay," Gabriel said automatically.

Sam shook his head and wrapped his arms around himself. "It's not okay. I don't know who he is." He pointed at the screen at an image of himself at an award ceremony. "He looks like me, but I don't remember him."

The pain in his voice broke Gabriel's heart. He hauled Sam against his chest and wrapped him in his arms. "It's okay." And he meant it this time. "I've got you. I won't let anyone hurt you."

Sam buried his face in the crook of Gabriel's neck. "I can't do this by myself." He felt hot tears slake his skin. Sam was obviously scared, and who wouldn't be, faced with such an unknown reality.

"I promised you weren't alone, and I mean it." Gabriel held on tight to Sam and waited for the tears to cease. He murmured soothing words into Sam's hair, the meaning unimportant. He just needed Sam to know Gabriel had his back.

As he held the shaking man, Gabriel was uncomfortably aware the clock was ticking. No way would Lisa and her family keep quiet on the biggest news story of the year. Sam was going to have to call someone soon and let them know he was alive.

Finally Sam pulled away and sat up, wiping his eyes with the back of his hand. "I'm sorry," he muttered, refusing to meet Gabriel's eyes.

Gabriel was confused. "What are you sorry for?"

"For falling apart over something so stupid." He sniffed, and Gabriel reached over to a side table and tossed him a box of tissues. "Thanks." Sam blew his nose noisily. "I find out who I am, and then I fall apart. I'm such an idiot."

Gabriel ran his finger down Sam's wet cheek. "You're not an idiot. You're just a bit overwhelmed at the moment. It's not as though you remember Storm Maitland, rock god."

Sam snorted. "I don't even know what kind of music I write."

Gabriel was embarrassed to admit he had no clue either, but he did have an idea. "You've got to be on YouTube or Spotify."

Sam nodded and gave a wan smile. "You'd think I'd remember something about my music if not my life."

Gabriel went onto Spotify and searched for Storm Maitland.

"Wow," Sam said faintly. "This is real. *I'm* real."

"Let's hear you." Gabriel played the latest album and leaned back into the sofa, pulling Sam against him, wrapping an arm around his chest and his hand over Sam's heart. He wanted Sam to know he was safe as he listened to himself.

Gabriel was more of a hard rock than pop fan, but he had to admit Sam was good, his voice soaring in plaintive melody. The song reminded Gabriel of early morning sunrises gazing out over the sea. "Is anything familiar?"

Sam tilted his head to look up at Gabriel. "It sounds stupid, but there's nothing. I don't recognise the words or the melody. It's all blank. If I write music, shouldn't I remember something?"

"I don't know anything about amnesia beyond what Toby told me, but…." Gabriel hesitated for a long time before he took Sam's hand.

"Your only memory is of someone trying to kill you. It's not surprising you don't want to remember who you are. You might be trying to blank it out."

The silence in the cottage seemed to stretch on for an eternity before Sam shuddered and held tightly on to Gabriel's hand. "If you're right and I make that call, what am I going back to?"

"You're not going anywhere until we both know it's safe," Gabriel insisted. "I don't care what your record company says. You can stay here until they investigate who's trying to kill you."

Gabriel didn't say that he didn't want Sam to leave him. He didn't have that right.

Sam gave him a grateful, if doubtful smile. "I need to talk to my brother. Tell him what happened. Maybe I need security."

"Don't all pop stars have bodyguards?"

Sam's eyebrow flew up. "You're asking me? The pop star with no memory?"

Gabriel grinned at him. "You have a point."

"I'm not going to be much use to the record company if I can't remember any of my songs."

"That's what lyrics and sheet music are for," Gabriel said.

Sam sat up, and Gabriel missed the warmth of his body. "Your guitar? Can I…., I mean…."

"I'll get it." Gabriel unfolded his length from the sofa and stood. "Is it in your bedroom?"

Sam's bedroom, not Michael's.

Gabriel swallowed hard as he realised what he'd said.

"It's on the bed," Sam said gently, brushing the back of Gabriel's hand.

"Okay." Gabriel smiled down at Sam. "Okay."

He left the room before he made a complete tit of himself and went into the small bedroom. The guitar was at the foot of the bed. He picked it up and held it in both hands. Michael had spent hours playing the guitar, resisting all Gabriel's attempts to replace it with a new one. Now Sam played it too, with the same care and devotion his son had shown. How could he have found two people who loved this battered old guitar?

Gabriel went back into the great room to see Sam staring at the photo of himself on the laptop screen. This was not a man who was happy to have discovered who he truly was. He looked scared, and

Gabriel wanted to shut the laptop and tell him not to make that phone call. He could stay here and be plain old Sam for the rest of his life. Then Sam looked up, and his smile eased some of the worry in Gabriel's heart.

"Let's see if I can remember any of my music," Sam murmured, taking the guitar from Gabriel as he sat down on his chair, this time to give Sam room to play.

Gabriel watched as Sam closed his eyes, his hands over the strings. He played a few notes and paused, his lips pressing together in frustration.

"It's okay if you can't remember, Sam," Gabriel tried to reassure him. "It will come back in time."

Discordant notes made him flinch, and he wanted to take his guitar away from the abuse, but then Sam sighed and placed his hand flat against the strings.

"I should know now," Sam cried out.

"You will do," Gabriel promised.

"It's there. I can feel it. Like there's a veil in place, and I can't tear it down." Sam ran his hand through his hair in frustration.

Gabriel sought for something to make Sam feel better. "We could go for a walk."

"No." Sam shook his head vehemently. "I don't want to go out there."

Gabriel understood. He wanted to shut out the world and forget it existed. He moved so he was beside Sam again and took the guitar out of his hands. Then he turned to face Sam, tucked one leg underneath him, and cupped Sam's jaw. "You are safe with me, I promise. In here no one can get you."

"You saved me once," Sam said. "You can't keep saving me. I've got to face the world at some point."

"Then you face it with me by your side," Gabriel insisted. "I know what it's like to be alone, Sam. I had Toby and Damien, and I still felt like I was alone forever."

A tear spilled onto Sam's cheek, and he impatiently dashed it away. "I've got to make that fucking call."

"I could call them for you," Gabriel offered.

Sam hesitated, and Gabriel could see he wanted to accept, but finally he shook his head. "I'll do it. May I borrow your phone?"

"Of course."

Gabriel picked it up from beside the laptop and handed it to Sam, who stared at it for a long moment. Jenny and Michael smiled back at them both.

"Sam?" Gabriel was afraid to know what he was thinking.

He turned to smile at Gabriel, and Gabriel ached at the pain clearly etched, although Sam tried to hide it.

"It's time I jumped off the cliff," Sam said and tapped out the number.

Chapter 16
Sam

"Coldstar Records. How may I help you?" A professional female voice answered the phone. Sam thought it sounded vaguely familiar.

"Hi... um... my name is Sam.... Storm Maitland. I think you might be looking for me." Sam stumbled over his name, not sure whether they knew him as Storm or Sam.

"All leads regarding Storm have to be sent to the police," she said in a bored tone, with the long-suffering patience of one who had said that many times before.

"We tried that already," Sam muttered. "I don't have a lead on Storm. I am Storm. I think."

"You think?" She sounded incredulous.

"I'm suffering from amnesia."

"Nice try, mate. Go to A&E."

She disconnected the call.

Sam listened to the nothingness for a moment and then stared at Gabriel. "She hung up on me."

"She did what?"

"The receptionist hung up on me."

Gabriel huffed and took the phone, redialling the same number Sam had a couple of moments before.

Sam heard the "Coldstar Records. How may I help you?" before Gabriel started to speak.

"Listen," Gabriel snapped, his eyebrows knitting together in a frown. "My name is Gabriel Pennant. I have Storm Maitland sitting beside me. No, this isn't a joke. He has amnesia, and we've just found out who he is. Now put me through to the CEO or someone with authority."

It was ridiculous, but Sam grew hard at Gabriel's dominating tone. He'd seen Gabriel in a number of moods, but demanding Gabriel was very sexy.

Unaware of Sam's sudden and inappropriate lustful feelings, Gabriel listened before he spoke again. "And who are you?"

Nerves curled through Sam as he waited, not sure who Gabriel was talking to. At least they hadn't hung up on him.

"Yes, it is. You want proof? Give me an email address or phone number and I'll send you a photo."

Gabriel scribbled something on a notepad on the table and disconnected the call after a terse "You have caller ID?"

He looked at Sam, who clutched his hands together. "I've just spoken to Graham Baines, the CEO. He wants proof it's you."

Sam furrowed his brow. "Like what?"

Gabriel held up his phone. "I'll take a photo of you."

Right. Sam ran his hand through his hair. That was stupid of him. Of course they wanted to see a photo to prove it was him. Gabriel snapped one and sent it. Two minutes later, the phone rang.

Gabriel answered it. "Hello. Yes, he's here." He held the phone out to Sam. "They want to talk to you."

Sam took the phone with trembling fingers. "Hello?"

"Storm. Is that you?"

The voice blasted down the phone at him, and he flinched. Gabriel put a hand on his knee. The touch was comforting and soothed him.

"Yes. At least I think so."

"Storm, baby, oh thank God. We thought you were dead."

"Not dead yet," Sam said tightly.

"Baby, Nessa's on the phone to Colin. Give me your address, and we'll get security down to pick you up immediately."

Sam shook his head, even though they couldn't see. He knew Gabriel would hate having his home invaded by people he didn't know. Who were Nessa and Colin? Colin sounded familiar. Then he remembered Colin was his brother. "I could come to you."

"You stay there. We don't want to lose you again. What's your address?"

"I don't know. I need to ask Gabriel." Sam looked at Gabriel. "He wants this address."

Gabriel held his hand out and took the phone again. "Hi. This is my address." He reeled it off, confirming it when Baines repeated it back. Then he handed Sam the phone. "Baines wants to talk to you again."

Sam nodded and took it, forcing himself to remain calm as he said, "I'm here."

"Colin is on his way," Baines said. "He's at your place so he's closest to you."

"My place?"

"Your home. You live in Devon, remember?"

"No. I don't remember anything about my life at all."

Except that someone tried to kill me and I can't remember who it is.

"It's okay," Gabriel murmured.

Sam wished Gabriel would stop saying that. Nothing was okay. "How long will he take to get here?" he asked Baines.

"A couple of hours. He's in a business meeting, but as soon as he's done, he'll be on his way to you."

So much for being concerned about his missing brother. Sam's fingers tightened around the phone.

"Okay, then. Can you ask him to bring clothes for me?"

"Sure, sure," Baines said. "God, it's so good to have you back, Storm. I've got a lot of people to tell. We'll need to get you checked out by a doctor."

That reminded Sam of Lisa. "I'm going to send you the name and number of a teenage girl and her mum. The girl is the one who kind of found me. She deserves the reward."

"How did she find you?"

"Kissing a guy on a clifftop."

If Baines had an issue with his sexuality, he could get fucked. Did he know Storm was gay? He must do. Lisa knew, therefore Storm Maitland had to be out of the closet. Then Sam saw Gabriel's eyes widen. Oh hell, would Gabriel freak at any publicity? He couldn't expose this private and grieving man to the tabloids.

Baines squealed in his ears. "That's fantastic. We can spin that one. I'll get publicity on it now."

"No. Wait!"

But Sam was talking to himself. Baines had hung up.

He cast a wary glance at Gabriel's closed-off expression. "I won't drag you into the publicity," Sam promised.

"I don't think that's a promise you can make," Gabriel said, his tone so icy it sent chills down Sam's spine.

"Why not?" Sam demanded.

"We were caught kissing in public. Lisa and her family will have exclusives with the tabloids before the day is out."

"Then we'll throw more money at them to keep them quiet."

Gabriel curled his lip. "Is that your answer to everything? Throw money at it to make it go away?"

"I don't know!" Sam yelled. "I don't remember."

Gabriel's derisive grunt made him narrow his eyes.

"You don't believe me? You think I've been faking the amnesia?" When Gabriel didn't answer, Sam got to his feet. "I guess that's my answer. What the hell did you think I was pretending to have lost my memory *for*? A holiday? A few days in a dead woman's clothes?" Gabriel flinched, and Sam flinched too, desperately wanting to apologise for hurting him, but anger was still coursing through his veins. He stepped away and shook his head. "I thought better of you, Gabriel."

He headed for the door, desperate not to show how betrayed he felt.

"Where are you going?" Gabriel said, his voice raw and angry.

"Outside, away from here."

Away from you.

Sam had almost reached the front door when Gabriel stopped him with a hand on his arm.

"You can't take off like this. We need to talk."

Sam fixed his gaze on the peeling paintwork of the front door, because if he looked into Gabriel's eyes, he would be lost. "I don't think there's anything to say."

Gabriel tightened his hands around Sam's bicep. "Don't go."

"Do you think I'm faking?"

Gabriel expelled a loud huff. "No, I don't. I'm sorry. It was a shitty thing to say."

"Do you want to be caught up in the publicity of my return?"

Just looking at the reams of articles about Storm—him—Sam knew his reappearance would be on the front pages of the media for days. Gabriel was a private man. How could he deal with such publicity? Gabriel's next words confirmed his fear.

"No, I don't. I went through hell with the press after Jenny and Michael. They all but implied I killed them and used the storm as an excuse."

Sam looked up and saw the pain and anger in Gabriel's eyes. "I will protect you. I don't know how, but I will."

Gabriel gave a wry smile. "Thank you. I don't think Toby could hold Damien back again. He nearly threw a BBC reporter off the cliff after he implied I'd killed them."

"Damien is fierce when it comes to protecting his family."

"We all are. We've been family for a long time. Even Jenny's death didn't break that."

Sam saw the gleam in Gabriel's eyes and drew his head down onto his shoulder. Gabriel stayed there for a while, but he raised his head and looked at Sam, his eyes dry now.

"I should be taking care of you, not throwing around false accusations and crying on your shoulder."

Sam cupped his hand around the back of Gabriel's neck. "It's been a hell of a morning."

"You're going to go home," Gabriel said, his expression clearly showing that was the last thing he wanted.

"I have to," Sam whispered.

"I know."

Gabriel bent his head, and Sam waited eagerly for his kiss.

Suddenly there was a flash of light from one of the windows and a pounding on the front door. Sam was so caught up in waiting for the kiss, for a moment, he thought it was thunder and lightning. Then he heard yelling.

"Storm Maitland? Storm, are you in there? It's the *Courier*. Will you give us an exclusive interview? Have you got a man in there? Who's the man? Are you in hiding? Did you run away?"

Sam was convinced the door was going to give way from the pounding it received. More flashes, and he realised someone was trying to take photos of them. He saw the anger building in Gabriel's eyes. "Call Toby and Damien. I'll handle them."

"We could just refuse to answer the door."

"They know we're here. I don't think they're going to go away," Sam said. "You stay here. I'll talk to them. Hopefully they'll fuck off when they have a soundbite."

He pushed Gabriel out of sight of the door and opened it, slipping out to be faced by a barrage of flashing lights. Instinctively he put a hand up to shield his eyes.

"Hey!" he protested. "Cut it out."

The flashes stopped, and he was faced by a strawberry blond-haired young man who barely looked as though he were old enough to shave and a middle-aged man with a camera.

"Storm?" the reporter asked tentatively.

"You tell me," Sam drawled.

The reporter blinked. "You really have got amnesia?"

"I don't remember a thing. How did you know I was here?"

"We got a tip off from a kid. I'm Will Peterson from the *Courier*, and this is Doug." Will pointed a thumb over his shoulder to the guy with the camera.

Doug mumbled a hello at him.

"Yeah, hi. Boy or girl?"

Will looked confused. "Boy."

Sam sighed. Fucking Alfie. "Yeah, we met him an hour ago."

"He said something about a reward?"

"My record company put up a reward for any information leading to my whereabouts. Alfie is determined to claim it."

Will smirked at him. "He said you were kissing a guy."

"I was."

Sam decided there was no point trying to deny it, as he was damn sure Doug had got photos of he and Gabriel almost kissing a few minutes before.

"So you weren't really lost."

"I didn't know who I was until Alfie's sister told me. She's the one you should be talking to."

Will frowned. "What's her name?"

"Lisa."

"How did you get amnesia? Isn't this Gabriel Pennant's house? Didn't he lose his wife and son last year? Were you kissing him?"

Sam ran his fingers through his hair. "Look, you can have an interview with me, but you leave him alone, do you understand, or I say nothing to you."

He caught Will's speculative look. Then the reporter nodded. "Just you, if it's an exclusive."

Sam shrugged. "Suits me. I don't want to do this again and again."

"Where do you want to do this?" Will asked.

He thought for a moment and then led the way to the rock. He wanted to get them away from Gabriel's place. Of course, the rock was still Gabriel's, but he hoped Gabriel wouldn't mind him using it if it got the journalist and cameraman away from his cottage. Sam sat down cross-legged on the sun-warmed rock, and Will perched awkwardly on the edge.

"Is it okay if Doug takes pictures while we talk?" Will pointed to Doug, who was taking pictures of the bay.

"Sure."

Will nodded at Doug, who seemed more interested in the view than in Sam. Reluctantly, he dragged his gaze away and smiled briefly at Sam.

"It's beautiful, isn't it?" Sam said softly.

"It is," Doug agreed. "I've been here before."

Sam looked at him warily. "Yeah?"

"When his wife and kid were swept away." Doug looked out at the silver-crested waves breaking on the shore. "I remember him. He was a wreck."

Sam nodded, but he didn't say anything. He didn't want to say anything they could use against Gabriel.

"They never found the bodies, did they?" Will asked.

Sam gave them a tight smile. "No."

Will pulled out his phone. "Can I record this?"

"Yep."

Sam hoped there was less chance of Will misquoting him if it was on tape.

Will fiddled with his phone and then smiled at Sam. "How did you meet?"

"Gabriel rescued me from a sinking boat in a storm."

Will's eyes widened with excitement. "He saved you?"

"Yes."

"What happened?"

"I don't know. I was unconscious when he found me."

"Why were you out in a boat?"

"I don't know."

"Don't know or won't say?"

Was Will leering at him?

Sam scowled. "Amnesia, remember? I woke up in Gabriel's cottage and couldn't remember anything, including my name."

"Convenient."

Sam's scowl deepened. He was starting to reconsider his offer of an exclusive to Will. Doug obviously caught his expression, because he nudged Will, who looked up and saw Sam's glower.

"Oh yeah, I didn't mean…. I just meant… tragic widower saves rock star from watery grave. It's a journalist's dream headline."

Jesus, the kid was young. He swore Doug groaned. Sam let him babble on for a moment. "Look, aside from the fact I like tea, not coffee, I don't know anything, not even my music."

Oh shit, from Will's excited expression, he shouldn't have said that.

"You don't remember your own music?"

"Not a thing. But that's what lyrics and sheet music are for, isn't it," he said, echoing Gabriel earlier that afternoon.

Doug whistled. "Damn, you must feel like you're in another world."

"Sam… er… Storm, your manager's here."

Relieved to have a distraction, Sam turned to see Gabriel and a man striding towards him. This must be his brother, Colin. He must have finished his meetings, because he was earlier than Sam expected. He didn't look much like Sam. Older than him, with thinning dark hair, stockier in body, and with permanent frown lines between thick, dark brows, he was shorter than Gabriel, but he seemed to have a long stride.

"Who are you?" he snapped, scowling at Will.

Sam expected Will to cower under the furious gaze, but the young reporter straightened his shoulders.

"I'm Will Peterson from the—"

"You shouldn't be talking to my client without me present."

"He agreed to give me an exclusive interview."

"I agreed," Sam said at the same time.

Colin turned on Sam. "This is not your decision."

"It's not?"

Colin blinked, as though he weren't used to Sam questioning his decisions. "I handle all your publicity. All interviews go through me."

Sam forced a smile. This wasn't how he expected his reunion with his brother to go. Colin was his manager, yes, but he was also his brother, and Sam had been missing for five days. Wouldn't that take precedence over business?

"You can work out the details with Mr Peterson, but he has the exclusive interview as agreed."

He caught the relief in Will's face.

"I think we're done now," Colin snapped.

Will looked mutinous, but for once he read the room and got to his feet. "I'll email you later," he said to Colin, who ignored him.

"We need to discuss how we're going to manage your return, Storm."

His return? How about "Thank God you're alive, brother," or some such shit?

Gabriel's cough broke the tension. "I'll show the guys from the *Courier* out and make coffee."

Sam smiled gratefully at him. "Thanks."

"Storm takes tea," Colin barked.

"We've worked that out," Gabriel said icily.

From Will's avid expression, Sam just knew this would also end up in the interview. Hopefully Colin would calm the hell down once the media left.

With one worried glance over his shoulder, Gabriel herded Will and Doug away like an overly large sheepdog, leaving Sam tentatively smiling at his brother. He started to say how good it was to meet him when Colin snarled at him.

"What the hell, Storm?"

Storm? He couldn't even call his brother Sam in private?

"What?" Sam asked, this whole confrontation making him confused and shaky. He hoped Gabriel made the drinks quickly, because he really wanted his steadying presence by his side.

"I get here and you're already giving interviews to some two-bit local rag? We could have sold your story to the broadsheets."

"Hello to you too," Sam murmured.

"Don't try and get cocky with me," Colin snapped. "I'm your manager. I organise your publicity."

"Did Graham Baines mention the amnesia to you?"

"He did. I thought it was a cover story." Colin studied him for a moment and then narrowed his eyes. "So you've really got no clue what happened to you?"

Flashes of the nightmares invaded Sam's mind, but he shook his head. "It's all a blank. I didn't know my own name until a few hours ago."

He felt like he was having this conversation over and over.

"Why didn't you call the police?" Colin asked.

It was Sam's turn to shrug. "We did. They weren't that interested, as I was an adult, unharmed, and with a bed for the night. They were overwhelmed with the aftermath of the storm and landslides here. Gabriel and I figured we'd wait a few days and then try again. I might have remembered something more by that time. Did you report me missing?"

"Of course I did. As soon as we realised you weren't in your studio or your bedroom. Your name was all over the news. Didn't you see it?"

"I slept most of the first couple of days, and the power was intermittent. We didn't watch the TV."

"I can't believe you survived the storm," Colin murmured. "Our boat wasn't designed for a storm like that."

Sam squinted at him. "The boat was ours?"

"Mine, technically. You didn't show much interest in boats. I used it for schmoozing clients."

"You knew it was missing?" Something niggled at the back of Sam's mind.

"We thought it had slipped its moorings," Colin corrected. "I fired Mitchell for incompetence."

Sam felt the blood drain from his face. "Mitchell?" he asked faintly. He remembered the two men talking over him.

Colin didn't seem to notice his distress. "Billy Mitchell. I'd asked him to take care of the boat."

"He…." Sam swallowed. "He tried to kill me."

"Yes," Colin said, so calmly they could have been talking about the weather. "He had one job to do, and he couldn't even manage that."

Fear, anger, frustration—everything mixed together and boiled up out of Sam. "It was you. You're the one who orchestrated this. You're the one who tried to kill me."

"Yes."

Colin stared calmly back at Sam, unfazed by his accusations or his anger.

"Why?" Sam demanded.

"Does it matter?"

Sam's jaw dropped. His own brother had tried to kill him, and he wasn't supposed to ask why?

Colin tilted his head and regarded Sam. "Why the hell didn't you die like you were supposed to?"

Frightened by the coldness in Colin's eyes, Sam turned to run back to the cottage just as Colin lunged at him.

Sam stumbled, and Colin caught him. "Let go of me."

"If you need a job done, do it yourself. That's what Dad used to say." Colin hauled him up and tightened his hands around Sam's neck. "Oh no. You don't remember that. Oh well."

He was strong, much stronger than Sam, who couldn't dig his heels into the ground as Colin pushed him inexorably to the edge of the cliff. Sam couldn't speak, not even to beg for his life. He felt the ground soften underneath him and knew the edge was close. He was going to die without ever getting to tell Gabriel he loved him.

Chapter 17
Gabriel

As Gabriel rounded the corner, he saw Colin dragging Sam by his neck towards the edge of the cliff. Sam flailed his arms, lashing out, but he couldn't get a grip on Colin or do anything to stop their inexorable progress.

"Get away from him," Gabriel shouted, but Colin didn't stop. Gabriel dropped the mugs and heard them crack as they hit the ground and he bolted towards the two men. What the hell was happening? He'd left them talking about managing Storm's return to his life.

Colin yelled something Gabriel couldn't grasp, his face distorted with rage and spittle flying in Sam's face. It was only as they got closer that Gabriel heard "You should have died then. Why didn't you die then?"

"Let him go," Gabriel bellowed.

He wasn't going to make it in time. He was at least twenty feet from them, and they were three feet from the edge.

Colin looked over his shoulder, his eyes wild. "You shouldn't have saved him. He's not worth it. He'll suck you dry just like he has me."

The man had snapped. For whatever reason, he'd lost his mind. Gabriel slowed, trying not to freak out the crazy man, and spoke as calmly as he could.

"Let him go, Colin, and we can talk."

Sam's face was crimson, his eyes bulging. He was able to make weak choking noises as he flailed at Colin's arm around his neck, but it was futile. Colin was a big, strong man, and Gabriel was petrified Colin would snap Sam's neck or strangle him before he threw him off the cliff.

"Walk away, Pennant," Colin snarled. "This is for the best. You'll see. You don't want to get involved with Storm. One minute he needs you, and the next you're old news. Only useful for what you can do for him. Stay where you are. Don't get any closer."

Gabriel had been edging nearer, hoping Colin wouldn't notice, but he was petrified Colin would carry out his threat, so he stopped. He tried to calm his pounding heart. "But why do you need to kill him? He's just about to make you a lot of money."

Colin gave a scornful laugh. "We've got enough songs for another five albums. I don't need him anymore. We release the tracks, his grieving fans will lap them up. As the sole beneficiary of his estate, I'll make millions. I'll find new stars and guide them into making the music I want. Not this folk crap he dreams up. He dies in a tragic accident, and he won't be a millstone around my neck. I'll inherit everything."

It was clear to Gabriel the man was off his rocker if he thought he was going to inherit anything now with Gabriel as a witness. Even as Gabriel studied his wild expression, it was clear Colin had snapped.

Sam was limp, consciousness fading fast. He was dying, and Gabriel was just freaking standing there. He had to do something.

Colin took a step back. Sam gasped out a warning, but it came out as barely a croak.

"Maitland, be careful." Gabriel barked, but Colin threw up his hand.

"Stay away, Pennant. This is between me and my brother."

Gabriel stopped, his heart pounding at the precarious situation Sam was in. "You're too close to the edge. You'll both go over if you don't move towards me."

"He needs to die. I told you that," Colin spat out. He seemed oblivious to the danger he was in.

Sam's gaze was locked on Gabriel's. Unlike his brother, he obviously didn't think he'd come out of the encounter alive. Gabriel had a horrible feeling in the pit of his stomach that he was right. Colin's grip hadn't lessened around Sam's neck.

"And you?" Gabriel asked. "You want to die too? Because you take one more step back, and you'll both tumble over. This isn't worth dying for, Colin."

He edged a little closer to them, hoping Maitland was too distracted to notice. He didn't care what happened to Colin, but Sam wasn't going to die at the hands of his brother. Gabriel focused his attention on Maitland when his heart was screaming to check on Sam.

Colin flung out a hand. "I said, don't move!"

Gabriel shook his head and edged closer. "I'm not going to let you do this."

Colin gave a scornful laugh. "You think you can stop me? Just because you saved him once? You've got a misplaced hero complex."

"It's not about being a hero. It's about doing what's right. Your brother doesn't deserve to die."

Colin's eyes were wild, bulging in his fury, sweat beading his forehead. "You don't know what he's like. You think he's Storm, rock god. I *made* Storm. He doesn't exist outside my mind." He tapped his head.

"He's Sam," Gabriel said. "He's your brother. You need each other."

Spittle flew as Colin shook his head. "I've done this once, I can do it again. I don't need Storm."

His arm around Sam's neck loosened, and Sam managed to gasp out, "I'm your brother."

For a moment Colin looked almost sad. "My brother died a long time ago."

"We're a team." Sam's voice was barely more than a whisper.

Colin shook his head. "I ran your life just so you could live inside your own head. What did you expect me to do, Sam? Be your puppet forever?"

"Hey, leave him alone!"

The cry came from over Gabriel's shoulder, and Gabriel cursed. He'd managed to get closer to them while the two brothers had been talking, but at the shout, Colin swung round. He took another step closer to the edge of the cliff and overbalanced. Gabriel hurled himself at Sam's legs as Colin's feet slipped over the edge. For a split second, Gabriel thought they would all plunge to their deaths and he thought how ironic it was that he'd die just as he found a reason to live.

He saw the shock on Colin's face as he realised the danger he was in, but by then it was too late. Colin fell, and thankfully his grip on Sam's neck broke as he scrabbled frantically at the cliff face. Gabriel held on as Colin's momentum nearly took Sam, headfirst, with him. Gabriel slammed onto the ground, Sam under him, both of them skittering towards the edge. He heard Sam moan, but they were still sliding, and he was sure they were both going to go over and follow Colin to the rocks below. Suddenly someone tackled Gabriel as he had Sam, knocking the air out of him, and there was the acrid aroma of sweat. They all stopped, Sam half over the edge, Gabriel looking down at the broken and twisted body of Colin Maitland. Then he caught the terrified expression in Sam's eyes, and nothing else mattered.

"I've got you," he said. "I won't let you go."

Sam clung on to Gabriel's arms, his fingers digging in painfully.

"We're going to pull you back," someone said from above him. "Don't move."

Gabriel kept his eyes on Sam's as the weight eased off him and they were dragged away from danger.

"You're safe now," the voice said.

Gabriel stayed where he was, sprawled half over Sam as he tried to get his breath back, his limbs unable to work for a moment. His brain hadn't caught up to the fact that he wasn't about to plunge to the rocks. Beneath him he heard gasps, and he raised his head to see Sam staring up at the sky, his eyes unfocused.

"Sam?" Gabriel said.

Sam didn't react, didn't even blink. Worry spread its icy tendrils through Gabriel.

"Sam—"

"Fuck. I thought you were goners for sure."

Gabriel turned his head to see a huge, almost bald man dressed in running shorts and a sweat-stained T-shirt, bending over him, his eyes wide and his face as sweaty as though he'd run a great distance. He swallowed hard. "You were the one who saved us?"

The man nodded and ran a hand over his shaved head. "I was just running past. You probably didn't notice me. I saw you drop the mugs and turned to see the man trying to kill your... friend." Gabriel stiffened, but the man continued. "I didn't think I was going to get to you in time." He looked sheepish. "Sorry about tackling you like that. Used to play rugby."

The man was built like a mountain, and Gabriel hurt like hell along his back and thighs, but that was okay. Gabriel could cope with a few bruises to still be here, and more to the point, for Sam to be alive.

"If you hadn't, we'd be dead," he reassured their saviour. "I can't thank you enough."

The man glanced at Sam, who was still on the ground, his eyes staring up to the sky, and furrowed his brow. "Christ, that's Storm Maitland."

Gabriel blinked. Was he the only one who didn't know who Sam was? Then again, he'd never been into music before Jenny died. She was the one who had music in the cottage, listening to the radio in the kitchen or the old iPod she'd had since university. Gabriel was more into video games and YouTube. Since they'd gone, his X-Box lay untouched as he spent all his days on the clifftop, waiting.

"You know who he is?" he asked.

"He's all over my daughter's bedroom," the man said. "Is he all right?"

Gabriel rolled off Sam, kneeled over him, and studied him anxiously. "Are you okay, Sam?"

Sam's face had lost the redness from Colin choking him, but his gaze was still glassy, and he took so long to answer that Gabriel was seriously worried.

"I'll call an ambulance," the man said, sounding concerned.

That seemed to stir Sam. He blinked and turned his head to look at Gabriel. "You saved me. Again."

He had to force out the words, and the red finger marks around his throat were darkening. Gabriel wanted to cover them with his own fingers, hide them until they disappeared. Anger started boiling in Gabriel's gut, and to distract himself, he pointed at the man now kneeling by them. "If it weren't for—" He paused and raised an eyebrow.

"Mick. Mick Powell," the man said hastily.

"Mick saved us both."

Gabriel helped Sam sit up. What colour was in Sam's face drained, leaving him ashen. But he managed to give Mick a wan smile. "Thanks, Mick. I owe you." He leaned against Gabriel who gathered him against his chest. Gabriel held him tightly as Sam shook in his arms.

"It's okay. I've got you," he murmured. "I won't let you go."

Sam shivered and nodded and held on to Gabriel, burying his face against Gabriel's chest.

Gabriel caught their rescuer eyeing them both, but he didn't care what Mick thought. He was only focused on Sam. But Mick's next words took him by surprise.

"Becky's never going to believe I saved her hero." He sounded starstruck.

"Don't look much like a hero at the moment," Sam muttered into Gabriel's chest, but Gabriel hushed him and smiled at Mick.

"Now you'll be the hero. You saved him."

"She's never going to believe me," Mick said again.

Gabriel heard shouting and turned his head to see Toby running towards them, consternation on his face.

"Gabriel, what the fuck just happened? What happened to Sam?"

Sam answered before Gabriel could open his mouth. "My brother tried to finish off what he tried before."

"Again?" Toby looked around. "Where is he?"

"At the bottom of the cliff," Gabriel said.

Toby blinked and then gave a grim smile. "Good."

Mick looked bewildered. "That was your brother?"

Sam nodded.

"Your manager?"

"Yup."

"Jesus." Mick thought for a moment. "No offence, but you're better off without him."

Sam snorted as though he were about to laugh, but then started to cough. "None taken," he managed finally.

Toby snorted too and then peered over the edge of the cliff. His expression was grimmer when he turned back to them.

Sam sucked in a breath. "Is he…?"

Gabriel had seen Colin lying on the rocks, but he wanted to check for himself that the bastard was actually dead. Sam shuddered, and Gabriel kissed the top of his head. It didn't matter. Morgue, hospital, or prison, Colin wouldn't be getting near Sam again.

"I'm sorry, Sam," Toby said, his voice as gentle as it had been to Gabriel after Jenny died. "I need to look at your throat, make sure the bastard hasn't done any permanent damage."

People were gathering to stare at them, and Gabriel was sure Sam didn't want this sort of attention. "Why don't we take this back to the cottage?"

He got to his feet, and between him and Toby, they hauled Sam up, balancing him when his legs wobbled. Mick stood anxiously by, looking ready to leap in if necessary. Once they were standing, Gabriel understood why he felt as though he'd been run over with a steamroller. The man was about Gabriel's height but would easily make three of him.

Sam managed to stand on his feet without collapsing, and held his hand out to Mick, who stared and then took it gingerly. "I can't thank you enough for what you did for Gabriel and me. What can I do to thank you?"

Mick shook his head. "You need to get medical help. The fact you're alive is enough for me."

"Let me take your phone number. When things have settled down, I'll call you and arrange a gig just for your daughter and her friends."

"I don't know what to say." Mick patted his shorts' pockets. "Uh, I don't have a pen or paper."

"Nor do I." Sam turned to Toby, who rolled his eyes and dug a small notebook and pen out of his jacket pocket.

Mick scribbled in it, pausing as he tried to remember his number, and then Sam took it and also wrote something. He carefully tore it out and handed it to Mick, who read it and looked dumbfounded.

Gabriel peered at the piece of paper, trying to decipher Sam's scrawl.

> *Becky*
> *Your dad saved my life. He's my hero*
> *Storm Maitland*

"Thank you."

Gabriel held out his hand. "You saved my life too, Mick. Thanks."

Mick shook it without the hesitation he showed Sam. "You're welcome. My morning runs aren't usually this dramatic."

"Someone must have called the police." Sam pointed to two police officers loping towards them. "You'd better call your family, Mick. This is going to take a while."

Mick looked almost pleased. "My mother-in-law is here for the day. The longer this takes, the better." He winced and cast Sam an apologetic look. "I'm sorry, mate, that sounded heartless. I know you just lost your brother."

Sam managed a brief smile and buried his face against Gabriel's chest. Gabriel brushed a kiss over his bright hair and held him closer. It was going to be a long afternoon trying to explain everything that had just happened. Then he took a closer look at the police officers.

Toby cast him a worried look. "Do you see—?"

"I see," Gabriel growled.

Sam tilted his head. "What's wrong?"

Gabriel forced a smile on his face. "Nothing. It's okay."

"It's not okay," Toby snapped. "We're just about to meet PC Arsehole."

"What?" Mick asked.

"Who?" Sam said at the same time.

Toby gave a grim smile. "PC Adam Riley. He thinks Gabe killed Jenny and Michael."

Chapter 18
Sam

Sam stared at Toby and then up at Gabriel and noted his hooded eyes and closed-off expression.

"You're joking," he said.

Toby stared grimly at the approaching policemen. "I wish I were. He caused a lot of trouble for Gabe, insinuating he had something to do with their deaths. He spread it around the village, and there are still people who believe it, even now."

"No smoke without fire," Gabe said harshly.

The two officers reached them, and Sam studied them carefully. It wasn't hard to guess which one was Riley—a thirtysomething man with small dark eyes and a wide forehead who scowled at Gabriel with vicious glee.

"Here we are again, Mr Pennant. Another death, and you at the centre of it again."

Gabriel's face couldn't have looked colder or bleaker. "Good to see you too, Riley."

The other officer was younger than Riley, probably no older than Sam. He looked between the two of them, his expression wary. "I'm PC Billings. This is my colleague—"

"He knows who I am," Riley said, his tone harsh.

Gabriel inclined his head at Billings, ignoring Riley. "Gabriel Pennant. This is Storm Maitland."

"Yes, I know."

Riley didn't look impressed, but Billings had the same starstruck look that Mick had worn.

"And this is Mick Powell," Gabriel said, indicating the man who'd been standing next to them.

Sam was pleased Gabriel took the time to introduce Mick, who had kept quiet during the whole exchange.

Mick nodded to the two policemen; his expression unfriendly. "I witnessed a man trying to kill Mr Maitland and this man save him." He pointed at Gabriel, who smiled at him.

"You saved us both," Gabriel said. "And you saw what happened."

From Riley's sour expression, he understood the repeated warnings that there were witnesses. If the officer thought he could blame this on Gabriel, he had another think coming.

Sam didn't move away from Gabriel's embrace. "Gabriel saved my life. If it hadn't been for him and Mr Powell, I'd have been at the bottom of the cliff, thanks to my brother. And he saved me from drowning five days ago."

"That's convenient," Riley snorted.

Sam frowned at Riley. "What do you mean?"

Riley curled his lip. "It's convenient that he happens to be there just in time to rescue you."

"I've watched the bay every day since my wife and child were swept away."

There was so much pain in Gabriel's statement that Sam wanted to hug him close and promise he could take the pain away, but that pain would stay with Gabriel until his dying breath. Sam leaned against Gabriel, trying to give him comfort. Gabriel didn't move away, and Sam was fully aware that both policemen noted the closeness between them. Just let them say something. Sam would have them up on disciplinary charges before they could take the next breath. There were some advantages to knowing the chief constable. He squeaked as a memory of entertaining the chief constable at a dinner party hosted by Colin popped into his mind. Gabriel gave him a confused look.

"I just remembered something," Sam said lamely. "I'll explain later."

"Where is the man who attacked you, Mr Maitland?" Billings asked, jumping in before Riley could make another acidic remark.

"He's at the bottom of the cliff," Sam said.

"Of course he is." Riley rolled his eyes, and Gabriel stiffened.

"Do you have something you want to share, Officer Riley?" Toby snarled.

"We need to take a look at him and then take statements from you," Billings said hastily.

Gabriel gave a short nod. "We'll be in the cottage. Riley knows where it is."

"Do you know who tried to attack you?" Riley asked.

Sam took a shaky breath, trying to hold back a sob. "My brother, Colin."

"Your brother tried to kill you?" Billings wrinkled his brow. "Isn't he your manager?"

"He is… was."

"What was wrong?" Riley snarled. "Didn't you pay him enough?"

Billings glared at his colleague. "Officer Riley, we need to look at the body."

He turned and headed to the steps without another word. Riley's scowl was just as fierce, but he stomped after Billings.

"The air is suddenly clearer," Mick muttered.

Toby and Gabriel laughed, although Gabriel's was a little shaky.

"Come on, Mick. I'll make you a drink," Gabriel said.

"Great." Mick shivered as the breeze suddenly picked up. "I wonder how long they're going to keep me. I could do with a shower and clothes. It's getting a bit parky now."

"The shower I can help you with," Gabriel promised.

"I might be able to find something to fit you," Toby said. "My husband's a big guy."

Mick eyed them all. "You all gay?"

Gabriel shook his head, and Sam held his breath.

"I'm bisexual. I was married to my Jenny for a long time."

It was obvious from his expression that Mick wanted to ask questions, but then he shrugged. "Coffee sounds good."

As they walked up towards the cottage, Sam slipped his hand into Gabriel's and was relieved when he didn't pull away.

"How are you feeling?" Gabriel asked.

"Like my brother tried to strangle me and then two big men fell on top of me." Sam gave him a wry smile. "I've got bruises on my bruises."

He was bruised from head to foot, and he felt as though he could feel every finger mark left by Colin around his neck and throat. Gabriel's expression clouded as he focused on the bruising around Sam's neck.

"It looks bad… huh?" Sam asked.

"You're not going to be doing any naked photo shoots for a week or two."

Sam rolled his eyes. "I'm a singer-songwriter, not a member of a boy band. I don't make a habit of taking my clothes off."

Ahead of them, Mick made a choking sound, and Sam realised what he'd said.

"Sorry, Mick," he called out.

Mick looked over his shoulder. "I'm glad you don't take your clothes off or my daughter and I might be having words."

"Is your throat sore?" Gabriel asked, lightly stroking one of the marks.

"Yeah," Sam admitted. "It's stupid, but all I could think of when he had his hands around my neck was that if I survived, he could wreck my voice."

He remembered that moment—the fear that Colin was going to strangle him and then the worry for his voice. It made him realise which he valued the most. He fought for his life, but also he wasn't going to let Colin take everything from him. Then it all became irrelevant as Gabriel tried to save him and Sam was scared for both of them.

"I'll take a look at you back at the cottage," Toby said.

"I'm fine," Sam assured him. Then Gabriel snorted, and Sam tilted his head to look at him. "What?"

"You're talking like you've got a choice."

"Finally he gets it," Toby muttered.

Sam opened his mouth to protest and then shut it again. Toby nodded in satisfaction.

"You're a quack?" Mick asked.

"Yes, local GP. My surgery is just over there." Toby pointed in the direction of the trees.

"I've run past here so many times but only stuck to the coastal path. I've never explored the villages."

Sam leaned into Gabriel, who slung an arm around his shoulder. He was suddenly exhausted and wanted nothing more than a nap in Gabriel's arms for the rest of the afternoon, but he knew the nap would be a long time coming.

Gabriel slowed down and let the others pull ahead. He stopped and turned to face Sam. "I'm sorry."

Sam looked up at him, confused by the sudden apology. "What for?"

Gabriel looked down at him, his dark brows knit together. "The next couple of hours is going to be horrible."

"Because the last couple of hours has been that great?"

"Yeah, but that was your shit. Now you're going to be caught up in my shit when all you probably want to do is nap."

"You must have been reading my mind," Sam said. "I just want everyone to go so I can cuddle on the sofa with you. But we have to give statements to the police."

Gabriel took Sam's hands in his. "This isn't going to be pleasant."

To Sam's surprise, he felt Gabriel's hands shake. "Riley's really got it in for you?"

"Yes. He tried to cause a lot of trouble for me." Gabriel shrugged his shoulders. "The thing he didn't realise was I barely noticed. I was in my own world for months. It was Toby and Damien who had to firefight all his unpleasantness."

"And now he's got a chance to start it all over again."

"You can bet he's going to try."

Sam gave him a vicious smirk. "If Riley tries any trouble, he's going to come up against my lawyers."

Gabriel managed a smile. "Are they good?"

"They eat minnows like Riley for breakfast."

"You're kind of scary when you smile like that."

Sam tossed his head. "My lawyers are scary. I'm the sweet guy singing about love."

Gabriel gave him a whatever-you-say look as they hit the gravel path and headed into the cottage.

Toby disappeared to get some of Damien's clothes for Mick, and Gabriel made tea for Sam and coffee for everyone else. Sam settled down in a corner of the sofa and closed his eyes just for a moment. He must have dozed off, because he was jogged awake as he felt the sofa dip and someone settle next to him.

"Wakey wakey," Gabriel murmured. "The big bad wolf is here to talk to you."

Sam reluctantly opened his eyes. Gabriel had switched on the lamp, and the fire crackled in the grate. The room was empty apart from them.

"Where are the others?" He clutched his throat. "Wow, that hurts."

Gabriel handed him a cup of tea. "Toby's gone off for evening surgery, but he'll be back later. I wouldn't let him wake you up. Mick and the other witnesses have been allowed to go home after giving brief statements. Mick wanted to act as bodyguard in case Riley tried anything, but I told him about your threat with the lawyers, and that seemed to pacify him."

"And the police?"

As if on cue, Riley and Billings entered the cottage and sat down opposite Sam and Gabriel.

Riley focused his attention on Sam, who thought that if the officer ever managed to smile, he'd be a handsome man. The sneer he aimed at Sam did nothing for him.

"Mr Maitland, why don't you tell us how your brother ended up at the bottom of the cliff."

"He tried to kill me."

"How?"

Sam gave him an incredulous look but kept his cool and answered the question. "He tried to strangle me—you can see the marks—then drag me and push me off the edge of the cliff."

"But he was the one who ended up on the rocks."

"He was too close to the edge and lost his footing. As Gabriel tried to save me, Colin didn't realise how close he was, and he slipped. Gabriel tried to warn him but he didn't listen."

"You didn't try to save him?"

"I couldn't save myself," Sam said bluntly. "If it hadn't been for Gabriel and Mick, I'd be dead too."

"Yes." Riley curled his lip. "It was convenient they were there."

Sam frowned. Gabriel had warned him Riley was going to get nasty, but he couldn't work out what Riley was driving at. "Mick was jogging past and Gabriel lives here."

"And why are you here?"

"Because my brother arranged for me to drown in a storm, but Gabriel saved me."

"But you don't know this for sure."

Sam licked his dry lips. How could he explain about his bad dreams? About the conversation over his head as Mitchell and Barrett discussed the reasons for killing him. Gabriel didn't feature in those dreams.

Billings interrupted, obviously having had enough of his colleague's tone. He knew who Sam was and had been handling the rock star with a wary respect, even if his colleague was oblivious. "Did you know Mr Pennant before he rescued you from the boat?" he asked Sam.

"I don't remember," Sam admitted. "I don't feel like I know him." He gave Gabriel a sideways glance in case he'd said something wrong. "My memory is patchy still."

"We'd never met before five days ago," Gabriel assured him and blushed a little. "I didn't know who you were before yesterday, and I never met your brother before today. And before you ask—" He gave the policemen a pointed look. "I haven't taken up homicide as a side hustle."

Billings nodded and scribbled something in his notebook, but Riley just gave a derisive snort.

Gabriel raised an eyebrow. "Is there something you want to say, Riley?"

His tone was icy. By contrast, Sam seethed next to him at Riley's obvious disbelief. What was this guy's problem? "My brother tried to kill me twice. Not Gabriel. My *brother*."

"Do you have any proof of this?" Riley asked.

"I remember the two men from my estate talking about it." He wasn't going to tell Riley that he'd thought it was just a dream. "And he tried to strangle me in front of witnesses."

"He could have been defending himself."

Sam leaned forward, his hands wrapped around his cooling cup of tea. "My brother was my manager, PC Riley. He wanted all my content, and there's a lot of it, so he could release it and keep the profits for himself. He would be extremely rich. Colin failed to kill me the first time, so he tried again, except he didn't bother to hide what he was doing. I think his mind snapped."

"Or this is just a convenient story, and you want all the money. You could have used Pennant to help you."

"But I didn't. You can check the witness statements. Billy Mitchell was hired to kill me. Have you got him in custody?"

He blinked. It was as if the fog in his mind suddenly thinned, leaving a brief gap he could see through. He shuddered as he remembered two men standing over him.

"Sam, are you okay?" Gabriel asked.

"Billy Mitchell?" Billings scribbled into his notebook. "You know who he is?"

"He works in security at my home. He was employed by Colin."

"You said the other man was called Barrett? Do you know his first name?"

Sam shook his head. "No."

"He also works on your estate?"

"He does."

He suddenly felt very alone and vulnerable and reached out for Gabriel's hand. Gabriel took it without hesitation.

Riley's expression darkened as he stared at their joined hands, but as he opened his mouth, Sam said in a tone so mild Gabriel looked at him in surprise. "I'd be really careful what you say next, Officer Riley. I'd hate to make a formal complaint. Think about how it would play out on social media."

Riley snapped his mouth shut.

Behind him, Billings rolled his eyes. "I think we've got all we need for now, Mr Maitland, Mr Pennant." He flipped open his notebook. "We've got your contact details, haven't we?"

The mention of contact details was an unwelcome reminder that his time with Gabriel was almost over. Sam stumbled over his address and phone number, unable to remember either fully, until Gabriel called the record company and found his contact there. From that call, they got his home address and phone number and a promise to send a car tomorrow to pick him up. They wanted to pick him up immediately, but Sam insisted on the following day. He needed at least one more night with Gabriel.

"Don't you go anywhere, Pennant," Riley snapped as he got to his feet.

Gabriel stood, ready to tear into Riley. "I live here."

Then Sam turned to him. "Why does he hate you so much? This is personal."

Gabriel ignored the two officers gaping at him. "He was Jenny's boyfriend before me."

"Ohhhhh." Sam dragged it out as insultingly as he could. "She picked you over him. No wonder he's being a prick."

"For fuck's sake," Billings muttered over his shoulder as he shoved a livid Riley out of the door. "Do you want him to arrest you?"

Sam smiled sweetly at him, and Billings sighed. "Just don't go anywhere, Mr Pennant."

Gabriel nodded and waited for the door to shut. "What the hell, Sam?"

"He's a bully. I hate bullies."

"He never forgave me for pinching Jenny from under his nose."

Sam kissed him on the cheek. "She picked the better man."

Gabriel sighed, pushed his hand through his hair, and grimaced at the grit lodged in it. "I'm lucky there was a witness to verify your brother was the one attacking you. Riley's not the only one who thinks I killed Jenny and Michael. And now here I am at the scene of another death."

Sam's eyes went wide. "What the hell?"

"They think I used the summer surge as an excuse to hide the fact I'd disposed of their bodies before I reported them missing."

"That's ridiculous," Sam snapped, wincing at the pain in his throat.

"Hey, be careful." Gabriel frowned. "How bad is it?"

"Bad. Don't change the subject."

Gabriel turned to face him, tucked one leg under his thigh, and took Sam's hand. "As I said, Riley's not the only one who believes it."

"No one in the village does," Sam said, his copper brows knit together. "I saw them. Everyone was worried about you. They all like you."

"You just see the best in everyone."

"No, I don't. I see things more clearly than most people. I'm a writer. I watch people for a living."

"I thought you hid away in your studio," Gabriel teased.

"The studio is my bolthole. I'm surrounded by people who want a piece of me. I'm watching them all the time. They think I'm just a musician, but I'm more than that."

Gabriel lifted Sam's hand to his lips and brushed a kiss over the back of his hand. "You're not *just* anything." He leaned forward to kiss Sam's cheek, but Sam moved so that they kissed on the mouth instead.

"Enough of that," Toby said as he walked into the cottage.

Sam sighed and pulled back. Were they ever going to get five minutes alone?

"What are you doing here?" Gabriel snapped.

"Checking up on Sam." But Toby headed towards the kitchen rather than coming over to the sofa. "Damn, I need a drink. It's been a long day."

Gabriel mouthed an apology at Sam, who shrugged.

"I'm fine," Sam called out.

"And once I've confirmed that, I'll leave you alone."

Sam heard the microwave ping, and Toby appeared in the kitchen doorway with a mug in his hand. He took a tentative sip and sighed in relief.

"You have fresh coffee at home." Gabriel's tone had moderated to mildly irritated.

"Your heated-up coffee is better than Damien's freshly made. You know that." Toby sat down where Billings had been moments before. "Thank God today is nearly over."

"Who's on call tonight?"

"Dr Willis. You're my last patient. Then Damien and I are shutting the door on the world and watching whatever horror flick he wants to inflict on me."

"You don't like horror."

"No," Toby agreed, "but I love Damien."

Sam swallowed back the sudden lump in his throat. Both these men loved as fiercely as the winds that battered the cottage. Did Damien appreciate just how lucky he was? Did Jenny?

"Sam?"

He blinked and looked at Gabriel. "Huh?"

"Toby asked if your throat was sore?"

Flushing, Sam tried to gather his thoughts together. "A little. I think it's going to be a few days before I can sing again."

Toby drained his mug and came to sit on the coffee table in front of Sam. He gently felt around Sam's neck. Sam hissed a couple of times as Toby pressed too hard on a bruise, but all in all, it could have been much worse. He knew Colin hadn't done any permanent damage to him. How his maniac brother would have loved it if Sam had survived only to never sing again. That would have been worse than death for Sam. Colin should have thought of that.

Toby dropped his hands and studied him. "You were lucky."

"Yeah, I was."

"Rest your throat over the next few days, and you should be fine."

Sam smiled at him. "Thanks for taking care of me."

"Between me and my idiot brother-in-law, you were in good hands."

"Thanks," Gabriel said dryly.

They both ignored him.

"I'll need to contact your own GP to tell them what's happened, but you managed to come out relatively unscathed."

"Apart from the amnesia, nightmares, bruised throat, and nearly being thrown off a cliff," Sam agreed.

Toby's lips twitched. "Apart from that." He sighed and got to his feet. "I think it's time I went home to my man."

"Bye," Gabriel said, obviously anxious for Toby to be on his way.

Toby rolled his eyes and grinned at Sam. "You're welcome to come watch the horror movie with us."

Sam shook his head and nestled into Gabriel's side. "It's my last night here. I think I'd rather spend it with Gabriel."

"Your loss," Toby said, "You could be watching the idiot blonde bird walk in the woods at night and get eaten by the monster."

"You know what you're going to watch?"

"There's always an idiot blonde woman running in the monster-infested woods," Toby said, and Sam nodded. It did seem like most of the horror plots Sam had ever watched.

Gabriel hauled Sam into his arms and pointed at the door. "Go away, Toby."

Toby rolled his eyes, but he was gone a moment later, leaving Sam and Gabriel alone for the first time since that morning.

Chapter 19
Gabriel

"I don't care if the cliff falls down. Someone else can deal with it," Gabriel said as he switched off his phone so no one could contact him while Sam locked the door and closed all the curtains.

"We might get some persistent paparazzi." Sam turned to smile at him. He looked exhausted, his thin face drawn and pale.

Gabriel really hoped not. He wasn't in the mood to deal with anyone else, and he didn't want Toby bailing him out of the police station in the middle of the night because he'd thrown a camera over the cliff. "It's due to rain heavily overnight. Hopefully that'll deter anyone."

As if on cue, he heard the first spatters of rain against the window, followed by a large gust of wind which rattled the front door.

"Thank you, British weather." Sam slumped into a corner of the sofa and yawned loudly. His stomach rumbled, and Gabriel remembered it had been a long time since either of them had eaten.

"I'm going to shower, because I'm covered in grit. Then I'm going to make dinner," he said. "Then we're going to sit by the fire and relax."

"Need a sous chef?" Sam asked.

"Can you chop?" Gabriel's question was serious. He didn't imagine Sam spent much time in the kitchen.

Sam's smile was sudden. "I managed before."

As it happened, Sam could chop, and he prepared the salad while Gabriel made fajitas. They didn't talk much as they prepared the food. Sam seemed lost in thought, and Gabriel wasn't sure what to say. Sam had shown little grief over losing his brother. Granted, Colin had tried to kill him twice, but he hadn't shown any signs of anger either. Gabriel knew from experience that grief would catch up with Sam soon enough, and he wanted to be there for him, but tomorrow he would be gone. He wasn't sure what to do for Sam except make dinner.

They retreated to sofas by the fire, and Gabriel sat next to Sam rather than taking his usual chair. Sam gave him a quizzical look but settled down in the opposite corner with a contented sigh, and they started eating.

Sam put his bowl on the coffee table with a contented belch. "I can't manage another mouthful, but it was good. Maybe later."

Gabriel looked down at his half-eaten bowl. He'd eaten more since Sam arrived than he had in months, but even he was defeated. They both ate far too much because Gabriel had made enough for six men rather than two.

"It was good," he agreed. Maybe he'd eat more later. Much, much later.

"I can't remember the last time I...." Sam laughed ruefully. "Of course I can't remember."

Gabriel glanced at him. "What were you going to say?"

"I can't remember the last time I cooked a meal for myself."

"You like cooking?"

"Yes. Maybe. I don't know. I have a memory of cooking with my mum, but it's so vague. I can't remember anything recent."

"Jenny and I shared the cooking," Gabriel said, and for the first time, saying her name out loud didn't stab him through the heart.

They sat in silence for a while, and Gabriel listened to the hiss and pop of the logs in the grate. Sam didn't seem to want to talk. His eyes were closed, his chin resting on his chest, and his hands folded over his stomach. He could have been asleep, but Gabriel had the feeling he wasn't. Still, it gave him the opportunity to study Sam, to memorise him before he left for good.

A thought occurred to him. "Sam?"

"Hmmm?" Sam didn't bother to open his eyes.

"Earlier, when the police were here, you remembered something, but Riley interrupted and got distracted. What did you remember?"

Sam sighed, and he opened his eyes. Gabriel wanted to take him into his arms to ease away the pain.

"I remember more about that night."

"What do you remember?" Gabriel asked softly. He didn't want to spook Sam, but his reaction had been so extreme it had to be important.

"It's still patchy like in the dreams, but I remember the dinner. It was chicken. Colin was in a great mood. He said it was because of a record deal he'd set up for me." Sam closed his eyes, then he pressed his lips together. "I didn't listen. I never listened. He made the deals; I made the music."

"Then what happened?"

"He gave me sherry to celebrate." Sam pulled a face. "I hate sherry. I remember gulping it down in the hope I couldn't taste it."

Gabriel chuckled. "I feel the same about brandy."

Sam gave a wry smile. "It was sweet. I mean, I like sugary drinks but not sherry. I just thought he was being a dick. Who thinks their brother is going to drug them?"

It was far outside Gabriel's thinking. "Is that all you remember?"

Sam's mouth pinched together. "I remember waking up and not being able to move."

Gabriel nodded, Sam had already told him that. "Do you remember anything else?"

"That's what I suddenly remembered. The two men talking over me."

Gabriel frowned, trying to remember the men's names. "Mitchell and...?"

"Barrett. Mitchell was something to do with security and Barrett worked on the grounds of our home. I remember talking to him as I wandered around the garden. I used to talk to his wife and children in the village. Mrs Barrett always looked tired, although I guess with a young family, that's hardly surprising."

Gabriel was amused to see Sam blush a little.

"We used to talk about who was on the front of the celebrity magazines. She liked soaps and begonias. I kept thinking how stupid this was. Begonias and soaps won't help me escape."

A tear rolled down his cheek and he dashed it away impatiently. Gabriel leaned forward and wiped the trace of water left on his cheek with his thumb.

"They talked about all the reasons for killing me like it wasn't important. Mitchell had gambling debts."

Another tear slipped down his cheek.

"Don't think about it anymore," Gabriel murmured, cupping Sam's cheek.

"Will you take me to bed." Sam leaned into his touch. "Make me forget this day even existed."

It was obvious he expected Gabriel to hesitate, to pull away and say he wasn't ready, but instead, Gabriel tugged Sam to his feet and led him towards his bedroom. Gabriel knew his hands were shaking as he closed the bedroom door behind him and left the two of them cloaked in the darkness, the only light from the moon outside. It had been a long time since he'd taken anyone to his bed except Jenny, and he wanted this to be right for Sam. He would only get the one night to show Sam how he felt about him.

Sam turned to face him and reached up for a kiss. They fumbled in the darkness until their mouths fit together, and Sam moulded against him, his hands going around Gabriel's neck to pull them closer together. His heady scent filled Gabriel's senses, and Gabriel threaded his fingers through Sam's hair. It was still damp from the shower Sam had taken, and he smelled of Gabriel's shampoo and shower gel. It was as though he were wrapped in Gabriel, and it wasn't as scary as Gabriel expected. Sam had been his from the moment he plucked him from a foundering boat. It just took him a while to realise it.

"You're thinking too much," Sam murmured against his lips.

"I'm thinking about you," Gabriel confessed.

Sam smiled against his lips. "You take my breath away with your honesty."

"What you see is what you get." Jenny had always told him he was too honest for his own good but he couldn't be any other way.

"My world is full of liars, fakers, and grifters. You stay honest, Gabriel Pennant."

Gabriel heard the pain in Sam's voice and dropped a gentle kiss on his forehead. "They've got no place here. It's just you and me."

"You and me," Sam echoed, and the sharp pain was dulled, if not gone.

It *would* be gone, Gabriel promised himself. By the end of the night, Sam would think only about the honesty he'd found in Gabriel's bed, under Gabriel's caresses.

He kissed Sam on the mouth—no fumbling this time, one hand cupping Sam's neck and the other on his arse—and focused all his attention on their kiss. Sam's lips parted under his, and Gabriel slid his tongue in to duel lazily with Sam's. There was no rush. They had all night. The tension and fear trickled away as they exchanged slow, tender kisses and Sam made sweet noises, little gasps that Gabriel loved hearing and captured with his mouth.

As they pulled away from each other, Sam sighed. "I need you in me."

It hadn't been discussed. Gabriel hadn't considered whether he would top or not. He snorted gently because it was a discussion he'd forgotten over the years with Jenny. He caressed Sam's cheek. "Are you sure?" He couldn't see Sam's eyes, so his words and tone would have to tell Gabriel what he needed to know.

"I'm sure," Sam assured him. "Maybe next time I'll take you."

Next time?

But Gabriel didn't want to think about whether there would be a next time. He bent his head to kiss Sam again, but tension suddenly flooded Sam's body.

Gabriel raised his head. "What's wrong?"

"Uh… condoms and lube?"

"In the bedside table."

"You had supplies?"

Gabriel heard the surprise and an element of suspicion in Sam's voice. "Toby must have put them there," he said sheepishly. "I discovered them a couple of days ago."

Sam rested his head against Gabriel's shoulder, shaking, and for one horrified moment, Gabriel thought he was crying until he heard a snort and realised Sam was shaking with laughter. Finally Sam raised his head and chuckled again.

"We should count ourselves lucky he didn't set up a hidden camera to check on our progress."

Gabriel grimaced because that wasn't so far from the truth. In the months after he lost Jenny and Michael, Toby had threatened to set up a baby monitor in case Gabriel needed him during the night. Only strong intervention on Damien's part had stopped that piece of idiocy.

Sam chuckled as he slid his hands under Gabriel's long-sleeved T-shirt. "If he *is* watching, let's give him something good to watch."

"I didn't know you had a kinky side," Gabriel grumbled, sucking in a breath as Sam's hands roamed over his stomach and then snaked up to thumb over his nipples.

"Doesn't everyone?" Sam said airily.

Gabriel's reply was cut short by a fierce kiss from Sam, followed by his top being tugged over his head. Sam's teeth nipped at a spot under his jaw while his hands slipped under the waistband of Gabriel's joggers to cup his arse.

Playtime was over, it seemed.

Gabriel tugged on Sam's T-shirt, anxious to run his hands over Sam's smooth skin.

There was a moment of flailing as Sam became entangled in the long sleeves, but then he was free and Gabriel threw the shirt to land somewhere unnoticed in the dark.

Sam's shoulders and torso gleamed in the soft light from the nightstand lamp. Gabriel stared at him for a moment and then ran his hands down Sam's torso, relishing the soft skin over lean muscle until he rested his hands on Sam's hips.

"You don't have to… if it's too different," Sam whispered.

Even now Sam was giving him the out, the chance to back away.

"Shut up," Gabriel said roughly and sank to his knees.

He undid the button on the fly of Sam's jeans, eased down the zip, and hissed at the sight of Sam's hard bare cock, framed by dark curls. He didn't want to be hampered by clothing, so he yanked the jeans down Sam's thighs. Sam rested his hand on Gabriel's shoulder as Gabriel slid the jeans off and pushed them to one side. Then there was nothing stopping Gabriel's access to his prick. It had been a long time since he had sucked dick, but it was like riding a bicycle, wasn't it? He leaned forward, licked a long stripe from root to tip, and then swirled around the head. Sam dug his fingers painfully into Gabriel's shoulder, and Gabriel smiled in the darkness. Oh yeah, he could ride that bicycle again. He repeated the motion, and Sam whimpered somewhere above him. Gabriel pressed a hand down on his own erection. It was as though Sam's little moans were connected to his own cock, but Gabriel willed himself to keep it together. This night was for Sam.

He cupped Sam's arse as he pressed kisses along the top of the curls and around Sam's thighs and did the same on the tight sac. Then he trailed kisses up the hard shaft until he sucked lightly on the head and lapped at the slit until precome burst across his taste buds, salty and good.

"Gabriel."

His name was a plea for more, and Gabriel obliged, wrapping one hand around the long shaft and sucking on the head—more flavour, more moans from Sam. Gabriel was going to come before he even got inside Sam. Then Sam tugged on his arm. Gabriel raised his head, but Sam's was in shadow. Only his husky words gave him away.

"I need you to fuck me, Gabriel. You can suck me off another time, but tonight I need you to fuck me until I can't remember my name—again."

His throaty laugh made Gabriel smile, and after one last kiss to Sam's dick, he got to his feet and buried his tongue down Sam's throat, wanting to share his taste. Sam hung on to his biceps as though his legs would give way without Gabriel's help, and Gabriel wrapped his arms around Sam's back and held him close. The kisses lasted a long time and grew more heated as their hard cocks pressed together through the soft fabric of Gabriel's joggers.

Sam wrenched himself away and stood back, chest heaving. "On the bed, now!" he growled.

Gabriel raised an eyebrow, though the gesture was completely lost on Sam in the darkness. "I'm still dressed."

With a growl that made Gabriel smile, Sam launched himself forward and tugged Gabriel's joggers down his thighs. His cock slapped onto his belly. From Sam's hungry stare, he wanted to feast on Gabriel's prick in spite of his previous words. Gabriel felt himself harden in anticipation of Sam's hot, wet mouth around him. Sam pulled the joggers off completely and threw them aside, not caring where they landed. He pressed his cheek against Gabriel's dick, kissed softly along its length and then got to his feet.

"Now fuck me."

Gabriel really liked confident Sam taking what he wanted. He held out his hand, Sam took it, and they fell messily onto the bed with Sam underneath. Gabriel straddled his lean hips, and their mouths sought each other in desperate need. Gabriel needed the closeness and intimacy almost more than the fucking, and it seemed Sam was prepared to give it to him.

For a while, at least.

Sam tangled his hands in Gabriel's hair and drew him closer. Gabriel kissed him, tongues sliding together, until his lungs burned for oxygen and he wanted his dick buried inside Sam's body. He raised his head, kissed Sam's cheek, and fumbled in the drawer of the bedside table for the condoms and lube. Then he sat back on his heels and rested on Sam's thighs.

Gabriel laughed as he tried to open the packet of condoms. "God bless Toby. He took the plastic wrapper off already."

"Thank him later. Fuck me now," Sam growled.

It took Gabriel a moment, but he undid the lube and smoothed gel onto his fingers. He moved, and Sam spread his legs with a contented sigh. Gabriel held his breath as he slid a slick finger behind Sam's balls to his hole and pressed against the muscle.

"Please," Sam begged.

Gabriel pressed a finger in and gently fucked Sam. He added more lube and then added another finger. Sam hissed in appreciation, and his thighs parted wider, as though he were begging for more. It was clear Sam was used to this, and when Gabriel curled his fingers and Sam arched off the bed, Gabriel knew Sam could take him. He pulled out his fingers, wiped them on the sheet, and reached for the condom. Sam moaned and tugged on Gabriel's hip when he was ready. Gabriel nestled between Sam's thighs, lifted Sam's legs over his shoulders, and pressed into the tight wet heat that had been waiting for him. Sam held on to his arms, and even in the pale moonlight, Gabriel could see Sam's eyes fixed on him with a need and desire that took his breath away.

Gabriel pulled back, and Sam clutched tighter. Then he pressed in again. Smoothly he repeated the motion and Sam let out a moan. Gabriel loved the noises he made and did his best to make Sam moan on every thrust. And when he leaned over and changed the angle, Sam yelled as Gabriel brushed his prostate.

"Close," Sam gasped out.

Gabriel grunted, his own climax coiling in his balls. He thrust again, harder, and they both yelled. Sweat dripping down his temple, he thrust and thrust until Sam stiffened and arched up, his channel clenching around Gabriel. Half a dozen thrusts, and Gabriel was there too, filling the condom with warm spurts, his orgasm drawn out by Sam's muscles around him.

"Sam," he murmured when they were quiet again. "Sam."

THEY LAY side-by-side, too hot to do anything more than entangle their fingers, their chests heaving. Gabriel felt the sweat trickle down his temples, and Sam laughed.

Gabriel turned to look at Sam. "What's so funny?"

"I never thought I'd get you into bed."

Gabriel snorted and smiled at him. "It was either going to be that or the wall."

"Not the sofa?"

"Never the sofa."

Gabriel wasn't possessive about most things, but the sofa was off-limits.

"Duly noted." The smile slid off Sam's face. "I'm sorry. I didn't mean… I know this is the bed you shared with Jenny."

Gabriel propped himself on one shoulder and stared down at Sam's worried expression. "It's okay, Sam. She would understand."

Sam cupped Gabriel's cheek. "You know I'd never try to erase them from your life."

"I do." Gabriel pressed a kiss to Sam's palm. "You respect her and Michael. Thank you." He kissed his palm again. "You're an amazing man, Sam Maitland."

Sam's face crumpled. "I think Sam got lost along the line."

"He got buried," Gabriel agreed, "but he's still here." Gabriel pressed a hand over Sam's heart. "I see *you*."

"I think you're the only one who does. Somewhere along the line, I became a commodity, even to my brother."

Gabriel held back the growl rumbling in his throat. *Especially* to his brother. The man had used Sam and then was prepared to discard him when he wasn't needed. Colin was out of the picture, but who was the next user lined up to take advantage of him?

"I'm okay." Sam reached up and smoothed out the lines of Gabriel's frown. "He can't hurt me anymore."

"Your brother can't, but what about the next arsehole?"

Sighing, Sam rolled onto his side, his pose mimicking Gabriel's. "I need to take charge of my career. I'm not a kid anymore. I let Colin make every decision for me. It's going to take a lot to unravel what he did, but it's down to me to sort it out. My next manager will be working with me, not in spite of me."

It was too dark to see Sam's expression, but he could feel the ferocious intent in his words. He wouldn't be caught off guard like that again.

Gabriel nodded. "I think that's a good idea. You need to get professional advice too."

"That's what managers, personal assistants, etc. are for."

"Then you need someone who has your back."

"I thought that was Colin," Sam murmured, and the crack in his voice was heartbreaking.

"It should have been," Gabriel said fiercely as he gathered Sam against him. "It should have been."

Sam sighed again, his breath warm against Gabriel's neck. "I should sleep. It's going to be a long day tomorrow."

Gabriel bit down on his lip. Sam was going to take a step back into his real life, barely remembering any of it. Gabriel wanted to beg… no, demand that Sam stay with him until his memory was sufficiently restored that he could protect himself against grifters. But he didn't have that right, so he wished Sam a good night and held him close until Sam's breathing evened out and he fell asleep.

Sleep proved elusive, despite the stresses of the day. Gabriel lay in the wreck of the bed and watched the shadows of the trees outside dance and play on the ceiling. His eyes were gritty, and he badly needed a shower, but he didn't want to leave the man at his side. Finally, the storm blew itself out. He rolled onto his side and watched Sam sleep, weak moonlight bathing the pale skin. Sam was on his back, his arms above his head and the duvet around his hips. No one ever got to see Sam like this, relaxed and asleep, an erotic study in white, with dusky shadows in his armpits, a patch on his chest and just above the duvet. Gabriel was privileged to see him just this once.

He had a few hours left before Sam left to resume his celebrity life, and he wouldn't waste it sleeping. Sam would wake up, the limo would come, and he would leave Gabriel behind forever. He was going to rock the world, and Gabriel would guard the cliff, alone again.

Tears prickled the back of Gabriel's eyes, but he impatiently blinked them away. This wasn't the time for tears. He leaned forward and brushed a kiss on Sam's cheek, light enough not to disturb him. "I think… I'm falling in love with you," he murmured. He could say the words in the cover of darkness that he couldn't say in the cold light of day. Then he held his breath, but Sam didn't move, and Gabriel relaxed.

He didn't want to put more pressure on Sam, who'd lost so much in such a short time, but he never expected to fall in love again. Gabriel had loved Jenny deeply and had thought he'd spend the rest of his life with her. He was a man who loved with all his heart, and he never expected to find someone else to hold it close. But what the sea had taken away, it had also given—a sweet, gentle man with a fiery heart. Gabriel couldn't hold on to him until they were old and wrinkled, but he could hold him close for this one night.

"Promise me you'll be happy. Reach for the stars, baby."

Sam sighed and rolled toward Gabriel until his head was buried against Gabriel's chest and his arm was over his waist. One tear ran down Gabriel's cheek to soak into the curls below.

He kissed the top of Sam's head, and the copper hair tickled his nose. "I love you, Sam."

Chapter 20
Sam

Sam stood on the clifftop, staring out over the bay at the white foam-tipped waves crashing onto the beach below. Despite the sunshine and blue skies, he shivered and the hair stood up on his bare arms. He was dressed in a thin white T-shirt and jeans, no match for the autumnal breeze blowing off the water. His jacket was in the cottage, draped over the arm of the sofa. He'd forgotten to pick in up in his haste to get outside. He was tempted to go back for the jacket and the guitar and pour out some of the hurt and grief through his music. Sam looked back towards the cottage and then at the sea. He didn't know what the hell he wanted to do.

It wasn't long since sunrise, and he shared the clifftop with a few dog walkers and one or two joggers. Sam sucked in a lungful of salty air and hoped it would clear his head. He'd had maybe four hours sleep and woken up with gritty eyes and a muzzy head. It wasn't hard to work out why he had insomnia. Sam had spent most of the night listening to the soft almost-snoring of the man sleeping next to him. This was the last time he would hear Gabriel whisper that he was falling in love with him when he thought Sam was asleep. Sam would return to his empty house, and Gabriel would spend day after day standing in this exact spot, monitoring the sea for anyone else in peril.

Last night had been special, but was that it? Was that all that they were going to share? Gabriel's fluttering hands had told Sam another story—his emotional turmoil and his need for something he thought he'd never have again, a love he felt he didn't deserve.

Sam had slipped out of bed as dawn lightened the sky outside the bedroom window. His head was full of cotton wool, and he needed fresh air before the drive home. The car was due in an hour, organised by the record company. They had promised him new management and a new team to take care of him, but they'd made it clear he was still under contract and he needed to get back into the studio as quickly as possible. How could he create music when he couldn't remember anything he'd created before? He was still reeling from the knowledge that his brother had tried to kill him twice, just for money. Sam dashed away the angry tears that welled up in his eyes.

"I ran your life just so you could live inside your own head. What did you expect me to do, Sam? Be your puppet forever?"

Colin's final words echoed in Sam's mind. Maybe his brother had a point. He'd let Colin take care of everything, just expecting Colin would deal with the mundane while he created music in his head.

They were two little boys who'd climbed trees and built sandcastles together. When had they stopped being close? His tenth birthday. Another piece of the jigsaw of Storm Maitland's life. He could remember it as clear as day, even as so much of his life was still a blank. His parents had bought Sam a guitar, and Sam's world had changed. He stopped playing with his brother and spent hours holed up in his bedroom, learning to play. He barely noticed his brother growing into a teenager, dating his first girlfriend, and then off to university to study economics and business. He didn't remember that. He'd read it in an interview about Colin. Bitterness had oozed from every word, and apparently Sam hadn't seen it because his whole world had been about music.

"I'm sorry, Colin," he murmured. "I should have been a better brother to you."

The words seemed hollow and empty as the wind caught them. It was hard to believe his brother was dead and Sam was now an orphan. They'd had no aunts or uncles, no distant cousins. Sam was alone in the world, and no one cared if he lived or died. More tears, and this time Sam let them spill and didn't wipe them away. He was allowed to grieve for the brother he barely remembered as a child.

And what about Gabriel?

They'd made love, shared confidences in the darkness. But Gabriel had made it clear that he'd never leave the cottage. He couldn't leave his memories of Jenny and Michael. That left Sam back to his rock star life. It should have thrilled him to be returning home, but Colin was dead, and two members of staff had tried to kill him. Were there others on Colin's payroll that he didn't know about? Was he safe going home? Gabriel hadn't asked him to stay here.

Sam shivered again, as much from fear as from the wind.

"You're cold," Gabriel said.

Sam didn't turn around, not wanting Gabriel to see him crying. He tried to wipe his eyes without being seen, and said, "I left my jacket on the sofa."

"Sam, look at me."

He turned, unable to refuse Gabriel even now. Gabriel looked sleepy, and his hair was tousled around his face. Clearly he'd just woken up. He wore a black sweater, the sleeves pushed up to expose his tanned forearms, and faded black jeans. He'd not bothered to put on shoes, obviously not affected by the stones on the gravel path.

Gabriel's eyes narrowed as he saw Sam's tear-stained face. He opened his arms, and Sam stepped into them, needing the comfort of his broad chest and muscled arms. Sam buried his face in the crook of Gabriel's neck and let the man rock him. Gabriel smelled of sleep and the lavender fragrance of the detergent he used. He muttered something Sam couldn't hear, but it didn't matter. All he needed was Gabriel's arms around him, keeping him together.

"I'm sorry he hurt you," Gabriel soothed, stroking Sam's hair. "He was your brother. He should have loved you."

Sam leaned against the solid fortress of Gabriel's chest and let a few more tears soak into his sweater. This man who had lost so much was offering him comfort, and he needed it. Let Gabriel think his tears were just for Colin. He didn't need additional pressure from Sam.

"It was my fault," he sobbed.

"The bastard tried to kill you. How the hell could it be your fault?"

"I spent all my time composing music. I never paid any attention to Colin. We used to climb trees together."

Gabriel held Sam even tighter, his fingers digging into Sam's skin. "He tried to kill you for money. There is nothing that will make me forgive him for hurting you."

"He paid the price." Sam shuddered at the memory of Colin falling over the clifftop and his horrified expression as he realised his impending fate, the same fate as he'd planned for his brother. "That's twice in less than a week you've saved my life."

"Do I get a cape?"

Sam looked up to see the smile playing around Gabriel's mouth and his eyes deep with emotion. Even in three days, he'd started to recognise Gabriel's moods by the colour of his eyes. Now there was a stormy intensity that made Sam shiver.

"I'd accept a kiss if you don't have a cape," Gabriel said huskily and bent his head to brush his mouth against Sam's.

There was no one near them on the clifftop, and at that moment, Sam didn't care. He wrapped his arms around Gabriel's neck, stood on tiptoes, and sank into the kiss. It was a brief press of lips at first. Then Gabriel captured his mouth in a searing kiss that melted Sam. He parted his lips under Gabriel's questing tongue, tentatively letting their tongues slide and play with each other. The kiss went on for a long while until he was breathless with need—for Gabriel and for air. Gabriel cupped Sam's arse with one hand and his head with the other. Was this a farewell kiss or an 'I want you in my life' kiss? Sam couldn't tell, but from Gabriel's moans, he wasn't letting go of Sam anytime soon.

A cough penetrated Sam's pleasure. He reluctantly raised his head to see Toby staring at them, one eyebrow raised.

Gabriel's arms were still a tight band around Sam's back. He scowled at Toby. "What do you want?"

"Sorry to interrupt." Toby looked as though he'd just woken up too. There were dark circles under his eyes, and he was dressed in pyjamas and a hoodie and—Sam blinked at the sight—unicorn slippers. "Sam's car has arrived."

"It has?" Sam licked his lips. "Already?"

I'm not ready to go. Don't make me leave.

"They tried your door," Toby explained. "Then they came over to mine. I thought you might be here."

Sam took a step back as Gabriel released him. "I... suppose... I ought to go."

Gabriel nodded, his eyes hooded and his expression unreadable. "Yes."

"Thank you," Sam said lamely. It seemed inadequate after everything Gabriel had done for him. He tried again. "Thank you for taking care of me."

Gabriel's hooded expression didn't change at all. "You're welcome."

Sam stared at him for a long moment, hoping, praying for any reaction, but there was nothing. After the passion of five minutes before, he might have not been there for all the emotion in Gabriel's face, but Sam couldn't tear his eyes away from him.

"Sam?" Toby asked.

"Yes, I'm coming."

Toby nodded. "I'll walk you to the car."

An acknowledgement that Gabriel wasn't going to. Sam smiled again at Gabriel, who didn't smile back. Then he took one last look at the bay and followed Toby back to the cottage. A Mercedes was parked outside, tinted windows obscuring his view.

He could feel the questions bubbling up inside Toby as Sam picked up his jacket. "Spit it out," he said wearily.

Toby gave him a long, cool look. "Are you coming back?"

"I don't know. Gabriel—"

"Forget Gabriel. I asked if you were coming back."

"I can't stay," Sam whispered.

Toby gave a curt nod. "I guess that answers the question."

"Toby, I—"

"You'd better go."

Sam stared at him, words hovering on his tongue, desperate to be spoken, but Toby opened the door, and Sam realised that was the end of the conversation.

But as Sam stepped over the threshold, Toby grabbed him by the arm. "Do you love him?"

"Yes." Sam owed Toby that honesty.

"Then you'll come back."

Sam shook his head. "I can't."

"Then you don't love him enough."

Sam wanted to protest. It was unfair of Toby to judge him like that. He had a life, one that required him to be in the studio and then away for months at a time. He couldn't settle down in cosy village life. He just couldn't. But before he could say a word, a balding middle-aged man with vivid blue eyes walked towards him, a huge smile on his face.

"Mr Maitland, it's good to see you looking so well."

Sam's fingers went to the bruising on his face in an unconscious gesture. "I'm sorry, my memory.... I don't remember your name."

The man didn't seem fazed or upset. "Dave Hughes. I drive you around when your chauffeur is busy."

A tendril of fear coiled through Sam's gut. Was he friend or foe? His feelings must have been reflected in his expression, because Hughes stepped a little closer. Sam took a step back.

"It's okay, Mr Maitland. I've been vetted by the record company's security, and there's a bodyguard in the car. I just thought you might like to see a friendly face first." He pulled a wry smile. "I forgot about your amnesia."

Sam licked his lips. "You weren't employed by my brother?"

Hughes shook his head. "You're not going back to your house immediately. The bosses want you to stay in one of their apartments until they've vetted all your staff."

"And the two men?" Sam struggled to remember their names.

"Barrett and Mitchell are in custody on a charge of attempted murder." Hughes gave a smile of grim satisfaction. "They're a little worse for wear."

He rubbed his knuckles, and Sam could see the bruising. The fear eased a little. He didn't have to go home to a place he couldn't remember and wonder if someone else was going to try and kill him. He studied Hughes and his open friendly expression. Maybe he wasn't totally alone.

"Okay." Sam managed a smile. "Okay, then."

He turned to Toby, who gave him a sudden fierce hug.

"Don't be a stranger," Toby whispered in his ear.

"Take care of him," Sam said.

"I will," Toby promised. "I always do."

Then there was nothing more to say, and Sam followed Hughes to the car. He slid into the back seat to discover a slim woman in a black suit sitting in the other seat. This was the bodyguard?

Hughes slid into the driver's seat and turned to face him. "Mr Maitland, this is Helen Stafford. She'll be taking care of your security from now on."

He blinked. "I… thank you?"

She was twenty-five tops, with short dark hair and dark brown eyes. She looked like she should be a CEO's personal assistant.

"Mr Maitland." Stafford inclined her head. "I'm sorry we're finally meeting under such difficult circumstances."

He went to answer and then realised what she's said. "You know me?"

"I've been in charge of your security for two years, but I always dealt with your brother."

"Friend or foe?" he demanded.

Her lips twitched, but she said, "Neither. I'm the guard between you and the world."

"Why didn't I notice you before? Wait, that's a stupid question. Have I met you before?"

"Yes, but we were never introduced. Mr Maitland…." She took a breath. "The other Mr Maitland insisted no one bother you about trivial details like security."

Sam nodded. "It's time I was bothered, Ms Stafford."

"Just Stafford."

"Call me Sam," he suggested.

"Yes, Mr Maitland."

Sam snorted. "Tell me about my security."

As the Merc pulled away, Stafford started talking. Sam listened, not looking back.

Except the one time, and he wished he hadn't.

Gabriel stood almost hidden in the shadow of the cottage, his hands in his pockets, his gaze locked on Sam's car.

Chapter 21
Gabriel

Gabriel watched Sam give Toby a hug and then get in the high-end car. He didn't miss the misery written on Sam's face. He looked alone and vulnerable. Gabriel wanted to rush forward and beg him to stay, to save him once more, but he held back. This was a good thing, he told himself furiously. Sam needed to resume his own life, and Gabriel could get back to his. He watched the car drive out of sight and then walked slowly back to the clifftop to resume his position, staring out at the bay.

This wasn't like losing his wife and child. Losing Jenny and Michael had torn apart his whole world. He'd only known Sam for five days, not even a week. He'd not had time to become a friend, let alone something more. Why did he feel so fucking empty inside?

The crunch of footsteps on the gravel told him he was not alone, but he didn't need to turn to see who had joined him.

"Why didn't you stop him?" Toby said.

Gabriel wasn't surprised Toby had sought him out. Toby would never have left him to handle this alone. "Sam has his life to live. He's a rock star."

"He's a young singer-songwriter who's about to make it big. His brother and manager tried to kill him, and there's no one who has his back. He's totally alone."

Gabriel glowered at him. He didn't need Toby making him feel bad. Sam's face had been enough of a guilt trip. "He has security. He has the record company."

"That's not what I mean."

Gabriel knew exactly what Toby meant, but he couldn't be that person. He'd barely managed to get out of bed for months after losing

Jenny and Michael. If it hadn't been for his vigil on the clifftop, he wouldn't have left the cottage.

"I can't...." Gabriel couldn't complete the sentence. He couldn't what? Be there for Sam? Be his rock? Love him? "I just can't."

Toby slung an arm around his shoulders. "You can. You just don't know it yet."

Gabriel rested his head on Toby's shoulder. "I can't take care of him. I can't take care of myself."

"You can, Gabriel, but do you want to?" Toby asked gently.

"Jenny—"

"Is gone, but she would have loved him. You know that."

Gabriel's hackles rose as they always did when Toby made him face the cruel truth that Jenny was dead. But for once he didn't confront Toby. Jenny *was* dead and she *would* have loved Sam. Those two facts were indisputable. He sighed and said, "I know."

"She didn't care that you'd loved guys before." Toby squeezed Gabriel's shoulder.

Gabriel knew that too. His beautiful wife had never had any issues with him being bisexual. He'd always been monogamous, and he loved his family with all his heart, including her brother and his husband. "I know that too."

"Then stop feeling guilty."

"It's too soon."

"Then forget about Sam."

Gabriel raised his head at the edge to Toby's voice. "You're giving me mixed messages here."

Toby shrugged. "I can't make up your mind for you. You either want Sam or you don't."

"I don't know what I want," Gabriel said helplessly.

"You do," Toby said. "You just don't want to admit it."

Katy Perry broke the strained silence between them. Toby pulled his phone out of his pocket and made a face as he looked at the screen. "Damien's asking if you're coming over for lunch."

Gabriel shook his head. "Tell him thanks, but I need to work."

"You mean you want to sulk here all day," Toby snapped. "Well, it's your choice. You know he's going to cook for you and bring it over, anyway."

Gabriel knew that. Toby's difficult, tetchy husband would never let him go hungry. He'd lived for months on Damien's cooking until one day he'd woken up knowing he couldn't face another toad-in-the-hole again. That day he went to the local store and bought groceries for the first time in months.

"Tell him thank you." Gabriel dragged Toby into a bear hug. "Thank you for stopping me walking off the cliff."

Toby hung on as though *he* was seeking comfort this time, and Gabriel realised that maybe Toby had been seeking his own support when he took care of Gabriel. He held Toby for a long while, until Toby raised his head, his eyes suspiciously bright. "It's time somebody else did that."

"You mean Sam."

"Or someone else."

Gabriel bit his lip. "I think there's a reason Sam was sent to me."

"You mean, aside from his brother trying to kill him?" Toby said dryly.

"Yeah, aside from the homicidal fuck who tried to kill him twice." Anger rose in Gabriel as he thought about it.

"No bitterness there, boyo. Okay, tell me why Sam was sent to you."

"I think Jenny was the only woman in my life. I don't think there could be another one to replace her."

Toby furrowed his brow, his expression troubled. "Do you see Sam as a replacement for Jenny? Because that's not really fair on him. He's nothing like Jenny, and you can't expect him to be."

"That's not what I mean," Gabriel protested, but Toby's expression didn't ease.

"I don't think you know what you do mean. You're right. You need to do some hard thinking about what you want from Sam. If you want anything at all."

Katy Perry sounded again, and this time she sounded distinctly annoyed.

Gabriel gave a wry smile. "You'd better go before he kills you."

Toby nodded, but he didn't move. Gabriel raised an eyebrow. "Tobes?"

"Don't throw away a good thing just because you're scared."

Gabriel didn't have a chance to respond, because Toby walked away, leaving him alone, shivering as a cold gust of wind whipped around him.

NOT SURE what to do with himself, Gabriel spent the afternoon in the dinghy, criss-crossing the bay, much as he had done when he searched for Sam. The sea was much calmer, although a stiff breeze whipped his hair around his face. He impatiently pushed it back, thinking it was about time he got it cut. Jenny used to cut his hair. He wasn't sure where he would go, certainly not to the salon in the middle of the village. They would eat him alive the second he stepped in the door. He'd ask Toby or Damien. They'd laugh at him, but he could live with a little embarrassment. Gabriel thought of Sam's bright copper hair, longer than his but neatly styled, whereas his was just a mess. Gabriel gave a wry smile. Sam probably paid Gabriel's monthly mortgage payments just to get his hair looking like that. Or maybe not. He hadn't seemed that precious about the way he looked.

The wind whipped up again, and Gabriel spat out a mouthful of hair. By the time he pulled the dinghy up the beach, he was still in a turmoil about Sam but he felt better. The fresh air had done him some good. He wished he'd taken Sam out in the boat, but then he reminded himself of Sam's narrow escape. Would Sam ever want to go in a boat again? He wouldn't know. Gabriel growled as he secured the dinghy. What the hell was he going to do?

Gabriel stomped up the wooden steps, angry at himself for his indecisiveness. He needed to grow a pair and make a decision. He charged up the steps, almost slipping once or twice on the damp decking, but needing the force to drive him forwards. He reached the clifftop, breathless and his legs aching from the exertion, but also feeling strangely triumphant. He would work, he would live, and he would stay away from the edge of the clifftop. That's what Sam had given him. Gabriel would always be grateful for that.

His resolve lasted as far as the cottage. It seemed empty without the vibrancy of Sam—not the soul-sucking emptiness after losing Jenny and Michael, but as though Sam had infused the place with joy again and now it had been taken away. Gabriel shook his head. He needed to get over himself.

Gabriel looked at the coffee maker and then reached into the fridge and pulled out a bottle of beer instead. He made himself a huge ham salad sandwich, found a packet of crisps, and took them both over to his chair by the fire. It was only as he bit into the sandwich that he remembered about Damien's offer of dinner. He looked at the sandwich, shrugged, and carried on eating. He could always eat dinner later.

It wasn't cold enough for a fire, but he lit it just for the comfort of seeing the crackling flames. He slumped in the chair, crossed his legs at the ankles, and watched the fire, his bottle balanced precariously on his belly. Copper, crimson, and yellow, the flames licked and curled around the logs, dancing higher as the kindling caught.

Sam was a flame, waiting to blaze and find his full glory. He was on the cusp of something big, and Gabriel couldn't be the one to hold him back. He would watch Sam shine and hope that one day he might want to come back to the man in the little cottage on the edge of the cliff.

Sleep was a long time coming. He finally managed to sleep, one arm wrapped around Sam's pillow, his scent lingering enough to sooth Gabriel to sleep. Gabriel woke early enough that the first pink flush of dawn was only just streaking through the sky. He rolled over onto his back and stared up at the ceiling.

"Fuck it," he muttered and sat up, scratching his belly.

Gabriel shuffled into the kitchen and made himself a cup of instant coffee. The coffee machine would take too long. He'd take the drink out to the rock and watch the sunrise, then he'd work for the rest of the day. He really needed to find something to do other than work and watching the bay.

"I'll get a dog."

He blinked. Where the hell had that come from? Then he remembered sitting on the rock with Jenny as she cooed over a mutt almost as large as she was. She'd tried to convince him to get a dog then, but he'd laughed and said there was plenty of time for that when Michael was older. Gabriel blinked back tears as he let himself out of the cottage. He'd not make that mistake again.

Then don't wait for Sam to come back to you. Go get him!

He needed to think, to make a decision about the man who'd turned his life upside down.

The sky had changed from mauves to blues to pinks, and now the sun peeked over the horizon. He walked the short gravel path, sipping at his coffee, only to discover someone was already in his place. His mood went from annoyance to shock as he stared at the lean man dressed in a thick cream jumper and tight black jeans, his bright hair whipped around his face by the breeze. Copper hair glinted in the morning's early rays.

Sam turned to smile at him, and it took Gabriel's breath away. "Is that tea?"

Gabriel rolled his eyes. "I don't drink tea. The kettle has just boiled, if you want to make a cup."

They were talking about something as mundane as a cup of tea when Gabriel wanted to know what the hell Sam was doing on his rock at sunrise. Which, if he thought about it, was exactly where he was the previous morning.

Sam nodded. "Don't run away." He slipped past Gabriel to the cottage.

Gabriel stared after him. "Run away?" Where did Sam think he would go? He ignored his traitorous brain, which pointed out Gabriel had made a habit of walking away from Sam.

Gabriel drank his cooling cup of coffee and tried not to be impatient for Sam's return. Maybe he should have asked for a second cup.

"Good. You're still here." Sam handed Gabriel another mug of coffee.

Gabriel accepted it with a bemused wonder. "Did you read my mind?"

"Maybe," Sam said cryptically before he took a sip of his tea.

"How long have you been here?"

"An hour maybe. I didn't check."

"Why didn't you knock on the door?"

Sam gave him a wry smile. "I needed to think, and your rock is a good place to do it."

Gabriel stared at him. "You drove through the night to sit on my rock?"

"I drove through the night to talk to you… and sit on your rock."

"Where is your bodyguard?" Gabriel looked around, but he couldn't see anyone apart from the two of them.

"I gave them the slip." Sam smirked at him. "They don't know I'm gone yet. I said I wanted to be left alone to write new songs."

"And they bought that?" Gabriel gave him a sceptical look, but Sam just shrugged.

"I'm a commodity. The record company expects me to write music, so it's not like it's a surprise."

"But you came here instead?"

"The view inspires me." Sam indicated the rock. "I think I could make a lot of music here."

Gabriel's mouth went dry, and he had to swallow a couple of times to get enough saliva to speak. "What are you saying?"

Sam bit his lip. "Can't you guess?"

"I don't want to guess. I need you to tell me, Sam. Why did you come back here?" He needed to hear the words out loud. If he was going to give his heart to someone again, he needed to know they felt the same way.

Sam took a long time to answer, and Gabriel didn't pressurise him. "I thought about it all the way back to London." He stopped and snorted. "They wouldn't let me go home. It has to be vetted, so I'm stuck in a sterile apartment with nothing to call my own. Even the clothes in the wardrobe were bought by someone else. I lay in bed and wondered what the hell I was going to do now."

"Write music, make songs, tour the world," Gabriel suggested when the pause went on too long.

Sam nodded. "I want to do all that, but…."

"But?"

"I want to do it with you."

Gabriel's heart skipped a beat, but he had to be honest. "I can't leave here."

"I know you can't, and I don't want you to. But I can write music here, on this rock. I can build myself a new studio. And I can tour the world, but I know you'll be here waiting for me when it's over.

"Please give us a chance." Sam reached out to take Gabriel's free hand and entwined his fingers. "I'm not expecting a promise of a happily ever after yet. We need to get to know each other first. But I'll take a happy for now."

Gabriel remembered Jenny talking about the differences between happily ever after and happy for now in the romance books she'd read. He'd always felt conflicted because how could you know you'd feel the same way about your partner in ten or twenty years? But then he looked at Jenny and knew he could see her by his side for the rest of his life.

He took a long look at Sam, who was waiting for his reply. Sam wasn't Jenny. His life wouldn't be the same as he'd expected. Could he see Sam standing next to him when they were elderly, his copper hair faded to ash, deep lines around his eyes, but his smile as bright as the sun?

"Are you sure it's me you want and not the rock?" he asked. "I could gift the rock to you with no expectations."

Sam placed their joined hands against his heart. "It's you I want."

Gabriel knew this was the moment. If he said no, Sam would walk away and never bother him again. He would make his music, and Gabriel would watch him on TV and wonder, "What if." Or he could take the step off the cliff into an unknown future. Sam wouldn't judge him for his decisions.

He looked at his left hand, tugged his hands free, and then slipped the wedding ring off and transferred it to his right hand.

"She'll always be part of you," Sam whispered.

Gabriel nodded and held Sam's slender hand in his. "Jenny and Michael will always have a piece of my heart. But you have my heart now. If it's all right with you, I think I'd like to work on our happily ever after."

Cranky middle-aged author with an addiction for coffee and a passion for romancing two guys, SUE BROWN loves her dog, loves her kids, and loves coffee—though which order very much depends on the time of day.

Sue can be found at:

Website: www.suebrownstories.com
Blog: suebrownsstories.blogspot.co.uk
Twitter: @suebrownstories
Facebook: www.facebook.com/suebrownstories

DREAMSPUN DESIRES

THE FIREMAN'S POLE

Sue Brown

The flames of passion rise for the lord of the manor.

The flames of passion rise for the lord of the manor.

It's springtime in Calminster village, but things are already heating up. Sexy firefighter Dale Maloney is new to the local station. When Dale backs the company fire engine into the village maypole, he attracts the ire—and attention—of Benedict Raleigh, the Baron Calminster.

Soon after meeting Dale, Ben breaks off his relationship with his girlfriend, and the sparks between Ben and Dale are quickly fanned into flames.

Unfortunately the passion between the two men isn't the only blaze in the village. An arsonist's crimes are escalating, and it's up to Dale and his crew to stop them. Meanwhile, as they investigate, an unscrupulous business partner attempts to coerce Ben into marrying his daughter. The May Day parade is around the corner, but they have plenty of fires to put out before Ben can finally slide down the fireman's pole.

www.dreamspinnerpress.com

Last Place in the Chalet

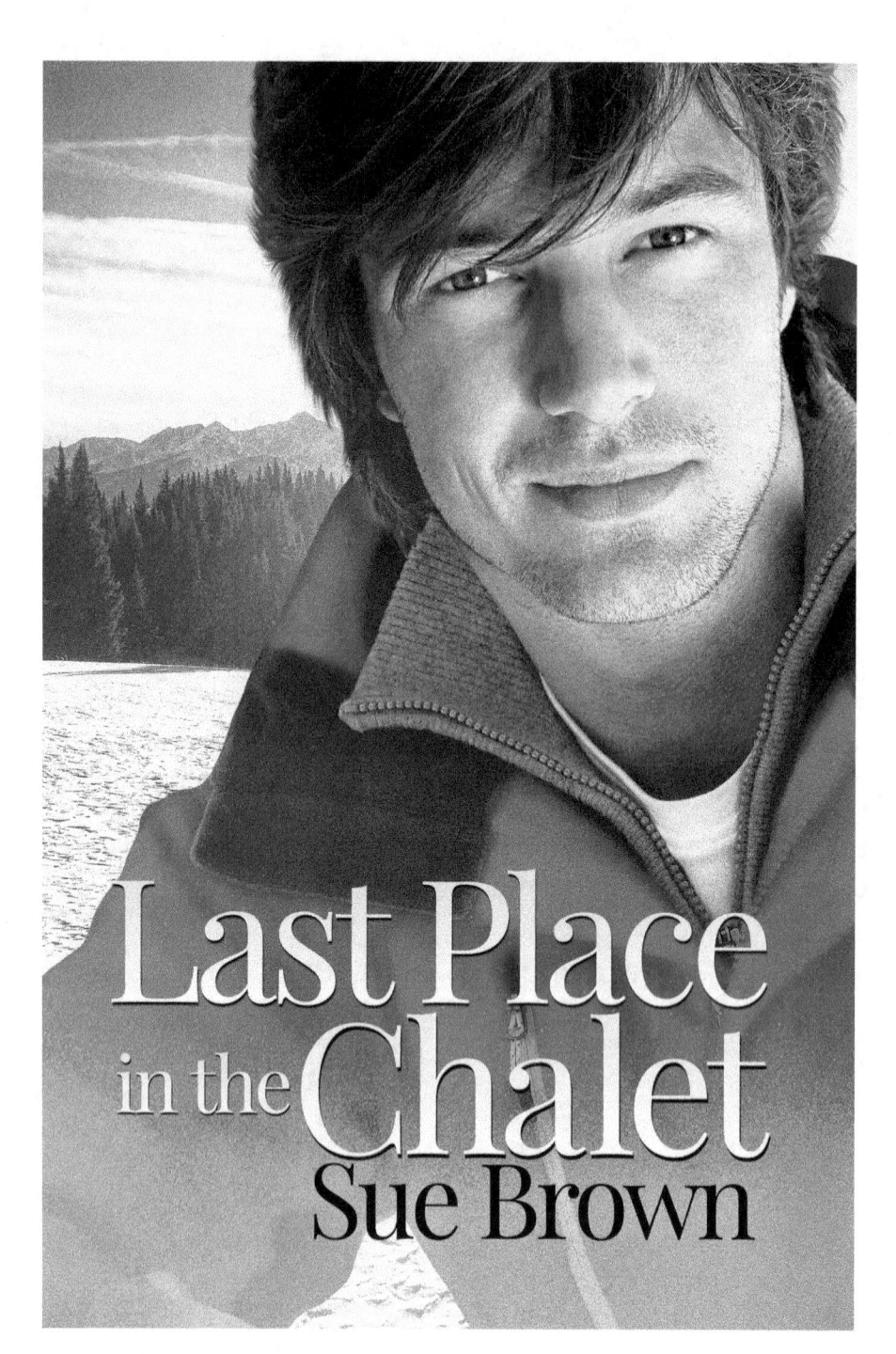

Sue Brown

Noel Garrett leaves for his Christmas vacation with an engagement ring in his pocket. But he boards the plane alone and with a broken heart when his boyfriend dumps him in the airport.

His seatmate, Angel Marinelli, takes care of him with gentle determination… whether Noel wants it or not, and Noel doesn't expect to see Angel again. But when an overbooking leaves Angel without a room and Noel is asked to host him, one night turns into the whole vacation and they settle into the chalet and mix with an eclectic group of guests, including the Wise Guys and a pregnant woman. As they ski and spend every moment together, Noel finds himself falling for Angel, and though his feelings are returned, Noel worries it's just a rebound romance. It'll mean taking a leap of faith, but Noel has to make a decision before he hurts Angel, and Christmas is fast approaching.

www.dreamspinnerpress.com

THE LAYERED MASK

SUE BROWN

Threatened by his father with disinheritance, Lord Edwin Nash arrives in London with a sole purpose: to find a wife. A more than eligible bachelor and titled to boot, the society matrons are determined to shackle him to one of the girls by the end of the season.

During a masquerade ball, Nash hides from the ladies vying for his attention. He is discovered by Lord Thomas Downe, the Duke of Lynwood. Nash is horrified when Downe calmly tells him that he knows the secret Nash has hidden for years and sees through the mask Edwin presents to the rest of the world.

And then he offers him an alternative.

www.dreamspinnerpress.com

SUE BROWN

SPEED DATING the BOSS

COWBOYS & ANGELS

Cowboys and Angels: Book One

Will a mix of privilege and blue collar be a recipe for love… or disaster?

Dan's pretty satisfied with his job at the working-class bar Cowboys and Angels. He enjoys his simple life, his apartment, and his cat, but he could do without the fights that break out in the bar, his boss's meddling daughter, Ariel… oh, and a brutal, unrequited crush on his straight alpha boss, Gideon.

When Dan's friend prepares to tie the knot, everyone insists that Dan needs a date for the wedding. Before he can protest, Ariel arranges a gay speed-dating event at the bar with Gideon as a participant. The unforeseen revelation that Gideon is bisexual raises Dan's hopes, especially when Gideon announces that he wants to accompany Dan to the wedding. Could Gideon really be interested in Dan?

When Dan needs someone most, Gideon offers his unconditional support, and with genuine commitment, he shows Dan the kind of man he really is. Teaming up to save the wedding from a hungover groom and intolerant parents, can Gideon convince Dan they're the best match since beer and pizza?

www.dreamspinnerpress.com

SUE BROWN

"A lively, emotionally satisfying story"
- *Publishers Weekly*

SECRETLY DATING the LIONMAN

COWBOYS & ANGELS

Cowboys and Angels: Book Two

Can a man burdened with family drama find his way into the arms of a happy-go-lucky stripper called Lionman?

Cris likes a drink at the Cowboys and Angels bar after his shift at the strip club—until one night when a trashed young guy named Mikey tries to kiss him. He's not Cris's type, but Cris is good enough to see the kid home safely. There he meets Mikey's handsome older brother, Bennett, and there's an immediate spark between them.

But Bennett might not be in a position to start a relationship, let alone with the carefree Cris. He's trying desperately to hold his family together, with a younger brother who's running off the rails and hostile parents who will never accept not just one, but two gay sons.

When Cris is unexpectedly fired and Bennett's family drama escalates, they turn to each other for support. But can a shoulder to lean on develop into something much closer, something they both deserve?

www.dreamspinnerpress.com

SUE BROWN

SLOW DATING *the* DETECTIVE

COWBOYS & ANGELS

Cowboys and Angels: Book Three

A gentle bartender might have what it takes to mend a relationship-phobic detective's broken heart… but first they have to admit they're dating.

Keenan Day could kick himself for letting the hot, dark-haired stranger he met outside a strip club get away. Instead of a phone number, he gets a punch in the face—from the boyfriend of his prospective employer at the Cowboys and Angels bar. When two cops come to check up on him, one is the sexy stranger, Detective Nate Gordon.

The initial attraction hasn't cooled, and though Nate is leery of commitment, one hookup turns into another until they're seeing each other in everything but name. After a recent nasty breakup, Nate balks at being part of a couple, and Keenan agrees, even though that's all he's ever wanted.

Just as they reach a standstill, a crisis shows them what their friends have known all along—they've already moved way past hookups. Now they just have to decide how to move forward.

www.dreamspinnerpress.com

FOR **MORE** OF THE **BEST GAY** ROMANCE

Dreamspinner Press

dreamspinnerpress.com

CPSIA information can be obtained
at www.ICGtesting.com
Printed in the USA
LVHW020115101220
673729LV00014B/1445

9 781644 055496